PIs

AN AJ CONTI NOVEL

PIs

JAMES A. BACCA

LUMINARE PRESS

WWW.LUMINAREPRESS.COM

Cover Design: Melissa K. Thomas

Luminare Press
442 Charnelton St.
Eugene, OR 97401
www.luminarepress.com

LCCN: 2021902446
ISBN: 978-1-64388-628-2

To K.L. and T.S.,
vastly different strengths yet excellent
investigative minds.

Thanks for your everlasting support
and friendship.

Acknowledgements

Thank you to the high-tech crime fighters and those willing to try and stay on the cutting edge. A couple of decades ago getting a detective or two assigned to a task force seemed sufficient. Today, it seems every detective must have some working knowledge of technology because the odds are it played a role, even if only a cell phone in the pocket of the criminal. Understanding technology helps solve crimes. More importantly, networking with others across the country and around the globe who have already worked similar cases has been instrumental in helping all agencies, regardless of size, to stay up with the fast pace technology world. I see it every day in the high-tech group I am fortunate enough to be a part of. To all of you in the group, thank you for your dedication.

CHAPTER ONE

F or the past three mornings, two men had watched the
woman step into her backyard pool for laps. Her pool,
an Olympic short course of eighty-two feet, provided them
time to slip in behind her unnoticed when she began her laps.
She routinely walked outside at 4:45 a.m. using only
ambient light around the shrubbery. She did five laps to
warm up, which usually led to a workout of thirty to forty-
five minutes. Having watched her they determined the best
time to move would be shortly after she entered the water,
her slowest lap. Swimming to catch up to her had never been
a serious concern especially compared to the difficulty and
timing needed to put the fabricated strap around her feet
while keeping her from screaming.

The three-inch-wide strap they fashioned had a loop on
one end with wool lining to minimize telltale markings once
they pulled it tight around her ankles. With the strap loop
preset to its widest point they slipped into the water after
she pushed off for the first length and made sure to keep a
reasonable distance while swimming under water. Her flip
under water and push off the wall propelled her directly
toward them…a jolt of terror seized her when seeing two
faces underwater staring at her.

Both men wore wet suits to prevent being scratched,
and the initial shock caused her to freeze for a split second

allowing them to get her in their grasps. To their amazement they slipped the strap over her feet and secured it in less than two seconds, despite her attempts to break free.

They both held the strap, their descent dragging her deeper from the surface. Her thrashing underwater created less noise on the surface than her laps while her gasps for air consumed water. When her flailing ceased one man let go, surfacing to check for any witnesses. Feeling secure he returned to the bottom, allowing his partner to surface for a breath. The best they could tell in the pool, she had no bleeding or marks, so they released her then surfaced, watching for thirty seconds to make sure she did not move or take a breath.

They exited the pool, sliding behind the filtering equipment to text their ride with a previously hidden burner phone. With the woman silently lying at the bottom and not having moved, they crossed through the gate onto the front lawn, and waited in the shadows. Their driver turned off the headlights several houses down, letting it slowly coast the last fifty feet so they could jump in without him using the brakes.

"How'd it go?" asked Thumper, the driver.

"Pretty smooth, except for the Australian cowboy back there having trouble lassoing her feet," Rock said, laughing.

"You're so full of it," Dingo said with a slight hint of an Australian accent. "It went off without a hitch, don't let him fool you."

"Yeah, a pretty easy job really," Rock nodded, "although I gotta say I'm glad we practiced it."

"Me too," Dingo said. "Her still being half asleep on the first turn might have helped. She had huge eyes when she first saw us, and she swallowed a mouth full of water, which put her in trouble right from the start."

"Pretty easy with her turning off the alarms, not lighting up the backyard, and her first lap being so slow. It seems odd they wanted us to take out the CEO's wife instead of him," Rock said. He looked back at Dingo who nodded in agreement.

"How many of these are we going to do?" Dingo asked.

"I'm not sure—according to the Colonel they want exclusivity through the elimination of their only competitor. They're smart though…they're in no hurry, and they want every job to look like bad luck or an accident, so nothing comes back to them."

"Not that anyone would ever ask my opinion, I mean it seems smart not to take out the CEO of the only competitor right away," Thumper said.

"You're right mate, nobody cares about your opinion," Dingo said.

He smiled when Thumper gave him the finger.

ANDY RAY SLID OUT OF BED AROUND 5:30 A.M., MUD-dling around until he stepped on his treadmill. He hated getting up early to exercise, although he knew it would never happen otherwise. How his wife Janice managed to get up even earlier to go swimming every morning remained a mystery. The importance to him of an extra hour of sleep could not be overemphasized.

After an hour on the treadmill he went to the kitchen, not paying the darkness a second thought…initially. While getting the coffee machine started and deciding on which K-cup he wanted, various inconsistencies started registering in his head…the biggest being he had not heard Janice. On mornings when he did not see her right away, he usually heard her in the downstairs bathroom showering after her swim. The small kitchen television where she watched the morning news sat dark, and the coffee pot had not been turned on, both of which she normally did before he came downstairs.

Andy carried his coffee while walking through the house, then out back on the deck to glance at the pool. Not seeing Janice anywhere, he started to turn when a nagging feeling told him to move towards the pool. He ignored it initially, almost scolding himself given Janice's swimming prowess. He slid the door open and got one foot across the threshold when the nagging feeling emerged again.

Initially he headed for the pool at a normal pace until an eerie feeling crept throughout his whole being which caused him to slow. The flash of inconsistencies bolted through his brain and fear engulfed him. He momentarily froze, then sprinted, oblivious to the splashes of hot coffee hitting his hand. When Janice came into view lying at the bottom of the pool, he slung his cup and dove in, piercing the water about the time the cup shattered on the sand colored cement pool deck.

Andy struggled getting Janice out of the water, her dead weight more of an obstacle than he ever imagined. Inability to remember details from his one CPR training course nearly derailed him. Somehow, he started, screaming for help in the fifteen minutes he did CPR until exhaustion enveloped him. He reached under her, pulling her into him, rocking on his knees and telling her how much he loved her.

He kissed her on the forehead before he gently laid her back on the cement. He called 911 and then his parents.

An hour later Andy sat in the porch chair, a large towel over his shoulders, staring at the deputy coroner pushing his wife's gurney towards the gate. His father stepped outside to console him while his mother stayed in the house shooing her three young grandchildren away from the sliding glass door.

Andy could not remember dialing his parent's number and vaguely remembered someone asking him if he needed anyone notified. His father stood next to him rubbing his back as he buried his face in his hands.

What will I do without her? he thought, through uncontrolled sobbing.

CHAPTER TWO

———◆———

I had stayed in Albuquerque for five months having gone there to help my good friend Judge Mac Murtagh. A group of rogue cops had targeted him, expecting his compliance or people would die…which they did. The Chief of Police and his Deputy Commander orchestrated the Asian Killa's gang attack on Mac and me at his house. We had been tipped off, so we made it through unscathed. Mac's house, not so much. Days later I killed one of their rogue cops after he shot me in the shoulder nicking an artery…a close call for me. Weeks later, authorities arrested the police administrators after their rogue cops who had not died began cutting deals.

Not having anywhere else I needed to be, I figured staying in Albuquerque might be good should the FBI have more questions in the course of their investigation. I also wanted to stay near my surgeon while I continued physical therapy with Sam, my good friend and Mac's brother.

Despite those valid reasons, Celia Howard, and her daughter Brooke, had become my strongest motivation to stay. Their husband and father, Albuquerque Police Sergeant Peter Howard, had been the victim of rogue cops who gunned him down six months before I arrived. I had grown quite fond of them, secretly hoping for a chance at a relationship with Celia someday.

Preparing for my usual morning run, I received a text from Kenny Love, a former high-tech detective with whom I had worked.

It's 4:00 a.m. in Phoenix, he's never up this early, I thought.

Feeling uncomfortable, I called him instead of replying to his text.

"Hey," he answered solemnly.

"What's up? This isn't a normal time for you to be awake, much less texting."

"I just got a call from the corporate office...my boss's wife had a drowning accident...she's dead."

I expressed my sympathy although having been in a similar situation I knew words of solace often fell on deaf ears when close to the initial moment of shock.

Kenny received assignments directly from the CEO of his company in Virginia. Even though Kenny never said exactly, I got the impression they tracked cell phones in sensitive or highly classified environments.

"AJ, I know you planned on coming to Phoenix to play around with this equipment, except I really need to bow out. I'm guessing the funeral will be sometime this week... I'd like to catch the first flight to Virginia...to be there for my boss."

"I understand. Don't worry about it. It's not like I have a busy schedule, you can show it to me anytime. Go."

Normally Kenny would have taken the opportunity to get a few jabs in about me not having a work schedule... not this time. Silence.

"If you need anything ...."

"Thanks, we'll talk later." Kenny disconnected.

Retired Colonel Rich Harbaugh left the Army disillusioned after the Gulf War. Along with many others, Harbaugh believed after defeating Saddam Hussein the military should have continued its march into other Middle East territories while the United States and its allies had the fighting forces in their favor.

After years of commanding mercenaries in foreign countries, he now spent time consulting, even becoming a guest expert on one of the national television news agencies. Harbaugh had come across many people who lost a loved one to violence in America where justice had not been done. The more he researched cold case homicides the more frustrated he became.

Harbaugh felt police chiefs, sheriffs and prosecutors across America had become so concerned about image they no longer legitimately cared about dealing with the dirt bags in society. Such lack of strength to defend the good people of America mirrored his reasoning for retiring from the Army.

Terrorist attacks on American soil brought about a clarity of purpose for him, understanding they would draw military and law enforcement resources for the foreseeable future. In his mind there would be an even greater number of Americans not receiving justice after the death of a loved one. He recalled the Clint Eastwood movie, Magnum Force, which dealt with cops killing people deemed bad for society. Even though he enjoyed Eastwood as Dirty Harry, Harbaugh quietly admired the young cops, who in his mind took bold steps to do their part to help society.

Harbaugh began searching for the personnel to

quietly step in and put a stop to weak governmental leaders failing to help good citizens. In less than one year he laid the foundation to what would become his personal mission to do the deeds others in law enforcement appeared afraid to do.

He named his business PIs knowing the implication of private investigators would be what the average person would presume, and hopefully the government, too. To add to the cover-up, Harbaugh employed two private investigators located in a small office in New York. Behind the scenes he put together a different team of PIs, private insurgents made up of former cops who despised soft leadership or had been let go for their transgressions.

The private insurgents side currently employed eight men and one woman, ready to tackle any mission Harbaugh gave them. He believed they each possessed the skills and attitudes to be killing machines with little conscience…if any. Only two previous employees could not stomach what Harbaugh wanted them to do. After implying they might tell authorities both ended up becoming fish food in the Atlantic.

While Harbaugh ran the insurgent business out of his home in upstate New York, those paying him dictated the location of the action, and few assignments had been turned down. The price per assignment had become steep over the years based on Harbaugh's employees being highly successful.

Success led to a better lifestyle for Harbaugh who compensated his employees well. For years Harbaugh turned down people willing to pay exorbitant amounts for unsavory, immoral jobs. In less than ten years, what started out to be the quasi-moral helping of victims receive justice slowly caved to greed…and contracts for hire.

CHAPTER THREE

Harbaugh had no expectations after receiving the initial call from a person at DALL Industries since countless contacts backed out after the first meeting. Over time he came to realize the lack of compatibility between people wanting someone dead and their willingness to pay for it to happen…except for those like Ava Lloyd.

He sat in his office reflecting on his first meeting with Ava before calling her with an update on the completion of phase one.

TWO MONTHS EARLIER, HARBAUGH HAD AGREED WITH the male caller's request to a face-to-face meeting in Virginia. Ten days later Harbaugh parked in the Denny's lot in Fredericksburg, Virginia. He shook his head, never understanding why people often wanted to meet at a restaurant under the belief it would not draw attention, when not eating what they ordered brought about the exact attention they wanted to avoid. Harbaugh had no issue with eating while discussing the demise of another human being, nor did he have a problem accepting a free meal.

Harbaugh went inside and hesitated when he saw a woman sitting alone in the corner booth. He started towards her when she waived him over with her index finger.

"Colonel, sit please," she said, "I'm Ava Lloyd, Danny's wife."

Harbaugh started to extend his hand, withdrawing it when she looked down at it and withdrew hers.

Sitting, he said, "Like I told the man I spoke with on the phone, Danny I presume, we never use the M word or the K word. Do you understand?"

Ava refrained from the words murder and kill, so she nodded, allowing the assessment of each other to begin. At first blush she looked to be late thirties, until he noticed the vanity work done on her face. Her dark blue Bottega suit spoke of money beyond average professional attire worn in the area. Her makeup and lipstick accented her blonde shoulder length hair, whereas the numerous diamonds only flaunted her status…out of place in his opinion for breakfast at Denny's.

The mid-morning lull between breakfast and lunch crowds provided the opportunity to talk privately, except for occasional service from the waitress. Harbaugh began eating while he watched Ava use her fork to play with the eggs as she contemplated how to proceed.

"You have a nice little vetting process," she said.

He reflected on her comment for a second.

"What do you mean?"

"It took me the better part of three months to actually locate you. You seemed to be a nameless person who many believed didn't really exist. The deeper I dug, those I spoke to who you've done work for, at least I think you have, became reticent to discuss anything about you. My guess is everyone is afraid of a squealer considering all of you have a great deal to lose…if discovered, of course."

"These people you think I've done work for, how did you come across them?"

Ava sat a little straighter with a self-righteous smile.

"We didn't get to where we're at by always playing nice and not hedging our bets," she said, her fingertips moving up to play with her diamond necklace.

The look on her face said she expected him to delve deeper into how well off she and Danny might be. He had no desire to give her the opportunity to flaunt her status again.

"So, back to finding me …?"

Her smile faded with the realization he did not care.

"Well, someone must have trusted me, although I have no idea who. I got a letter in the mail with your information. Nothing else. It looked like one of those kidnap for ransom letters you see on TV where words appeared cut out of some magazine and pasted on a sheet of printer paper. No return address and I presumed clean of any forensic evidence. To be safe I shredded it in case you wanted to know."

Harbaugh paused, staring briefly before he loaded another bite on his fork.

"Are you always this…this quiet?"

He knew she wanted to say "rude," which would have been somewhat accurate. A certain enjoyment existed in making the rich uncomfortable for a bit. He decided he had said enough.

"Yes, actually I am, Mrs. Lloyd."

"Ava, please. Mrs. sounds too old."

He nodded once.

"Look, Ava, I come to a meeting like this presuming you have an agenda. You know what my company does, what we charge, and I would prefer we get this over with in a timely manner. I mean, let's be honest, this is not a restaurant you frequent or feel comfortable in. So, idle chit-chat only drags out your uneasiness."

For the first time since he arrived Ava relaxed her shoulders and sat back, sipping her coffee.

"Very astute, Colonel." She paused to take another sip before she continued. "Let's clear up a few things, shall we. Being the face of the company, my husband Danny perceived being seen with you could be too great of a risk for him. From this point forward all contact will only be with me. To put your mind at ease, or rather mine, I slipped the restaurant manager enough money to guarantee our privacy in this God forsaken corner for two hours."

Harbaugh looked around before nodding.

"I do have one question for you, Colonel," she said with a stoic face, her eyes focused on his. "Do we get any kind of a cut rate for multiples?"

"Now I know why you're well-off," he said trying to make a joke, to which she didn't flinch. "I'm not sure how many we're talking about. I'll consider it contingent on my hearing exactly what it is you're looking for us to do. The first two are full price. The third and fourth will be ten thousand less. The rest are back to full price, and nothing beyond six months."

"Fair enough. Let's get started."

Harbaugh wiped his mouth, slid his plate to the edge then pulled out his notepad and pen.

The waitress walked up and grabbed his empty plate, her eyes scrunching when Ava slid her plate full of food over without making eye contact.

Once the girl departed Ava said, "A-Ray Corporation is our only competitor in a niche market selling to …."

Harbaugh raised his hand to stop her. "I don't really care about your niche market. All I care about is what you want from us."

Ava tilted her head and stared through squinted eyes. People seldom cut her off, and those who did generally received her wrath. The lack of groups available like PIs along the east coast left her biting her tongue.

"Very well. Moving on, what I want, what we want, is for you to create a disruption in A-Ray hobbling them enough we will have won the big contracts before they can sufficiently recover."

"Go on."

"So, it seems like the obvious solution would be to eliminate the CEO, Andy Ray, alternatively...I kind of think you should try something else."

Harbaugh saw an evil look in Ava's eyes and a grin to go along with it. Despite the signs, hair on the back of his neck standing and his gut telling him to make a break for it, the potential profit made him nod for her to continue. Harbaugh had become accustomed to a lifestyle only large volumes of money could provide.

"Maybe if Andy's wife is no longer in the picture he would mentally check out for a while, you know, consumed with their young children's overall well-being."

The evil in Ava's eyes had been confirmed. Oddly, Ava's personal reasons for wanting Janice Ray dead, albeit unknown to him, exposed an opportunity for Harbaugh to pounce. He set his pen on the pad and sat back, pausing for effect.

"Mrs. Lloyd," he began, his formality a means of showing control, "to accomplish what you want eliminates any possibility for a *cut rate* as you put it. Disposing of an innocent mother of young children does not sit well with me, nor will it sit well with any of my personnel, so if you insist we start with her I will double our normal fee for her. Any beyond her are subject to the full fee or more if I deem them to be equally immoral to that of disposing of Mrs. Ray."

Though Ava tried to act flustered, the slight lift of her cheeks gave away her joy in his willingness to fulfill her request. Upon the completion of her plan the one hundred fifty thousand fee for Janice and the subsequent seventy-five thousand fees for the others would have been well worth it.

When she felt she had adequately feigned enough surprise Ava told Harbaugh to start with Janice Ray, then to do three others of his choice within the A-Ray Corporation.

"When you're done with those, we will meet again so I," she hesitated, clearing her throat, "so Danny and I can tell you how we want to wrap up the deal."

Walking to his car Harbaugh could not stop thinking about nearly four hundred thousand dollars, not counting wrapping it up which could bring in another seventy-five thousand at a minimum. For the kind of money the Lloyd's seemed willing to pay, Harbaugh could sidestep his personal disdain for Ava.

CHAPTER FOUR

———◆———

As the CFO of A-Ray Corporation, one of only two companies trying to fill the void in a unique alcove of the technology industry, Laird Spencer's days often amounted to long and arduous hours and he looked forward to Fridays. The CEO, Andy Ray, understood the psychological benefit to casual Fridays, something Laird used to his advantage.

Laird stood five foot ten, appeared to stay in shape, and liked showing it off on Monday through Thursday in his expertly tailored suits. On casual Fridays he rose earlier to go for a twenty-five-mile bike ride before work. His long rides ended at A-Ray where he always had a clean pair of knockoff Gucci jeans hanging in his locker along with accessories. He would shower, don his casual clothes, grab coffee and head to his office.

With Andy taking time off after the death of his wife, Laird had been working longer days to maintain the status quo. He had difficulty shutting his brain off at night since Janice's drowning, desperately wanting things to run smoothly at work so Andy could focus on his family. Craving stress relief, he planned a shorter fifteen-mile ride this Friday.

Laird got up an hour before his alarm, killing time making coffee and checking emails. He left the house at his normal 4:30 a.m. without waking his wife and kids. He enjoyed the peace in the beginning of his Friday rides before having to be mindful of the early morning Quantico commuters. Laird never feared getting hit at those early times with all his head-to-toe reflective attire and his bike well equipped with appropriate lighting. He punched in the code on the garage keypad then mounted his bike.

The initial half a mile through residential areas would reach Monument Drive bordering the golf course until hitting the main route, Courthouse Road. Despite never encountering a car at the T-intersection at such an early hour Laird slowed to a coast, darting a precautionary glance. Not seeing headlights, he began to pedal again roughly twenty feet before the intersection.

Laird failed to see the dark F150 truck idling with the lights off, parked backward along the curb to his right, nor did he see it starting to creep forward. He completed three revolutions of his pedals, starting his lean into the left turn when something struck the rear tire. The impact sent him flying to the pavement, his left hand reflexively extended to break his fall. Instead, both bones in his wrist fractured and the ulna punctured through the skin simultaneously with his helmet bouncing off the asphalt. The low impact had not killed him, his helmet preventing a major head injury as advertised. The intense pain in his wrist initially grasped Laird's attention, somewhat giving way to his need to see what hit him. He pushed the bike off with his feet and rolled onto his right side and sat up.

His mind registered the constant low hum of an idling engine, the smell of engine exhaust replacing the fresh morning air. The front of a stopped truck without headlights a few feet beyond his bike drew his eyes in. Looking above the grill he saw the silhouettes of two people in the truck, neither making a move to get out. Laird began groping for the bag with his cell phone attached to the rear of his bike seat. He grasped the zipper at the same time his peripheral vision caught the truck moving toward him. The grill struck his outstretched right hand a split second before the left front tire crushed his torso.

The driver let the truck creep forward until the rear tire climbed on Laird's chest then dropped off, coasting down the street another forty feet. Both men focused on their side mirrors hoping for no movement from the cyclist. If necessary, they could back up to do it again, although they knew it would then look like a definite homicide. They waited twenty seconds, convinced they had not been seen after no movement or witnesses rushed to the cyclist's aid. The men fist bumped as the vehicle accelerated, the driver turning on the headlights once up to speed.

Laird's internal injuries would later be deemed massive. His wide-open eyes had locked onto the dark sky, unblinking for the twenty-five minutes he laid in the intersection before being discovered.

NICKNAMES USUALLY CAME ABOUT NATURALLY FOR COPS. Ben Rockford's had been Rock since his academy days in Pennsylvania. Nobody at PIs, except for Harbaugh, ever knew Dingo's real name. Being considered a dog for sleeping with hordes of women and the hint of his Australian accent, he acquired the nickname back in his early twenties.

Rock and Dingo preferred killing people with stolen handguns then tossing them in some river or lake. Still, their training from police academy cadre in their past lives had been to follow orders without question, especially from a leader they respected. More exciting ways existed to kill people besides drowning a woman in her swimming pool and running over a guy on a bike, except for the bonus per kill the colonel offered above their regular pay made it hard to argue with not using a handgun.

The moderate commuter flow on I-95 of those hoping to avoid the soon to be bumper-to-bumper traffic replaced the minimal side road traffic. Rock went northbound on the Interstate, obeying all laws and staying with the flow of traffic. He took the Garrisonville Road exit and turned left to go to the car wash they had scouted out earlier in the week. The only video cameras had been directed at the coin machines for each of the eight bays. In any case, both men wore hats and plain dark hoodies with no logos.

Rock began putting quarters in the machine while Dingo pulled up the front passenger floor mat to retrieve the trucks two original plates. They had not wanted to risk a police officer seeing two different plates and they knew most officers would not stop them for a single infraction of a missing front plate. Dingo went to the rear to remove the stolen plate from an F-150 manufactured in the same year, replacing it with the truck's original rear plate. While Rock began washing the back of the truck Dingo moved to put on the front plate.

Rock chose to operate the hose knowing he had the most patience of the two. He wanted to make sure the undercarriage had no evidence left behind, so Dingo added quarters on two different occasions despite considering it overkill in his mind. When Rock finished Dingo slid the stolen plate under the floor mat while they let the truck drip dry before getting in.

They drove towards the Interstate and the road changed to Washington Drive after they crossed under the highway. Knowing the route to the Aquia Harbour Marina from previous recon, Rock headed there to get rid of the stolen plate knowing only a few people would be walking around in the early morning hour. Dingo replaced his hoodie and boonie hat with a pulled-up collar on a polo shirt to help him fit in before he made his way into the area. When he felt comfortable, he slid the plate from the back of his waistband and into the water in under three seconds.

The drive to the junkyard on the southeast side of the Aquia Harbour Golf Course took almost twenty minutes. Despite the empty parking lot, they saw a man inside behind the counter.

Apparently, nobody gets up early to find parts for their car, Rock thought.

Colonel Harbaugh had previous dealings with Dutch, the owner of the junkyard, who cared more about easy money than he did about what illegalities may transpire with the cars he let the colonel's employees rent.

After wiping down the inside of the truck, the handles and the license plates Rock went inside while Dingo used a burner phone to call their ride.

"You boys are here early," Dutch said.

"It's always best to do what we do when there are minimal witnesses, or when there are so many people nobody knows you're there."

"I hope you got done what you needed. Personally, I think being a PI waiting for some guy to be seen with his mistress so you can snap a couple photos would be boring."

Rock figured what Dutch didn't know wouldn't hurt him. He appreciated Dutch doing what they told him to do without asking questions, unlike other junkyard owners they used in other states.

Handing Dutch the keys, he said, "You might want to hide the truck for a little while."

"Not a problem. I'll put it inside the fence, take off a couple tires, throw a couple of greasy handprints on it to make it look like it's been there a while. Nobody will give it a serious look."

"Has Colonel Harbaugh taken care of the details?" asked Rock.

"Yep. He always pays up front. Makes it easy to trust you guys."

"We appreciate it, Dutch. We'll be in the area for a few more weeks so we may need to borrow something else. The Colonel will let you know."

"Not a problem. Give me twenty-four hours' notice if you can."

"Will do. Thanks again."

Rock headed for the door.

Dingo knew Rock hated sitting in the back seat. He had already decided not to give up the front seat this time and flashed a broad grin at Rock. To Dingo's surprise, Rock got in the back without saying a word.

"Where to?" Thumper, their driver, asked.

"Wherever Dingo wants to go for breakfast. I'm buying."

"Dang, I ought to take the front seat more often," Dingo said.

"Yeah, right. Enjoy it while you got it."

CHAPTER FIVE

———— ••• ————

Kenny got in touch with me when he arrived in Virginia, yet I had not heard from him since. I spent the time helping Sam and Mac try to repair the damage done to Mac's house from the Asian Killa's drive-by attack months before.

Kenny called at 9 p.m. on Friday, the night before Janice Ray's funeral. I could hear the stress in his undulating pitch, a discernable nervousness in his quick speech.

"Kenny, what's going on? Something's wrong, I can tell."

The silence lasted a good thirty seconds before he said he would call me back, telling me to answer even if I did not recognize the number. I had been around Kenny long enough to know he always had a stash of burner phones for times like these.

Less than ten minutes later I put his call on speaker.

"You alone?" Kenny asked.

"No, Mac is here and I'm on speaker. You remember me telling you about Mac; he's the retired judge I'm staying with in Albuquerque."

"Yes. Hello, Your Honor."

"Hi Kenny. Please, call me Mac."

"Nobody else is there?"

"No, only us. Kenny, what's up man?"

"Dude, you're not going to believe this…the CFO of the

company rides his bike to and from work...he died this morning in a hit and run."

I shot a look over at Mac whose wide eyes mirrored how I felt. In our careers we had seen a few coincidental deaths in the same company within days of each other being legitimate bad luck...although nothing close to the number turning out to be foul play.

Even though I knew the answer, I asked, "Is something bothering you about the two deaths being so close together you're not telling us?"

"Exactly. Nobody here seems to agree with me...except for my east coast counterpart Ric, who used to do a lot of highly classified missions for the military. He pretty much doesn't trust anyone though, so I'm not sure how much weight to give his support."

I often tried to think from a defense attorney's point of view forcing me to look for evidence-based reasons when something does not look right instead of relying solely on my gut instincts.

"Hit and runs happen all the time, especially in high traffic areas like where you are. We'd need a whole lot more to really justify something isn't lining up."

Kenny and I knew each other well enough he would not take offense to my not jumping on board with him right away. I understood he did not pause out of anger, he needed time to formulate his thoughts before he spoke.

"I agree, so here's why Ric and I are concerned. Friday's are casual at the office, meaning the CFO usually gets up earlier to go for a long ride, arrives to work slightly later than normal, and showers there. The rest of the week he rides straight from home to work in his suit. Probably around 5 a.m. he got hit in a residential area near a plush golf course where the speeds of vehicles there would likely be around fifteen to twenty. He had pretty extensive damage to his bike...and he had been run over."

I raised my eyebrows when I looked at Mac who nodded.

"Plus, my boss's wife...Dude...she's like an accomplished swimmer, trust me. It took some serious schmoozing before I got the ME who examined her and signed the death certificate to tell me it appeared to be a straightforward drowning accident...except for a faint red mark on one of her ankles. Not enough for the ME to definitively say foul play, so he signed off on it. Here's the kicker, it took him two days, and he still doesn't act convinced."

"Okay, you've piqued our interest, only you're still going to need to help us out here. You've never really told me what your company does. Is it highly sought after? How competitive is the market for whatever they do? I mean, why would two people be killed if it's some run of the mill company?"

"I can't explain in detail what it is we do, a lot of it is highly classified. Suffice it to say there used to be one major company out of Texas having the attention of law enforcement and military buyers for what we do. The Texas company bowed out about two years ago and we picked up where they left off, except now there is another company we are competing against. To say there are billions of dollars to be had is a conservative statement."

People have killed for way less, I thought.

My brain flashed back to a homicide I worked where a rich guy had the car repair owner killed for bilking him out of three hundred dollars. Greed can kick in regardless of a dollar amount. Typically the difficulty in proving murder increases right along with the payoff amount considering the expertise of the killer increases.

"This may sound crazy," Mac said, "but isn't billions of dollars enough to share between two companies? I would almost think a third party would want in on some of the action before your opposition would kill their sole competition and jeopardize everything."

"Not crazy at all, Mac. I do know our boss has always felt there's enough room in the market for both companies to become quite wealthy. He's never said the other company needs to be eliminated. The strange part is, when Ric did some digging, he heard the same thing about the other CEO. It's like they both realized regardless of each other they stood a good chance of becoming filthy stinking rich."

"It's possible the other CEO is sincere," I said. "It's also every bit as likely he didn't get to where he is without knowing how to act sincere while being ready to do something underhanded. Not saying he did so here, although …."

Despite the fact Kenny agreed with me, I heard exhaustion in his voice. I decided we could talk more in depth once they all made it through the funeral in the morning. I wished him luck before he disconnected.

"You're going out there, aren't you?" Mac asked.

I tilted my head and hesitated when I looked at him.

"You know it's true, so admit it."

"Alright, yes. The way I see it if it's nothing I should be back here in less than a week. If it turns out to be something, hopefully I can help prevent a third person in the company from dying."

"And Celia? How you going to break the news to her?"

"Helping Kenny find some criminals if they exist seems easy compared to telling her what I'm doing. Sometimes I think it would be best for Celia and Brooke if I left the picture so they could move on without having to worry about another important person in their lives getting killed."

"Something tells me there's a *but* in there."

I hesitated, admiring Mac's ability to read me so well.

"I don't want to throw away the possibility of us being a family either."

"Your sense of loyalty to others in need is admirable, AJ. What you have to ask yourself is, is it the right thing if it means not having a family of your own considering the woman you love, at least I think you love her, is afraid you might end up dead and she can't face that again."

We both knew Mac nailed it. Still, I could not quite bring myself to throw in the towel. Instead, I did the next best thing…I left the room despite hearing my former friend and police psychologist, Dr. P, saying inside my head, "Avoidance is never the answer."

CHAPTER SIX

I called Celia about going over to her house after Brooke finished with gymnastics. When I saw them come around the corner I got out of my car and walked toward the driveway carrying a large pizza.

Brooke walked around the back of the car with her backpack draped over her shoulder and smiled as she gave me a quick hug.

"You trying to suck up with the pizza? Mom's nervous about you wanting to talk to her," she whispered before Celia got out of her car.

Brooke rolled her eyes before taking the pizza and running for the front door.

A perceptive girl with a good sense of humor, I marveled at Brooke's being so relaxed with everything, including me. She had been through a lot, yet seldom did I see tension.

"Hi, AJ," Celia said, closing the car door.

I went to her and we hugged a typical good to see you hug. I sensed she too wanted a relationship beyond friends, though I also sensed something holding her back, so I never pushed for more.

No surprise Brooke had nailed it…Celia had a nervousness about her. Heading for the door without another word, I followed.

Once inside Celia went toward her bedroom. When the door shut Brooke raced into the kitchen, sliding on her socks into me.

"She's worried you're going to go off and do something dumb like put yourself in danger again," Brooke whispered.

As I reached for plates in the cupboard, I hesitated.

Brooke said, "You are…aren't you? I mean, I'm okay with it. The counselor I'm seeing, we've talked about all of this, so I get it."

I tilted my head to look at her, admiring her sharpness.

"What, just saying," she said, shrugging her shoulders.

"How'd you get to be so smart?"

"My counselor says I'm like my dad. If I have enough time to think about something where I can understand it, then I accept things without a bunch of emotion, unlike mom."

"Really?"

Such candidness from an eleven-year-old intrigued me.

"Yep. I don't want you to get shot again, or worse…but my counselor helped me to understand. She explained we're kind of alike because I really like gymnastics even though I might get hurt and you're always helping people who really need you, even though you might get hurt. She said you don't want to die; you just feel you need to do the right thing and make sure other people are okay. You're kind of a bad-ass, aren't you?"

I chuckled. "No, sweetie, I'm nowhere near. Navy Seals and Army Rangers, those people are bad-ass, they could run circles around me. All I try to do is the best I can with what little training I've had."

Closing the cupboard with plates in hand, I saw Celia in the doorway, leaning against the frame, a settled look on her face instead of the upset one I half-expected.

"Oh, hi," I said to clue Brooke in about her mom. "We have been having a nice little conversation."

"Yes, I heard. For the record, she's right, Brooke is a lot like her dad instead of all emotion like me."

I looked at Brooke who had not yet turned to look at her mom. She opened her eyes wide and did one of those coy little smiles only a little girl has, which made me laugh. Brooke chuckled, turning to give her mom a hug.

Eating dinner, we listened to Brooke tell us about all the girl drama with her friends at school. When she finished, she went off to her bedroom for homework and a shower.

The silence after Brooke's departure lasted for what felt like an eternity with Celia staring at her plate. When I reached for it to clear the table, she put her hand on top of mine and raised her eyes to look at me.

"The counselor and I have been talking about a lot of the same things."

Silence accompanied my raised eyebrows and prompted her to continue.

"I don't like the idea you are always willing to go put your life on the line for others…still, I realize it's selfish thinking on my part."

She paused long enough to take a deep breath before going on. "Look, AJ, my biggest concern has been how Brooke would handle it if something happened to you. The truth is my eleven-year-old daughter is much stronger than I believed. So…where is it you're going and what are you looking for?"

As Celia's last words came out, I saw a little thumbs up poke around the corner, bringing a smile to my face. When Celia saw my smile, she jumped up to scare Brooke who screamed and laughed all the way down the hall. I silently said a prayer of thanks for the way the evening had gone… surpassing anything I could have asked for.

I began to rinse the plates when I felt Celia's arms wrap around my waist, her head lying in the middle of my back. I sensed her saying *please be careful but I'm not going to hold you back.* Turning, I took her face in my hands, promising I would be careful. She laid her head on my chest turned away from the kitchen doorway where Brooke stood smiling and squeezed tightly. I winked and nodded for her to come participate in our hug.

When Brooke went to take her shower Celia and I sat at the table sipping coffee.

"To answer your question from earlier, I am going to Virginia. My buddy who used to be the high-tech guy in our detective bureau now works for a company based out of Virginia. I told you earlier in the week about the CEO's wife drowning in their backyard pool, well this morning the CFO died while riding his bike before work in a hit and run."

"Let me guess…you feel something is suspicious?"

"I'd be lying if I didn't say yes. If I'm right, maybe we can stop someone else from being killed. If I'm wrong, then I'm only out the cost of a flight out there."

"I'm hoping for the latter, of course. Still, if your suspicions are correct, please do everything in your power to come back to us. We've grown kind of fond of you."

"Careful now, talk like that might lead to you saying the L word," I said with a slight grin.

"You never know," she replied, a slight grin of her own. "And for the record, I'm not sure if you are a bad-ass like Brooke thinks, though I am sure your ass looks pretty good to me."

We both chuckled.

I loved our interactions throughout the evening, yet I could not shake the feeling she needed to tell me something. I chose not to push her, instead settling solely for the enjoyment of her company.

CHAPTER SEVEN

———◆———

Not knowing how long I would be gone I picked a flight to Ronald Reagan airport in the Washington D.C. area late on Sunday so I could spend time with Celia and Brooke at Brooke's gymnastics competition.

Kenny picked me up shortly after 9 p.m. Eastern and it took us quite a while to get past the Springfield interchange going south on I-95. The remainder of the drive took another forty-five minutes to his hotel near the company office. Most of the drive I sat quietly listening to Kenny talk about the sadness of seeing Andy and his kids at Janice's funeral.

At the hotel Kenny kicked off his shoes and flopped on a bed. My internal clock ran a couple hours behind his so I went out on the balcony right after I heard the low grinding gravely rumble preceding what would soon be all out snoring. I knew the time would give me a chance to text Celia and Brooke to see how the competition ended.

———

As a homicide investigator at Turlock Police Department I learned to function without sleep, like homicide investigators everywhere. After one of the suspects in a case I worked murdered my fiancé, sleep became short naps to avoid nightmares and haunted me for months.

Gradually I worked my way through it, although I never got beyond learning how to sleep for more than five hours with any consistency.

I used my run in the early morning hours to get a feel of the Stafford area. The drop in altitude from Albuquerque took away some of the strain allowing me to look around and take things in during my run.

I did not want to run past Andy and Janice's house figuring I could get a feel of everything when Kenny took me there to talk with Andy. Instead, I decided to run to the intersection Kenny had told me of where the CFO had been killed. During my approach, the stillness in the darkened early morning hours stood out.

I got to the area at roughly the same time in the morning the CFO had been killed and I'd only seen one newer SUV pass.

A golf course ran along one side of the road and two-story houses lined the other. The T-intersection where the accident took place appeared well lit and nothing occluded the three stop signs.

I stopped when I saw what looked like evidence from where the bike pedal initially dug into the pavement, along with blood evidence left near the gouges in the asphalt. I could picture the CFO approaching at roughly the same time of the morning, not seeing any lights coming from his right before he began to make the turn, and probably not coming to a stop himself. Seeing the evidence clearly showed the CFO had to have been struck on his right side, meaning the vehicle would have been in the wrong lane.

As a person who often ran in the early morning dark hours, I could not believe a regular bike rider at the same hours did not have my same beliefs…drivers never see you.

Regardless of the great number of drivers who are always observant, runners and riders feel like they must always be prepared for the one who doesn't.

Lying in wait, the driver sat in a darkened-out vehicle on the wrong side of the road, I thought.

I felt my suspicions turned out to be confirmed when I looked past the intersection at the first house on the right at the corner. Three newer looking vehicles sat in the driveway, two side-by-side and one behind them...nothing parked along the curb in front of the house, or the next one.

People are creatures of habit. I'd bet their cars sat in the same spots at this time last Friday.

WHEN I WALKED IN THE HOTEL ROOM, I SAW THE BATH-room door closed and could hear Kenny brushing his teeth. I pounded on the door hoping to scare him, or at least make him think I needed in.

"Always wanting something I possess, aren't you," Kenny mumbled. He opened the door, his toothbrush in his mouth and a huge grin allowing white bubbly saliva to show in the corners. Holding up his index finger he said, "Almost done," catching the saliva before it made it all the way down his chin.

"Ai, yai, yai," I said, shaking my head.

I settled in one of the chairs on the balcony, thinking back to what I saw at the intersection.

Stepping onto the balcony, Kenny said, "I'm hungry. Hurry it up. I know this little hole-in-the-wall diner...you'll love it. It's a lot like the one at the Chandler airport."

I did not move, instead thinking of our good friend and former detective, Seth, who always teased Kenny the world did not revolve around him, despite Kenny's belief it should. I stared off in the distance for another ten seconds for effect.

"Went to the intersection where your CFO got killed."

"Really," Kenny said, his eyebrows raised. "And?"

I paused another ten seconds for fun before I said, "No way to prove this conclusively…I could feel the vehicle ambushed him, which I believe had to be parked idling on the wrong side of the road in front of the corner house… waiting for him. Your CFO probably had a lot on his mind given the situation with the boss' wife, and his instincts to ride defensively had yet to reach full capacity, especially since he had not even made it out of the residential area. An experienced rider like him would know to look for head-lights, when he didn't see any his mind likely reverted back to all the work stuff on his plate. A darkened-out vehicle on the wrong side of the road would be the last thing on his mind so early in the morning."

Kenny smiled.

"What's that for?"

"I know you. When you start saying you feel someone got 'ambushed,' I know you're bought in."

"It's one feeling, nothing more. I'm curious, not bought in."

Kenny laughed as he walked away.

"Yeah right!"

Buying a plane ticket to go help my friend dig a little deeper into the tragedies befalling his company spoke of my support. Feeling like the CFO had been blindsided at o-dark-thirty less than a mile from his house in a residential neighborhood caused the hair on the back of my neck to stand. We both knew Kenny nailed it.

I'm in!

CHAPTER EIGHT

K enny took me to breakfast two blocks off the main road in a corner house turned into a small restaurant. He parked on the street since the parking lot in what used to be the backyard lacked open spots. Walking to the front we saw a well-manicured lawn with a wooden sign painted in patriotic colors and the name The Nook in large scrolled white letters, while underneath in small block letters it said Breakfast Only.

On the drive over Kenny described Tom and Luci, the owners, as an older couple who retired from their corporate positions and followed their dream of a small restaurant. Kenny being Kenny, it did not take long for him to become friends with them.

Apparently, some scamming went on when they first opened and served varying meals throughout the day and early evening, which meant a much bigger staff. Kenny offered his services, identifying three employees skimming within a week of setting up his high-tech equipment.

Kenny always had an opinion at the ready, so when they asked his guidance about what they should do, he said since both had decent corporate retirements he wondered why they didn't limit the hours to the one meal they liked serving best. In less than a month they transitioned to Breakfast Only, closed at 1 p.m., dropped the staff down to those they truly trusted, and Kenny had never paid for a meal there since.

When we stepped inside Luci ventured toward us with a big smile.

"Hi sweetie," she said, kissing Kenny on the cheek. "You must be AJ," extending her hand.

She had a firm grip, her eye contact never breaking, important features in the corporate world where first impressions often lasted indefinitely.

"Yes. I feel like I already know you and Tom with all Kenny has told me. I'm honored to be a guest in your restaurant."

Luci smiled as her grip relaxed. Patting the back of my hand with her free hand she said, "A friend of Kenny's is a friend of ours."

She turned and said over her shoulder, "C'mon sweetie, your table in the back is ready. I know you like your privacy."

I looked at Kenny and mouthed "Your table," to which he grinned, his head bobbing side-to-side, seemingly proud of himself. I flicked my left hand twice to get him moving and shook my head at his standing taller like he had importance.

If Seth could only see Kenny now.

The table sat diagonally with one corner almost touching the wall, directly opposite the entrance. The abnormal positioning allowed both of us to sit somewhat facing the door, something I believed Kenny had them do for his benefit.

"Kenny, if it's okay I think I have Tom convinced to talk with you about something. If you have the time?"

"Absolutely, anything for you two," Kenny said.

The corners of Luci's lips turned up in appreciation. She

patted his shoulder once then took off, heading straight to the coffee machines and grabbing a pot along with two heavy pure white mugs.

She returned, poured my coffee, and said to Kenny, "I'll get your tea in a second."

"They don't have menus here?"

"Of course, they do," he said defensively. "I told her the last time I visited if you came out, you would have the same breakfast I have. You always follow my lead, hell, you can't even think for yourself."

I tilted my head and raised my eyebrows giving him my *you're full of crap* stare. He started laughing, got up and went to greet people he apparently knew at three different tables while I sat drinking my first cup of coffee.

Seconds after Kenny returned Tom and Luci walked up to the table. Luci put Kenny's tea and extra hot water down before she looked at Tom and said, "Go ahead, they won't think you're stupid. Tell them."

Tom pointed at one of the chairs with his open palm, looking at Kenny for approval before he sat. Kenny nodded and Tom put his hand on the back of the chair, looking at Luci, who patted him on the shoulder. Tom sat while Luci went to get a coffee pot and a cup for Tom.

I thanked Luci before she walked away figuring we might be awhile, considering I sensed she would not put our food order in until Tom finished talking with us.

Tom's discomfort seemed genuine as he fidgeted with his cup, unable to look Kenny in the eye for long. Not having any idea what he wanted to talk about, neither of us said a word to prevent leading him, something experienced investigators like us knew to be a good tactic.

Finally, Tom said, "I overheard something the other day

I didn't pay much attention to at first…until I read in the paper about your CFO being killed."

Tom recognized our interest in what he had to say, helping him to relax a little. He winked at Luci for being correct about us not looking down on him.

"I happened to be sitting over at the table in the corner," leaning his head to the left, "working on scheduling, and three guys sat two tables away in front of the big window. At the time we did not have many customers so I could overhear some of what they talked about."

It took Tom a couple of seconds to continue after realizing we had no intention of asking any questions right then.

"This happened last Friday morning, about 7:30 a.m., and they had already finished eating when I sat down to start working. They probably only had one more cup of coffee before they took off."

I took a sip of coffee and sat back.

"In this area you hear lots of talk. Most of the time you dismiss it knowing the area is swamped with federal law enforcement, local law enforcement, people coming from all over to do training at Quantico, not to mention lots of military personnel. You generally figure people are talking about training exercises and you kind of get numb to it."

We nodded, easily able to picture it happening.

"The youngest guy sitting next to the window caught my attention when he said something like, 'Now that the bicyclist is gone, who do you think the boss wants to go after next?' Right away one of the two admonished him with a couple of expletives for talking so loudly. It sounded like the one sitting next to him…he had an accent, foreign, you know?"

Kenny did a quick glance at me, probably thinking the same thing about a bicyclist and the inference of going after someone else. We looked at Tom waiting for more.

"Now I know this may be nothing…the next day I knew you planned on going to the funeral for your boss's wife, and when I read the morning paper I saw an article about a bicyclist being killed in a hit and run. Later in the article it mentions he worked for your same company, along with the tragedy of the CEO's wife dying earlier in the week. To be honest with you, it made the hair on the back of my neck stand as I recalled those guys the day before."

"Have they been in since last Friday?" I asked.

"No. I've been watching closely; in case they did I planned on getting a description of their car."

"Do you think you could identify them again if you saw a picture of them?" Kenny asked.

"Pretty sure. Well, maybe not the guy facing away from me, the other two I could, I think."

"It's probably nothing, Tom," I lied, "thanks for sharing it with us. If they do show up again call Kenny, if we are nearby, we will swing over this way."

Tom apologized for inconveniencing us, relaxing some after we both assured him he did the right thing.

CHAPTER NINE

———◆———

Danny Lloyd's tranquility on the back porch shattered when Ava burst through the door telling him about her day and of all the things she planned on doing.

"When I finish a round of golf with the girls, I thought I might sneak in a massage. What do you think?"

Ava broke the five seconds of silence. "Uh, I'm waiting."

"Oh, sorry. Sure, whatever."

"What are you so down in the dumps about?"

"I'm thinking of Andy and his kids. I feel bad for him."

Opening Fully Operational Military Communications (FOMC), another one of his businesses under the DALL Industries umbrella, went smoothly for Danny, a long-time entrepreneur. DALL Industries began shortly after Danny and Ava married over twenty years ago. Ava thought they should mix the first letter of their first names and the LL from Lloyd. At the time he took pleasure in Ava wanting to be part of their new adventures—now he wished she hadn't.

"Why do you feel so bad for him? I mean he is our competitor for heaven's sake."

Ired, Danny slowly turned his head to stare at her for several seconds after her comment. He took a deep breath to compose himself.

"Andy got into this industry six months before us. When he heard we might be opening F-O-M-C *he* called me, even took me to lunch. He said what we wanted to do sounded great. Andy said the money available in this industry would be enough for both of us and if we played our cards right, we could work together without stepping on each other. He was, and still is, a great guy…apparently you forgot."

"I'm sorry dear, you're right. Forgive me," she said with little in her tone to validate whether she really cared if he did or not. "I've never taken to him or…or …"

"Janice."

"Yes, Janice, thank you dear. They never seemed to like me being around, which is why I haven't attended any of the dinners you three have gone to in the last few months."

What a surprise, you're a bitch compared to Janice, he thought.

He stood, walking to the door. "I have to go, I have a meeting in forty-five minutes," he lied.

When she thought she heard his car leaving she pulled out her cell to call one of the girls in her foursome.

"Yes, dear. Something is coming up soon and I won't be able to make the round of golf today. I promise I'll be there Wednesday."

She disconnected then punched in another number. "Meet me at the hotel. I'm horny and he's been all poor, poor pitiful meish, for days. Besides, he never takes care of me like you do. I'll be there in thirty minutes." She hung up before Keith Dignam could say anything about how he barely got to the office and question her about him slipping out this early unnoticed. She did not care. She owned the company, and no one would fire him until she approved it.

Ava loved the irony of Colonel Harbaugh choosing to take out Andy's CFO while she happened to personally be using Keith, Danny's CFO.

WE WAITED FOR TOM TO DO WHAT MOST NERVOUS PEOPLE do, look over his shoulder. Once Tom went about his business we began.

"Are you convinced yet?" Kenny asked.

"Three guys, one with a foreign accent, only four days after your CEO's wife…yeah, I'm pretty well there."

"Why Janice, then Laird? It doesn't make sense."

Reflecting on it for a second I asked, "What will this do to the company? I mean, is it enough to make it go belly up?"

Without hesitation Kenny said, "No, no way. Andy's parents live in the area, so he has enough people to help him on the personal front. And, he trusts his board so I'm sure he'll be able to continue without Laird. There will definitely be a hiccup until they replace him, on the other hand I can't imagine someone on the board doesn't know a good replacement who can hit the ground running."

"Okay, so what do you think …" I saw Luci heading our way with our breakfast, "the Nationals chances are in their game today."

Kenny looked at me strange until Luci entered his peripheral vision.

"Fifty-fifty. We should catch one of their games while you're here," he said.

"That's a great idea boys, go catch a little baseball and relax. First you need to have a go at this breakfast so you can have a good start to your day. Eat up," Luci ordered.

When she got out of earshot, I finished my question, "What do you think the chances are there's a neutral party out there who wants in on the action, so they are eliminating one of the two players in the industry?"

Kenny did not think about it long. "I'd say pretty slim. If they tried to take out a little of both companies so one of them would fold and then they could slide in, maybe. Realistically, how would you choose one company over the other to start killing personnel so they would fold?"

"Okay, using that logic, who stands to gain the most from your company being eliminated?"

"F-O-M-C, Danny Lloyd's company."

"How adamant is Andy that Danny Lloyd would not have anything to do with it?"

"Very, for several reasons. He says they are friends. Danny is likely wealthier than Andy already, and Andy has been in business long enough to spot people with ulterior motives, which he doesn't believe Danny has."

"You ever met Danny?" I asked, trusting Kenny would have a good assessment if he had.

"No. When I come to Virginia it's to help the tech guys solve problems through my insight into what I'm experiencing when demoing the product to law enforcement agencies. I usually have dinner once with Andy and Janice at their house, I never deal with the suits, not even Laird. Something tells me you want to meet Danny."

"You learn fast, Grasshopper," I joked.

Kenny gave me the finger off to the side so no one else would see it…he thought.

"Kenny, knock it off," Luci barked. She approached the table with a fresh pot of coffee and more hot water, although Kenny only noticed the scolding stare.

As a light skin-toned black man Kenny's face did not hit the same red on a color chart mine would have, nonetheless his cheeks changed color. I had seen the identical look on his face before when his wife Mary used the same tone.

Luci and I laughed while Kenny tried to regain composure.

I gave Kenny time to recover and start eating his breakfast.

"What about meeting Andy this morning, do you think he's up to it?"

"Pretty sure we can. I spoke with him yesterday before I went to get you at the airport. I told him about you and said we would like to talk with him. He seemed good with it. Let me text him."

While Kenny started the text, I looked at the two tables Tom spoke of and decided the odds of him accurately hearing bits of the conversation with the tables being relatively close and few customers seemed decent. Thinking about the one man's comment about *who is next* after the bicyclist gave me an eerie feeling.

To make matters worse the eerie feeling had a twin. The hair on my neck rose while thinking of Kenny and I being thousands of miles from our normal domains, neither having any authority as former detectives. Added to it, nobody in law enforcement in the area had pieced the puzzle together so far like we had…and why would they, the two deaths happened in different jurisdictions within the same county.

CHAPTER TEN

————◆————

Ava left the hotel door ajar with the swinging latch and pulled the covers down. Lying seductively with several pillows propping up her head, she wore a sheer black negligee and a red thong, neither of which she expected to remain on for long.

Keith Dignam had long been known to be a player and kept himself in excellent shape. She knew no other woman had made love with him more in the last two years than her since anytime a woman started getting serious, he dumped her. She never asked why he kept meeting her, she simply figured he enjoyed knowing she had no intention of leaving Danny, therefore no getting serious…that is until she strategically lured him into her plans enough so he would go to prison with her if he said anything. His phone calls to Colonel Harbaugh to set up her first meeting locked him into conspiring to hire a killer. She relied on the fact intelligence did not keep men from thinking with the wrong head.

Keith tried to shut the door behind him fearing someone passing could see her. He pushed the door hard twice into the latch before he realized why it would not close. Once closed, deadbolted and latched, he walked further into the room, stopping ten feet from the edge of the bed.

Ava could see the stress in his face. Since she told him of his involvement to hire a killer, he had trouble relaxing around Danny. He often had trouble relaxing around her, at least until she had his clothes off.

Slow to take off his suit jacket, Ava decided to help him. She gradually raised her left leg, the heel of her foot never leaving contact with the sheet. Her knee bent, the bottom of her foot flat on the sheet, she slowly began to do the same with her right leg. The process took close to a minute and when she had his eyes locked onto hers, she smiled and raised her eyebrows. At the same time, she gradually began to spread her legs, making sure the negligee fell toward her waist enough for him to get a good look at the already moist thong.

Lust replaced stress and he took less than a minute to be standing at the foot of the bed in his boxers, waiting for her first command.

WE ARRIVED AT ANDY'S HOUSE AROUND TEN O'CLOCK like he had asked, allowing enough time for his parents to pack up the kids and head to the zoo. Despite never having met before, the instant he opened the door I could see the overt signs of stress.

A bone-chilling sadness ran through me as the memory of my fiancé's murder rushed into my brain, along with the recognition of the signs I displayed for months. Andy's cheeks appeared slightly sunken, his dress shirt and pants had already started to look a size or two off, and his swollen red eyes from crying nearly made me sick.

You work enough homicides and you start to get a feel for which of the survivors deeply loved their spouse—Andy appeared to be one of them.

Andy and I had been thrust into the same club, one neither of us asked to be in, one whose dues had been paid for with the murder of our lover.

I did not relish extermination, and I always had concern for not wanting to become the very person I sought to bring to justice…a stone-cold killer. Still, I could not turn a blind eye to the wrongfulness of the fallacious and unjust actions of others. I knew right then I would do everything in my power to ease Andy's suffering in the only way I knew how… to dispense with those responsible.

Kenny entered and gave Andy a caring hug, not the bro-hug which seemed to envelope the country. I waited until Andy invited me into his house, whereupon I took his extended hand in both of mine and offered my condolences. Having gone through a similar experience I knew nothing beyond straightforward condolences would be acceptable from a total stranger.

"My mother made a pot of fresh coffee; she doesn't care for the K-cup machines of today. Would either of you like a cup?"

Even though Kenny declined I figured I might as well be comfortable, and coffee most definitely fit into my comfort category.

I heard a familiar hum coming from the kitchen with a loud ding close behind. Andy walked in with one cup full, the steam rolling off the top.

"I remember Kenny telling me you like your coffee extra hot, so I put it in the microwave for forty-five seconds," Andy said, setting the cup on a coaster near an accent chair in the living room.

Sitting, I grabbed the cup and took a sip, nodding approval to Andy who tried to smile. He went to the couch and sank into it with the weight of burden on his shoulders, while Kenny took the chair opposite me.

Janice's death occurred less than two weeks before and I knew from experience Danny had been overwhelmed with visitors and people trying to engage him in conversation. I also knew he would not initiate anything substantial...so I did.

"Has law enforcement or the coroner said anything to you about your wife's death having a hint of being anything except accidental?" I asked.

He shook his head.

"Do you think she accidentally drowned in your pool?"

Andy looked directly at me, turned his head toward Kenny, and turned back to me after Kenny nodded. I presumed he wanted to make sure Kenny believed he could trust me. I knew Kenny had told him about our friendship and having worked together, then again, I also remembered not listening to many things people said to me after Bethany had been murdered.

"Absolutely not. Janice had long been an accomplished swimmer. She put herself through college on a scholarship. Getting to the edge of the pool even if something medically had taken place would be something she could have easily done. The answer to your question is no!"

The obvious next question would be to see why he thought law enforcement passed on it being a possible homicide, although I already knew the answer. Shootings, stabbings, gangs going after other gangs, and obvious homicides easily swamped most homicide bureaus, so looking into why a woman drowned in her backyard pool without any evidence beyond a slight redness around one of her ankles would be summarily dismissed as an accident.

"Do you think someone is targeting you or your company?"

"I didn't want to at first, although the more I thought about what Kenny said I began to. When Laird got killed, it felt like …" Andy's head dropped for several seconds before he stood and left the room.

"I'm not sure we need to ask much more right now," Kenny said.

Kenny had firmly planted his feet in the quandary between doing what we needed to do versus looking out for his boss.

Andy sat, looking at me like he could handle more questions.

"Do you think the CEO, Danny Lloyd had …."

"No. Definitely not. My mom would say he and I are like two peas in a pod. We think alike and have become friends."

"Would you have a problem setting up a meeting for us to talk with him? I have no reason to not believe you, so I really want to get a feel for anyone he thinks might be trying to eliminate one or both of your companies. I mean, according to Kenny, there's a lot of money to be made in this niche you two have."

"True. Danny had done quite well financially before this, which is part of why I don't think he would do this to us. He and Janice got along well."

He had not answered my question about a meeting, so I waited and stared.

"Yes, I'll text him and see," Andy said, walking to the dining room table.

Within minutes we had a time of 11 a.m. to meet Danny at the country club.

Kenny gave Andy another hug and I extended my

condolences once more after thanking him for letting us talk with him.

Walking toward the car Kenny said, "Told you, he's pretty emphatic Danny Lloyd would not do this."

"Yeah, well, if it's okay with you I'll wait to pass judgement until after we've had a chance to talk with Mr. Lloyd ourselves."

CHAPTER ELEVEN

———————◆◆◆———————

Colonel Harbaugh had searched A-Ray Corporation's website many times. The Leadership section listed eight positions: CEO, CFO, Lead Director, Distribution Manager, Human Resources Director, East Coast Sales, West Coast Sales, and Safety Manager. All had a picture along with the person's name in the respective position, except for East Coast Sales, where only the name, Riley Ian Chesterfield, III, existed and West Coast Sales, where Kenny Love's name existed.

It had not taken the colonel long to discover a former Army Ranger also named Chesterfield, and with minimal digging he discovered the Ranger went by the name Ric. Harbaugh knew no serious special operations guy would let anyone call him Riley Ian Chesterfield, III, and most used a short simple name or nickname once inside a unit. Ric seemed a natural modification and the short one syllable would have been perfect to minimize radio chatter.

As a retired colonel for over a decade he no longer had access to Ric's dossier, although he knew people who did, and before long he had a thorough picture of the number of missions in Afghanistan of which Ric had been a part. Harbaugh now understood why Ric dealt with sales given his background he could connect with military leaders who needed to be convinced about the usability of A-Ray's products, and more importantly reliability. He also understood why Ric did not have a picture.

Harbaugh decided to meet his team of insurgents at The Founders Hotel, his favorite in the D.C. area. Plush enough to make him appreciate the wealth he had attained, yet not stuffed full of attitudes from those who acquired their wealth through birth and not through hard work.

Their stay in the area would be long so Harbaugh separated them into pairs to eliminate all being seen together daily in one hotel. The remaining three worked on a separate mission in Nashville. All six knew dressing in business attire would help them blend in.

Once in the conference room Harbaugh got straight to the point. Without a reservation he had to pay the Concierge handsomely to get the room for forty minutes between those who had reserved it.

"As you all know we have two more people to take out at A-Ray," Harbaugh said. "I've been doing quite a bit of research and I think we should target a lesser known person who I believe would be one of two who could create a problem for us. This guy is a former Army Ranger with probably more kills than you all put together. He's highly trained and won't go down easy. I want to make it look like someone ransacked his apartment and he happened to die. It can't be with a gun or knife—those are too obvious."

The fidgeting from several of the insurgents became the only sounds in the room.

"I'm pretty sure I can poison him if we can get him incapacitated enough for me to stick him," Lou said.

More than all the other insurgents, Lou most liked to plan their kills using various methods besides the normal shootings. He had come up with the original idea on how to kill Janice Ray.

"We ain't gonna get in his apartment easily," Carli said, the only female in the room. "I wouldn't be surprised if it's alarmed."

"Maybe we use that to our advantage," Dingo said. "We know from the time the door is opened we have at least forty-five seconds before the alarm goes off. If all of us have a role in it, we can pull it off."

"You can't forget this guy is highly trained," Harbaugh said, shaking his head in disbelief. "One wrong move and one of you might be dead, or worse, only injured and sitting in an interrogation room at some law enforcement agency."

Vic, the newest member snidely asked, "What's worse than dead?"

"The op takes too long, meaning witnesses, who are willing to talk to any news reporter who will listen. We would have no choice except to unass the AO."

"The AO? What the hell?"

"It means leave the Area of Operation, Rookie. Now, shut up," Dingo said.

Vic shot Dingo a hard stare with narrow eyes, his jaws clenched.

Unimpressed, Dingo rolled his eyes before looking back at Harbaugh.

"Colonel, relax," Rock said. "Let's hear them out." He knew the colonel likely had anxiety over the target being a decorated soldier, not for the reason he lacked trust in his team.

"You're right," Harbaugh said. He walked to the table holding water bottles nestled in an ice bucket, rubbing a cube he snatched out on the back of his neck before tossing it back in the container. Taking one of the napkins he dabbed the mixed sweat and water off his neck and asked, "How do we incapacitate him so Lou can do his thing?"

All heads turned when Thumper cleared his throat. Up to this point he had mostly been the driver on missions, although his name came with his reputation after being fired from his police department for using his baton nearly three times more than the next closest officer.

"I know how we can do this in thirty seconds flat, assuming we get the drop on him right as he opens his door."

When nobody questioned him, Thumper went to the front of the room, a huge smile on his face and light in his eyes at his opportunity to finally do something besides drive.

LYING NEXT TO HER ADMIRER, AVA COULD TELL SHE HAD him where she wanted him— staring at the ceiling with a satisfied expression. The time had come for him to satisfy her need. She enjoyed the sex for what it was, simple physical pleasure. He did nothing more for her than Danny did, when she could convince Danny to have sex. What she wanted went beyond orgasms.

Reaching under her pillow she grabbed the USB voice activated recorder and slid it toward the edge of her side of the bed. She had no idea what it would have captured from under the pillow while they had sex, only now she needed it to capture everything. Getting him on tape acknowledging his helping her would lock him in to doing more when the right time arrived.

"I appreciate you making those calls to Colonel Harbaugh and pretending to be Danny. It's important for Harbaugh, and for everyone really, to think Danny wants to rule the industry so badly he hired people to eliminate A-Ray."

"I didn't like it," Keith said sternly. When she tilted her head and smiled, he said, "You're welcome."

"Can't you picture yourself as the CEO of our company? I can. I know you want the power…the prestige…and who wouldn't want the money owning the industry would bring."

"I have to admit, I think about it often," he said. "What if the structure no longer included Danny? You and I could be together and who knows how big we could make this company."

"Is it what you really want?" she asked, trying to add an inflection of uncertainty in her tone despite knowing him better than he knew himself. She slid her hand under the sheet, moving it within touching distance of his phallus, slowly running the backside of her fingernail along it.

He took the bait.

"You know it is. I want nothing more than for him to be out of the way so we can be together."

"Wow. I never really knew," she lied.

She rolled onto her stomach keeping one hand on him while the other grabbed the recorder and slid it back under the pillow.

"Take me," she said, a seductive grin on her face.

CHAPTER TWELVE

Recognizing our names, the hostess took us straight to Danny Lloyd's table. After handshakes and introductions, I took the seat directly across from Lloyd so I could watch his body language from the table up.

"I knew Andy had a former detective working for him, I didn't know he had two," Danny said.

"AJ doesn't work for Andy, he's a good friend of mine who came out to see if he could help in any way."

Danny looked at me, "Were you a high-tech detective, too?"

I chuckled. "Sorry, if you saw me around a computer you would understand. No, I worked violent crimes."

"Homicides?"

I nodded.

"Is that why you're here, you both think what happened to Andy's wife and CFO are homicides?"

"Do you?" I deflected.

Danny started to say something and stopped suddenly.

"Hi ladies," Danny said to the two women in golfing attire approaching our table. "Is Ava coming in?"

The women stopped, looking at each other uncomfortably for a couple seconds.

"No, sorry Danny," the taller one said. "She called about twenty minutes before tee time and said …."

We all could see she did not want to say anymore, nonetheless Danny nodded approval for her to continue.

"... she said something would be coming up soon and bowed out."

The women did not wait for things to become even more uncomfortable and started to skip out. I heard the tall one whisper, "I didn't want to have to tell him it's the third time this month."

My eyes locked on Danny and when his eyes broadened, I knew he heard it, too. His eyes shifted to see me staring, lowered his head and grabbed a menu.

"Now, let's see ..." Danny hesitated, unsure of where he left off.

"You started to tell us your thoughts on Janice's and Laird's deaths," Kenny said.

Kenny knew I would have asked more directly like I did the first time before the ladies walked up. I like the element of surprise and turning a question right back around on someone. Since we lost the element of surprise Kenny's way would have to work.

Danny alternated looking at us for several seconds and I noticed his eyes got a hint of moisture on them.

"Janice is...was a wonderful person. I feel so bad for Andy and the kids...excuse me."

He stood and walked away with urgency.

Kenny's head canted, his eyebrows raised, and his lips closed with one cheek slightly elevated. I had seen that look many times before, Kenny's way of saying he tried to tell me. I had always told myself working around other good detectives like Kenny and Seth made me better, so I could not get around what needed to be done next.

"You called it, I apologize."

"Thank you," Kenny said, a Cheshire cat grin taking up most of his face.

We didn't need to beat a dead horse, so I changed the subject to the beautiful country club until Danny returned. "Sorry. I'm not afraid to admit I cry sometimes, nonetheless I didn't want to lose it here with the room full of people I know, yet would never be friends with," Danny said.

I looked around the room while Danny settled back in. I started feeling even better about him considering I internally appraised most of the people in the room to be fake and pretentious. He seemed genuine to me.

"I would consider Andy a friend, and truthfully, probably the only real friend I have. The three of us often spent time together, a great deal in their backyard while we watched their kids play and swim in the pool."

Kenny caught the same thing I did in Danny's statement and asked, "The three of you?"

"I really loved everything about my wife, Ava, when we first met. Somewhere along the way we began to be successful in our business adventures, which brought about a change in her. She started becoming one of these people." His head hardly shifted while his eyes did a sweep of the room.

"So, she didn't hang out with you and the Rays?" I asked.

He shook and lowered his head. "Janice had always been too grounded for her. Janice never felt the need to be flashy, to hang out here, or go to the numerous parties so the hosts could show off their wealthy homes while claiming to be supporting some cause as the means to get people there. Even though I used to follow Ava to those places I knew… I'm different I suppose. Not many people are your friend when you are at the top. Friendly, of course—not a friend.

59

When I met Andy, I admired him for not getting caught up in the extent of his wealth. The more our friendship grew, the more I began drifting from the club and most of the people. I suppose Ava might have resented Andy and Janice a little, so she always found reasons not to meet with us…kind of like I started finding reasons not to go to the fake parties."

"Did you know Laird, Andy's CFO?" I asked.

"Not really. We had briefly met on a couple of occasions."

"So, your thoughts on their deaths are …?"

"Unfortunate accidents. I've sat with Andy for hours and I know he can't wrap his head around Janice dying in a swimming pool given her being a strong swimmer. The truth is, accidents happen, even to special people like Janice. I haven't said anything to Andy so please don't tell him. I'm a sounding board, I'm there to listen to my friend. I think he'll realize it one day, and until then I'll be there to support him, even if it means biting my tongue."

"And Laird?" Kenny asked.

"Pretty much the same thing. Look, around here there are lots of Type A personalities, driven people who don't sleep and go to their offices at all hours. Most of them drive their cars on rote memory, not thinking about driving really. It's kind of like these parents who leave their kid in a car seat and forget they didn't take them to daycare. Their minds are on a million things and I'd bet they drove to the office on rote memory. The part that bothers me is whoever hit him panicked instead of getting him help. Sadly, I'm not surprised."

"You're not surprised?" Kenny asked, his eyebrows scrunched.

"Not really. Look around this room. How many of these

people would risk the lifestyle they have when they hit someone in the blackness of the early morning, not a single witness around, yet they would call 911? Many of these people are highly successful for the exact reason they lack high morals, so I think under those conditions it's more likely they would drive off, sell their car and get a new one. They would not tell a soul and they would move on."

"Kind of a grim picture you paint of your peers," I said.

"Just trying to be honest with you guys. Look, people here have no clue about the gang mentality and why they get caught up in killing each other before they even had a chance to live life. The same goes for most people not understanding highly driven people like most of this room."

"So, I take it you haven't felt the need to increase your personal security."

"No," he said, a pronounced crevice between his eyebrows. "Why would I? There's no need."

"Everything you said makes a lot of sense," I said, standing and extending my hand. Danny stood and shook both of our hands before we headed for the exit.

"You think he knows?" I asked.

"You mean about his wife having an affair? The look on his face said he does."

"I think he set up the meeting here to check on her."

"Why do you say that?"

"He talks about the people in the country club like all they care about is money and their image, not like him or Andy. Chances are he does not come to the country club unless he has to. I think Danny set the time so he could kill two birds with one stone, check on her at what should have been the end of her round of golf, and meet with us in a neutral place."

"Who knows, he may end up killing his wife for screwing around on him, which is a lot different than killing Janice and Laird. I still say Andy is right, Danny didn't have anything to do with their deaths."

"At the risk of your ego getting out of control, I think you're right. We can probably eliminate him from our suspect pool unless something pops up to make us reconsider."

Kenny's grin told me ribbing him about his ego did not bother him, considering I admitted he had been right. He chuckled when I shook my head.

CHAPTER THIRTEEN

———◦———

Ric had been with A-Ray Corporation for almost the entire two years they had been in operation. Most considered him somewhat of a loner, never one to strike up a conversation. Still, Andy saw in Ric what many did not, he could communicate effectively when necessary. One of Ric's specialties in the Rangers had been communication devices, in all facets. Andy felt Ric would be the perfect liaison to sell their goods to the military. His ability to speak knowledgeably about their products and the instant respect he got from having been a special ops soldier proved Andy's instincts right, getting A-Ray Corporation in many doors which would otherwise be closed.

Few people at A-Ray knew of Ric's background, and he preferred it that way. He never spoke of his experiences or military missions with civilians; he even maintained vigilance about sharing much with someone in a military uniform unless he knew them well enough to trust them. Still, for the sake of saving soldiers' lives, Ric worked hard on being well versed and spoke eloquently about the difference A-Ray products could make.

The last time Ric had been on a date, things did not end well. The date's ex-boyfriend showed up at the restaurant and created a scene, culminating in him slapping the woman in the face. Ric had tried to remain neutral and calm the man down, until he struck her. Within seconds Ric pummeled the man until several customers pulled him off. When his date jumped on his back screaming and started hitting him for hurting her boyfriend Ric walked away from the dating scene.

He enjoyed movies, especially at theaters, and lifting weights. He always included cardio in his workouts knowing stamina could come in handy when strength did not carry the day. Still, nothing replaced his love of pumping iron. Both had dropped off considerably after Janice died, then Laird's death added to his depression. He had lost several friends in battle and losing people he knew well stateside threw him off his game.

Kenny being around seemed to help, especially since they both admired the other's strengths and accomplishments. He felt at ease talking with Kenny, sensing he could trust him. He even felt comfortable sharing with Kenny his suspicion that Janice and Laird's deaths had been orchestrated, knowing he would not be looked at like a fool. Kenny's detective background gave him the understanding of listening to all possibilities without rushing to judgement, something Ric admired.

It had been a couple weeks since Laird's closed casket funeral and almost five since Janice's. Ric decided he needed to get back to working out again. He had gone twice this week already, although neither reached his normal two-hour workout. Still, he felt satisfied about getting started again. PTSD haunted many soldiers returning from the Middle East, a large number with worse symptoms than Ric's. Working out helped him to maintain mental stability.

Although Ric liked the city of Stafford for its amenities, he preferred living on the outskirts. He knew from being a special-ops soldier bad things could happen even in relatively secure environments. His apartment sat in the unincorporated smaller community of Roseville where crime seldom happened, a location where he enjoyed the slower pace and tranquility. He had reached a point where he would relax as he approached Roseville. Every time he thought of needing to keep his guard up, he would dismiss the idea, often thinking to himself, *it's Roseville.*

Ric pulled into the parking area in his covered spot on the far side of the lot. The lot had uncovered visitor parking close to the building, although some of the residents used them, too. Ric did not pay much attention to the blue panel van backed in at his eleven o'clock position, figuring someone must be moving in or out.

Scanning towards the building he saw a young black woman who looked to be in her mid to late twenties walking toward him. She had her hair pulled back, wore a white thin strapped shirt and tight short jeans. His eyes drifted to her unrestrained nipples pushing the fabric out, and when he looked up, she had an, *I saw you looking* grin. Ric jerked his head, trying to look away as he felt his face getting hot.

Ric rented a bottom floor apartment in the building closest to the parking lot. He fumbled with his keys while he looked over his shoulder towards the girl now walking in the direction of a car parked several spaces down from his. When he heard some male voices, he looked back and saw two white guys walking towards him, both dressed in what looked like softball attire. One had a glove tucked under his armpit and keys in his other hand, while the man closest to him punched the glove on his left hand several times. He noticed the one with the keys had an earbud in his left ear with a cord running down and around his waist out of sight. Figuring the guy had a phone in his back pocket he turned back to the door, inserting his key into the deadbolt.

Ric had not noticed another man walking towards the ballplayers, nor had he noticed the black girl work her way back up toward the van. The instant his door unlocked and started to open the unseen man ran and jumped on Ric's back and jammed a stun gun into his neck. The force of the man pushed Ric inside where he slipped on the tile floor when he lunged for balance. His body jerked when his foot went out from under him causing the man to shift and the stun gun connection to be broken. Ric reached behind, grabbing a handful of hair, pulling the guy off his back and slinging him to the ground.

Ric turned in time to see the ballplayer who had been punching his glove rush in and the second one five feet behind. A split second after they stopped, the first guy had an extendable baton at full length, rearing back to swing. Ric closed the gap in two quick steps, allowing him to do a combat Jujitsu throat strike.

Thumper dropped the baton, both hands reflexively moved up to his throat, his eyes wider than ever before. Thumper thrashed around, unable to breath, his mind registering the continuing fight meant he had no help. He dropped to his knees then slowly laid to one side as unconsciousness approached, his hands still around his throat.

Out of his peripheral vision Ric saw another person entering the room, the woman he ogled earlier coming into view. The thought, *trust no one*, raced through his brain a split second before someone jammed the stun gun prongs into the back of his leg. Ric felt the shock from the stun gun, still adrenalin pushed him to reach down for the guy. Before he could grab him the full weight of a solid swing with the extendable baton struck him in the upper right arm and chest. The humerus bone shattered, and together with the shock to his right lung Ric's adrenalin rush had been brought to a temporary standstill. Before he could move to defend himself someone with a weighted-knuckle sap glove caught him under the chin and Ric collapsed like the fighters he often watched on television.

Carli rushed past the fight and began ransacking the bedroom looking for any quick money or guns to take. Lou had made it in and closed the front door where he waited with his syringe full of nicotine for the fight to end. The instant Ric flopped on the carpet Lou ran over and put the needle into his jugular vein, swiftly dumping all 60cc's in. Dingo set the stun gun down and went through the pockets of Ric's gym shorts coming up empty. Carli raced back into the living room waving a wad of money and one black semiautomatic handgun.

"The alarm should go off any second," Vic said into the radio from inside the van.

Rock left the sap glove on and raced over to Thumper. He knew he did not have time to resuscitate him there, so he jerked him to a sitting position and threw him over his shoulder.

"See if it's clear," Rock told Dingo.

"Thumper's hurt. Is it clear for us to carry him out?" Dingo called out into the mic.

"Yes. Go NOW!" Vic replied on the radio from the van.

Lou opened the door and stood back letting the other three out. He locked the deadbolt with the keys still hanging there and took them with him.

The van took off the instant Lou's butt hit the front passenger seat. Once the door closed, he looked over his shoulder and saw Rock doing compressions on Thumper's chest.

"Rock, I can't get any air in," Carli said. "Somethings wrong with his throat."

"On top of being strong, that bloke had some training," Dingo said. "He nailed Thumper's throat, probably crushed his windpipe."

"Rock?" Carli said, laying her hand on his shoulder.

Rock stopped and looked up, a hint of moisture in his eyes. He looked at Carli, then at Dingo who slowly shook his head. Rock sat back on his heels for several seconds before he slid to the side and sat, his elbows perched on his drawn-up knees and his head in his hands.

CHAPTER FOURTEEN

W ith no family in the area the apartment manager did not know who to call about Ric. Someone from the sheriff's office got ahold of Andy who called us. When we learned of what happened we raced to Stafford Hospital and found out Ric had been there for almost four hours.

As we walked down the hospital corridor Andy appeared to be having a rough time. His face looked drawn, his eyes red and puffy. He almost lost it when he saw us walking up, so Kenny threw his arm around Andy's shoulder and led him down the hallway.

"Corporal Svenson, Stafford County Sheriff's Office Major Crimes Unit," a voice from off to my left rear said. "You Kenny?"

I looked over and saw a woman in her early thirties walking toward me with a business card extended in one hand and a small note pad in the other. She wore dark slacks, a polo shirt and a grey suit jacket, and her blonde hair had been pulled into a tight ponytail.

The blond hair and the Swedish name go together, I thought.

"No," I said, sliding my wallet with my retirement badge and ID out of my back pocket. "AJ Conti, retired homicide detective from California."

Most people do not know a great deal about California so trying to identify a city other than LA or San Francisco tends to be a waste of time, especially back East.

"That's Kenny down there, trying to console his and Ric's boss."

"Any idea why Ric, as you call him, would make a statement to the ER staff to tell Kenny a specific message?"

"Kenny used to be a detective with me before he went to A-Ray Corporation out here. I think they have a good bond; they trust one another. Why, what's the message?"

"Normally I wouldn't say …."

"Of course not, I understand."

She hesitated, then said, "Since you are both retired officers, I guess there's no harm."

I nodded, my silence hopefully encouraging her to get to the information.

"Ric told the staff to tell Kenny he saw a blue van, a black chick, and three white guys. They told me he passed out and never said anything else."

"So, no interview?"

"No, apparently they poisoned him, after they beat the crap out of him. Shortly after he made the statement he went into respiratory arrest. He's in critical condition and from what they tell me, he's in a medically induced coma so his body can try to fight through this."

"Poisoned? What the hell with?"

"Officially they are saying I need to get a search warrant since it is a person's medical record. Unofficially, a certain person told me nicotine."

"Gotta love nurses who appreciate cops, right?"

She nodded.

"So, what are you thinking, straight robbery?"

"Yeah. They only ransacked his bedroom, the other bedroom looked untouched. Can't say what all is missing until he comes around, but it couldn't be much. When the alarm went off people started coming outside. Most people around here don't alarm their apartments, houses yes, apartments no. Anyway, the perps closed and locked the door. Someone looked in a window and saw Ric on the ground, then we got called. My guess…they did not stay in the apartment for more than a minute."

"Injuries?"

"Looks like a broken right elbow and a couple of cracked ribs underneath a serious contusion to his right chest area. The doc said something thin and round, like maybe a tire iron, hit him. They all seemed surprised he didn't have a punctured lung. And then, oddly, a puncture site in his neck where they stuck him with a needle to inject the nicotine. He's not a smoker and the amount in his system could have been fatal to an average size man, and still might prove to be for him. Like I said, he's in critical condition."

"You the lead investigator on this?"

"Yes," she said, her eyebrows drawing close to one another.

"Can you get us in the room so I can look at him a little closer?"

She hesitated again. I surmised she gave in knowing I had investigated more homicides and violent attacks than she ever would.

As we passed the nurses station, she whispered something to one of the nurses who nodded.

Ric and I had never met, yet even in a hospital bed I could easily tell he had to be over six feet…and muscular.

You would have given your attackers a run for their money, I thought. *So then, how'd they get a needle in your neck?*

I went to Ric's right side and took a few seconds to get an assessment. The bruising to his chest had become pronounced and I could see why the doc told Svenson it looked like a tire iron. I could see a mark in his right neck area near his jugular and figured it to be the injection site. I had been around enough injured people in hospitals to know somebody with beautiful veins like Ric's, no medical staff would use the jugular vein. Something caught my attention behind the mark.

"Got a flashlight?"

"Yeah, a small mag lite," Svenson said. She retrieved it from the inside jacket pocket, then handed it over to me.

I shined light on the backside of Ric's neck without moving his head.

"Know what those two marks about a quarter of an inch apart are?" I asked.

"Holy shit, excuse my French."

I chuckled.

"Those are stun gun marks, right?"

I nodded. "If I had to guess someone came up behind and tried to zap him. The marks don't look deep though, almost makes me think the connection didn't stay on long. Things like tasers, rubber bullets...that crap doesn't work on everybody. I can't imagine Ric giving in to one jolt and not putting up a fight."

I turned the light off. "No hospital staff told you about those marks, correct?"

"No. Why?"

"From the time the door opens to the time the alarm

goes off, how much time did they have to work with?"

"I'm guessing forty-five seconds, maybe a minute. What are you getting at Mr. Conti?"

"Please, call me AJ."

"Okay, AJ. The question still stands."

"You wouldn't want to let him get turned around to defend himself, at the same time you wouldn't want it to take place outside so there are witnesses. Only one person could come through the door behind him and that's probably when he gets zapped first. They had to get well inside to be able to swing a tire iron or whatever hard enough to cause such damage," I said, pointing to Ric's chest and arm. "Not to mention, with all the crap Kenny says Ric has been through in Afghanistan, I say he would have put up a fight. My point is, if you attacked him, how many times would you hit him with the stun gun?"

"He's not a small man…twice, maybe even three times."

"Me too. And his arm looks like a defensive wound, like he tried to block the swing and took some of the oomph out of the end of the connection."

"You're wanting to see if there are more prong marks from the stun gun."

I smiled, appreciating her ability to reason.

"Yes. Paramedics would have done a quick assessment, probably didn't see anything beyond the major issues and passed it along to the ER staff. A couple of little burn marks, not their priority."

Svenson really had no desire to look at Ric naked once I pulled the sheet down, so she stood at the door watching for any approaching nurses. It did not take long to find a second set of burn marks on the inside of Ric's left leg, much deeper than the first set.

"You're going to want to get the different prong marks photographed for evidence, and soon, before they start healing," I said pulling the sheet back up over his legs.

"Will do. Let's get some coffee. I know, a little presumptuous, though odds are as a former homicide investigator you drink coffee. Plus, it's actually decent here."

I raised my eyebrows and grinned.

CHAPTER FIFTEEN

After Lou came up with the plan on what to do with Thumper's body, Rock contacted Dutch at the junkyard for assorted items.

"I didn't expect it would take him three hours to come up with a compound bow, some arrows, and a metal detector," Lou said.

"That shit's not just lying around," Dingo said. "It takes time to find, much less the right person willing to part with it."

"Yeah, well, whoever Dutch found must have seen an opportunity to score big, making sure they got paid handsomely for them."

Dumbasses, Rock thought. *Not even considering Dutch made sure to add on his cut.*

"Whatever, it's better than one of us getting caught on camera going inside a store to buy stuff," Rock said.

Pulling into the Chancellorsville Battleground almost four hours after Thumper died, Dingo said, "Damn good thing we didn't take any longer. Another hour and rigor mortis would make it hard to move him."

"What makes you think it's easy moving him now," Lou grunted when they lifted Thumper to start heading for the canopy of trees. "And we ain't done, we still have to hold him upright and hope Carli hits what she's aiming at instead of one of us."

They carried Thumper thirty feet into the woods and laid him down to catch their breath. Carli had already examined the beginner compound bow with a twenty-pound draw weight, like the one she started with years before. She paced off the steps she knew would work best for the type of bow she had, while Dingo and Lou tried to determine the distance Thumper would be if he took one step and fell forward after being shot, landing on the two foot stone wall. They knew if they could make it look like the wall crushed Thumper's larynx the investigators might be thrown off for a while.

When Carli said, the two lifted Thumper upright, holding him relatively straight while Rock shined his light from his phone onto Thumper's back. The light silhouetted them, so she knew they could not see her in total darkness or know when she would release the arrow preventing them from flinching out of fear and messing up the entire plan. She raised her bow arm into position, and in one continuous motion she smoothly drew the string to a full draw position. Even though she had vast experience with bows a year had passed since she last shot, so she mentally took stock of her posture.

Head's straight, relaxing my shoulders, squeezing my shoulder blades, perpendicular, wrist is flat, finger near my archer point, take a breath.

Without a word she released the tension in her bowstring fingers and the arrow departed, penetrating Thumper's back on the left side. The others heard it thwack Thumper before anyone saw it, the fletching already touching Thumper's shirt with most of the shaft sticking out the front, evidence from his destroyed heart clinging to the broad head point.

The release of the arrow blended with forest sounds and went unnoticed, the sound of penetration startling both men, each taking a step back, struggling to keep Thumper upright.

"Man, no wonder it kills an animal," Dingo said. "I never saw it, I only heard it, and barely for a split second."

"You don't hear it, arrows are quiet," Carli said walking towards them. "The sound of the arrow tip touching and penetrating is so fast it tricks your mind into thinking you heard the arrow."

She inspected the result of her efforts, pleased with the location.

"The broad head point hitting his heart should make it harder on the ME. Can't change lack of bleeding though, so they'll figure it out."

"Nice shot is all I can say," Lou said shaking his head. "And in the dark. Impressive."

The corners of Carli's lips went up a hair and she shrugged.

Carli set the bow down and positioned herself between Thumper's legs, holding his waistband. The three leaned him over with his throat somewhere around three feet above the wall like they planned. When Rock reached the bottom of the countdown, they all let go. A thud from his body and a snap of the arrow shaft mixed as Thumper's body crumpled into somewhat of a backward C position, the wall scraping skin from his chin and face when they slid down.

Staging began with Lou placing the band from the top of the metal detector handle over Thumper's right wrist, letting it fall to look more natural. Most people looking for artifacts have a knife or digging tool of some kind, so Thumper's knife in a sheath on his waist meant one less staging item Rock needed to worry about. To finish it off they wiped a plastic water bottle clean and used Thumper's left hand, wrapping his fingers around it to make it look like he had been holding it when he got killed.

"What made you think about this place?" Carli asked Lou while they used fallen branches to brush away evidence of their shoe prints.

"Read about two poachers getting arrested for killing a deer in here. Can't hunt on federal property, and you can't use a metal detector and dig up artifacts in here either. Both would have to be doing this at night, so it worked out perfectly. A hunter killing some schmuck on federal land means another law enforcement agency. It's not a terrorist attack, so odds are they won't share any information with local law enforcement."

"The best part is, no cameras," Rock said. "All we got to do is hope no one sees us drive out of here and we're good to go."

Rock pushed the button to activate the radio mic and said, "We're getting ready to leave now. Come pick us up."

Hearing a double click to acknowledge the order they all headed towards the road.

Carli's nerves started to settle once they waited near the road to be picked up. She liked the money Colonel Harbaugh paid, conversely, she had not signed up for killing innocent people. When they killed violent dirtbags who deserved to die for what they had done she felt a sense of accomplishment, especially when the system had let the grieving family down. She could not mentally or ethically invest in missions to kill people solely based on another person's greed and ability to pay the expenses.

The option to leave never existed. Harbaugh made it perfectly clear when he had Rock and Dingo kill an employee trying to quit and turned him into chum bait for the ocean dwellers.

The paper she slid into Thumper's pocket simply said, *PIs-insurgents-NY*. She wrote it with her left hand knowing nobody had a clue about her being ambidextrous. Regardless of who might question her she could deny it, backing it up with what everyone would expect, a right-handed writing sample…absent someone seeing her slide it into the pocket.

Carli sensed nobody saw or she would have seen them retrieve it. Still, Rock would not do anything right then, he would plan a hit when she least expected it. She reasoned it best to have her hand next to her gun for the next several days.

CHAPTER SIXTEEN

Corporal Svenson and I stood together paying for our coffee when Kenny walked in. He dropped into his chair like he had a huge load on his shoulders, and I introduced the two.

"Where's Andy?"

"I convinced him he couldn't do anything for Ric right now and to go home to his family."

Even though Kenny wanted to say more, he stopped due to Svenson. Not surprisingly she could tell Kenny had more to say, too.

"Corporal Svenson here—"

"Why don't you guys call me Ellie. I get enough of the rank and last name crap at the department, it's kind of nice to hear my first name."

"Fair enough. Ellie said Ric gave some info on his attackers before going unconscious."

"Good for Ric. The part I'm struggling with is how fast it went down though. He had to have been ambushed. I can't imagine he didn't hurt any of them."

Now it appeared to be Ellie's turn to look like she had something to hide when she turned sideways and draped one leg over the other. I looked at Kenny, then we both stared at her.

"What?"

"You're holding something back," I said. "Understand-able, considering good investigators seldom share every-thing with unproven people, and you have no reason to trust us."

"Other than we've been in your shoes more times than we care to count...and Ric is a friend of mine," Kenny said, the hint of a quiver sneaking in at the end.

Ellie hesitated, alternating her eyes between us. She unwrapped her leg and turned forward, leaned her fore-arms on the edge of the table, then clasped her cup with both hands.

"Okay, I'll tell you something. Then it's your turn to tell me something you've been holding back, since I can tell Kenny has more to say."

Lightly backhanding Kenny's shoulder, I said, "Way to go, she reads you like an open book and you barely got here."

Ellie laughed, which helped to relax Kenny...a little.

"You might be right about Ric hurting someone. We do have a witness who looked out her window and saw one guy carrying another guy over his shoulder and plop him down in a van in a hurry, not gentle like. She did not get a plate; the good news is the color she gave is the same as what Ric said. And before you ask, no, she can't ID anybody."

"Any blood in Ric's apartment?" Kenny asked.

"None. We did the Luminol thing and came up negative."

After seconds of silence Ellie tilted her head and flared her arms out, palms up, waiting for our information. I had already decided we probably needed Ellie's assistance in the future more than she needed us, so we had to give her something to help build some trust.

"Ric is the third person from the company Kenny now works for who has been attacked or killed in the last month."

"You're shittin' me?"

I leaned forward to make sure we had good eye contact, and then shook my head.

"And the sheriff's office is working all of them?"

"No, one took place in Aquia Harbour's jurisdiction," Kenny said.

She stood, her chair screeching across the tile drawing looks from people, not that Ellie seemed to care.

"I need another cup of coffee," she said.

I raised my cup and she took it with her.

"I like her."

"Yeah, for two reasons…she's easy on the eyes and she drinks a boat load of coffee like you. Never mind what her detective skills are," Kenny said, with a slight chuckle.

"Right now, her liking coffee is enough. At least she's not a teetotaler like you."

"You dumbass, that's for alcohol, which incidentally I am not opposed to having. It's coffee I won't drink."

"You say potato, I say potato. You say teetotaler is no alcohol, I say teetotaler is no coffee. *Capish*?"

Kenny shook his head, and said, "Whatever?"

"Besides, who else do we know capable of legally accessing police information and computers to help us? I admitted being wrong about your gut feeling Danny most likely isn't a suspect; well, I have a gut feeling Ellie might turn out to be a good detective."

"What are you going to do about not exactly telling her the truth?"

"I'm going to lay it all out in about ten seconds when she sits down. And hope she doesn't get pissed about me misleading her."

Kenny got his Cheshire cat grin and the instant Ellie

got within earshot he said, "The only reason you like her is she's not a dude."

"What the hell's that supposed to mean?" she said, staring at me.

I shot a look over at Kenny with squinted eyes, which only served to make his grin bigger.

"Relax, Kenny likes to create havoc for fun," I said, shaking my head at him before turning to her. "I have a history of working well with women detectives. Long investigations are nothing like the streets where you often need brawn. Good investigators definitely need patience, reasoning and passion…which is why I like working with women."

Her glare softened and she sat, sliding over my cup of coffee.

"AJ has something he needs to share with you," Kenny said, chuckling as he left to go fill his cup.

You shit stirrer, I thought.

"Some of what I said about three people being attacked or killed is speculation, although it's not far-fetched or beyond a reasonable possibility."

Displaying two of the qualities I described, patience and reasoning, Ellie said, "I'm listening."

Yeah. So far, my gut feeling is right about her.

"The CEO's wife drowned in their backyard pool. She swam laps every morning and according to everyone who knows her, she is an accomplished swimmer."

"I remember reading about it in the paper. Ruled an accident if I remember correctly."

"You do. She is the speculation I referred to. She had a small red mark on one ankle. This is a woman who's strong and in shape, plus their pool is not overly deep. More of a lap pool. The bottom line is, there is almost no reason for her not to be able to make it to the edge if she experienced trouble."

"Who else besides her and Ric?"

"The company CFO, Laird Spencer. Your agency worked his death, a hit and run of a bicyclist near the golf course west of the highway."

She nodded like she had heard about it.

"Dark, almost no moon, early morning, and no traffic to speak of in a residential neighborhood at a three-way stop. I've been to the scene and I'm fairly confident there had to be a vehicle running, darkened out on the wrong side of the road waiting for him. Once he started to round the corner like any number of riders would do who did not see oncoming headlights, they nailed him from the back."

"Our Crash Investigation Unit worked it. During one of our weekly briefings the CIU First Sergeant in Charge came in and told us a little about it. He said they sent the rider's body to Richmond for a forensic autopsy at the Central District. Apparently, they crushed the guy's organs."

"And now Ric. Something tells me he's not the last one."

"Really? What do you think the motive is? I mean, seems to me if your speculations and gut feelings all pan out, which I'm not totally bought into yet, greed tops the charts."

"Oh, you should buy into his gut feelings," Kenny said. He turned his chair around to sit backwards, his elbows resting on the table.

"You being serious this time?"

"Dead serious. Most cops develop a decent sixth sense, AJ has a…it's like a seventh sense, well beyond the average cop. His gut's right way more than it's wrong. Which is why I wanted him to come out here, figuring he would be able to give me a neutral perspective. Ric and I both had our suspicions, and now with AJ's gut saying somethings wrong…well, let me make this easy for you, we aren't going away without a fight."

The corner of her lip lifted at the same time the eye on the same side squinted. After several seconds she sat straight and took a deep breath. I thought we lost her until she stood and said, "We might be here awhile. I need a fresh cup of coffee."

CHAPTER SEVENTEEN

———◆———

With no traffic in sight, they pulled out from the battleground and headed back towards Fredericksburg. Other than Thumper being killed, Rock felt pretty good about how it came together after the difficulty in getting the guy subdued in his apartment.

"Great idea about the battlefield, Lou," Rock said.

"Thanks. It kind of all fell into place after I remembered the article about the poachers being arrested. We had to come back to Fredericksburg to turn the van in and the battlefield is close."

"I saw a do-it-yourself type carwash kind of behind the 7-Eleven up on your right in a few more miles," Rock said to Vic, the driver. "Pull in there, we need to put the plates back on and make sure this thing is clean."

"What the hell for?" Vic asked, a brashness in his tone. "A place where you can buy run down cars and rent old ones, I mean c'mon, it's a frickin front for something else. This van is a piece of crap, they won't even check it out."

"Do what he told you and shut up," Dingo said.

Rock slightly dropped his chin to thank Dingo. He struggled at times with some of the newer guys Colonel Harbaugh brought in, only preferring half the insurgents they had now. Thumper and Vic always wanted to cut corners, never believing it could lead the cops back to them. He knew all the growth had to do with Harbaugh wanting to make more money, and since insurgents only got paid for the jobs they did, Harbaugh's income had more than doubled compared to the times with only the original four PIs.

"Stop behind the 7-Eleven," he said to Vic. "Carli, go in and get a standard cleaner spray bottle and a roll of paper towels, then meet us at the car wash."

Rock handed her a twenty-dollar bill.

They no sooner stopped in the wash bay and got out when Vic started walking towards Dingo.

"Nobody tells me to shut up and gets away with it."

Dingo grinned, hoping the punk would try to back up his words.

Lou started to step forward like he might try to get between them when Rock grabbed his shoulder and stopped him. Rock looked at Vic and dipped his head towards Dingo and shrugged his shoulders, letting him know he would not put a stop to it if the kid wanted to take the chance.

Here in a second we may end up going back to the battlefield, Rock thought.

After Vic stood still for several seconds Dingo chuckled and went to the machine to put in quarters.

Rock shook his head, thinking, *No time like the present since he's already proven he's a pussy.*

"You ever question me again … you won't have to worry about Dingo," Rock said. He turned to leave and said over his shoulder, "Change out the plates."

Vic looked at Lou who whispered, "Be careful. They're not opposed to killing you."

Thirty minutes later they drove into the heart of Fredericksburg, stopping at the Fredericksburg Shopping Center where they all got out except for Carli. She drove to Eddy's Used Cars and Rentals nearby on Falls Hill Avenue. She put the keys in the visor and locked all the doors before walking back to where the others waited.

Approaching the parking lot she saw them all standing outside of their vehicles. When one of them moved she saw Harbaugh, his finger bouncing like a parent lecturing his kids.

Carli made it to within ten feet of the group when she heard Harbaugh say, "How the hell could this have happened?"

Up to then nobody in the group had said a word, everyone hoping Rock would do the explaining.

"You ready to listen and quit flying off the handle in a public parking lot?" Rock asked.

Harbaugh stood erect and took a deep breath, although the crimson color in his cheeks did not change. Nobody else could talk to Harbaugh like Rock could, nor would they try. Still, he trusted Rock more than any of the others realizing Rock tended to see the big picture.

Harbaugh nodded.

"We had a good plan and prepared for contingencies. There's no way to know he would slip going in the door sending Dingo flying before he could stun him good. Overall, we recovered well. Thumper forgot him being a highly trained, battle tested soldier. He wanted to hit the guy so bad he got tunnel vision, allowing the guy to close the distance, and hit him in the throat before he even got a swing in. Thumper didn't bleed so he didn't leave any obvious evidence behind, and we got out at the same time the alarm went off."

"You got the nicotine in him?"

"Yeah, Lou did great. Hell, we all did great, except for …."

Harbaugh turned and started pacing, something he did while processing information. The insurgents remained quiet.

"What about the battlefield? Will it throw the feds off the attack?"

"It should. There's no doubt they'll figure the staging out, not right away though. The likelihood of some agent thinking his own guys staged him is slim, I mean you'd naturally think it had to be whoever killed him. Right?"

"Plus, the feds won't talk with the deputies, at least not right away," Lou added.

Harbaugh nodded several times, still pacing.

"And we're sure he's going to die, from the injection? I'm telling you, the client will become even more of a bitch than she already is if he doesn't. Not to mention the inherent risk to all of us if he ever recovers enough to give a statement."

The pause caused Harbaugh to stop pacing, turning to them with wide eyes, his index finger turning rapid circles like winding them up to give him more information.

All eyes turned to Rock. Nobody wanted to be the one to go on record saying the guy would die and be wrong. Who knows what Harbaugh might do then?

"Look, you need to relax, have a little faith. We'll do some recon at the hospitals in the area and watch the papers over the next couple days. It'll all work out. You watch."

Rock's confidence bled out to the others who started nodding in support.

"Besides, didn't you say we need to do one more?" Dingo asked.

"Yeah, except for …."

"Except for what?" Vic said, a nasty emphasis on the last syllable and his hands flaring like he considered himself a badass.

Rock locked eyes with him and his jaw muscles protruded enough for Vic to see. When Vic looked away Rock's eyes slid over to Dingo who faintly nodded once.

Vic's days became numbered.

"Nobody gave you permission to talk, Shithead," Harbaugh said, staring at Vic.

"Who the fuck do you guys think you are? I'm tired of you acting like you're all better than me."

On-the-spot Vic numbered his own minutes.

Vic never saw Dingo slide behind him, and worse yet, nobody else's eyes gave Dingo's movements away.

"Well, Vic. Let me tell you who we are," Harbaugh said calmly, sounding like the consummate teacher while drawing Vic's full attention to him.

Dingo's left hand wrapped around Vic's mouth, pulling to expose his neck in less than a second. The blade of Dingo's knife went in at a forty-five-degree angle and destroyed everything in its path. Vic's arms barely made it up to his chest before instantaneous death caused them to flop back down.

Without prompting Lou took two quick steps and put Vic's arm around his shoulder like helping a drunk walk. Dingo took his other side and together they led Vic back to his car. Carli opened the door, and they set him in his driver's seat, letting him fall toward the center console like a sleeping drunk.

On the other seat Carli saw the cleaner and paper towels. She went and grabbed them while Dingo worked to get Vic's legs inside. She had the areas they touched wiped clean in under a minute.

Two minutes later she and Lou finished wiping up the blood droplets on the asphalt parking lot and sprayed the area with the cleaner to help create confusion for forensic work in the future.

"There's a café right around the corner," Rock said. "Maybe you should take us to dinner for a job well done."

"Might as well," Harbaugh replied. "Can't stay around here."

CHAPTER EIGHTEEN

———◆———

Ellie agreed to see if she could get the manager's approval to look at Ric's place. The apartment had been released to him once evidence collection had been completed. When we arrived, the manager stood watching a handy man fixing the door frame EMS personnel had shattered to gain entry.

Hanging back about ten feet while she spoke with him, I looked around the parking lot and the exterior of the building. I noticed some uncovered parking spaces close to Ric's apartment, although tenants had designated spaces in the covered parking across the lot. I sensed the van Ric saw would have been parked almost right in front making the suspects exposure time minimal.

Ellie approached and almost said something, and then she stopped.

"What's on your mind?"

I took a deep breath. "This attack's well planned. With his size and strength, there had to be several of them. I'd bet the van parked right there, probably backed in for a quick getaway. Who would even think twice about a van backed in to move a tenant in or out? The players had to do something besides milling around to make Ric comfortable enough to open his door, otherwise it would be a red flag for a guy hard-wired not to trust anyone. Something tells me they knew about the alarm; they got in and out so quick.

Even though they didn't quite make it, they got damn close."

"Ric hurting one of them slowed them down," Kenny said.

"Wow, and we haven't even gone inside," Ellie said surprised.

"We can look around in there, although everything we really need to know is out here. These people are an experienced team."

"I'm not saying I don't believe you guys, even so it's going to be hard to sell my first sergeant on this not being a simple home invasion type robbery. And without his support I'll never be able to convince the major.

"You'll see, the bedroom is ransacked and we're pretty sure stuff is missing, exactly what remains a mystery until Ric regains consciousness. I'm telling you, my boss will say it's simply a coinkydink. His term, not mine."

"Let's go inside," I suggested.

The remains from the paramedics working on Ric inside the door still cluttered the floor. A stool had been knocked over and a lamp laid on the ground, giving the appearance Ric had been subdued right there. The master bedroom had been ransacked like Ellie said, with the dresser drawers rummaged, the mattress sat canted on the box springs and the closet had been rifled.

When I looked over my shoulder, I noticed Kenny gone.

"Detective?" a man said from the front room prompting Ellie to excuse herself.

I found Kenny in the clean and tidy spare bedroom. He nodded sideways, opening the closet door. When I looked a closet safe sat staring right at us with the door ajar. I peeked inside without touching the door and saw at least five handguns, some rifles, several boxes of ammo, a small stack of cash with the top bill being a fifty, and what appeared to be Ric's important papers underneath.

"What prompted you to look in here?"

"He showed me his guns on a visit once—told me he trusted me. When we finished, he didn't lock the safe, he hardly closed the closet door, and at the time I told myself he would lock it up after I left."

"Let me guess, the cleanliness of the room made you wonder if they even saw this safe?"

Kenny nodded. "Exactly. I figured they probably got the gun under his mattress, and maybe the one in his gym bag, I hoped they didn't get these. Totally surprised me to see it open and untouched. I'd bet Ellie and her gang never even saw this."

"Yep, probably peeked in, saw how clean it is and never even came in here, much less checked the closet."

"What do you think we ought to do?"

"If we point it out to Ellie, she might be able to convince her brass there's a connection in the attacks."

"And if that happens our chance of digging into who's doing this and taking care of them is almost zero."

I had never heard Kenny speak about taking care of people like I had in Albuquerque when I dealt with corrupt cops and administrators authorizing their actions. My past view of always believing in the system and trying to color inside the lines changed in Albuquerque where doing the right thing took on a new dimension for me. Kenny on the other hand...I had to make sure I heard him correctly.

"Are you suggesting ...."

Kenny stared me in the eye and said, "I'd prefer alive... I'll accommodate them either way. I'm not going to sit idle and do nothing while they eliminate everyone in Andy's company, including me."

"And Ellie?"

"I've got a plan. We don't have time so you're going to have to trust me."

Seriously, I thought, canting my head. He knew I trusted him.

"Sorry. Play along and keep her out of the bedrooms."

We went into the living room and Kenny waited for a pause in Ellie's conversation with the manager.

"Since you guys have cleared your investigation in here do you mind if I grab a few things for Ric when he wakes up, maybe some clothes for him to come home in?" Kenny asked.

I could read Ellie's thought, *Really?* She looked at me so I shrugged, hoping she thought I even believed Kenny might be overly hopeful.

Ellie looked at the manager who had no clue the extent of Ric's injuries, so when he nodded, she turned to Kenny and did the same.

Kenny went to the kitchen, found some paper bags and fortunately nobody paid attention to how many he grabbed. He could double and triple bag to hold the weight of the items in the safe.

I made eye contact with Ellie hoping she would think I wanted to talk with her and headed outside.

Just outside the door I paused. I could not see where the sidewalks on either side went to and thought, *Good places to hide so they could blind-side him when he opened his door.*

"Where's the witness who saw the guy carrying a body?" I asked, palms out.

"Up in Ric's building opposite of his," Ellie said. "She thought she heard noises and when the alarm went off, she walked to the window. Barely got there in time to see the one guy sling the other into the van and jump in behind him. From up there she couldn't ID anyone and she admitted she did not look at the van's license plate."

I saw Kenny come out of the apartment carrying one bag partially rolled up under his arm and holding the handles of the other one.

"Any video cameras in this place?" I asked to keep Ellie distracted.

"Not in the complex itself …."

Kenny used his fob to unlock his car and open the trunk, which got Ellie's attention. From where we stood in the dark, I had a hard time seeing anything beyond Kenny putting a couple of bags in the trunk and presumed she could not make them out any better than I.

"Video?"

I wanted to get her attention back on me, plus I really did hope somewhere they located a picture of the van.

"Oh, yeah. We did locate a couple of places with security cameras on the fronts of their businesses and I assigned one of the newer detectives to look into those."

Kenny walked back and thanked Ellie. She and Kenny exchanged business cards, and she wrote my cell number on the back.

"Well, what all did you bring?" I asked once in the car.

"I got his five handguns and the ammunition for each of them. At least three hundred rounds. I wanted to take the AR-15 except I knew I could not get past the manager with it. I left the rifles, the money and the papers locked in the safe, and then wiped it down with one of Ric's shirts."

"Now we have to decide if we tell Ellie or not?"

CHAPTER NINETEEN

After my morning run, I returned to find Kenny reading the newspaper. He said, "Ric's attack made the front page. The writer played up the angle of no similar attack like it in any of the smaller outlying towns over the last decade."

"Anything from Ellie?"

"Mentions her as the lead investigator and how to contact her if anyone has any info. This next part pisses me off. Some Major Potts infers a home invasion in a small town is most likely Ric's being involved in something he shouldn't be."

I had no idea of the sheriff's office exact structure, although my gut told me the major probably oversaw the entire investigations bureau and had already started political maneuvering in case they did not solve the investigation. Sheriff's offices across the country are almost all political in that the sheriff must be voted into the position. Every sheriff I had ever met knew some administrators below them constantly prepared themselves for a takeover, or at a minimum to run when the sheriff retired. Unsolved attacks like Ric's raised red flags during elections unless people like Major Potts could explain it away.

"No wonder Ellie didn't get quoted," I said. "I'm kind of wondering if we need to rethink our decision from last night."

"Let me guess, you want to tell her, 'Oh, thought you should know, we stole some guns and ammo from Ric's apartment last night. Hope you understand.'"

"Not exactly, smart-ass. Answer this first and then I'll explain what I think we should tell her."

Kenny nodded.

"Do you think Ellie's administration wants to hear anything about the possibility of a connection?"

He paused and shook his head. "So?"

"Maybe the spin we put on this is to say we found his safe open and locked it. We stay away from mentioning his weapons or the ammo…we tell her if Ric had been involved in something nefarious, like narcotics, why would his bedroom be the only room ransacked and why did they leave so fast? We show her we will work with her while at the same time showing her the major is an ass."

Kenny went outside to the balcony leaning on the railing with both forearms.

I followed and took a seat, giving him time to process while I cooled down from the run.

Finally, I said, "Look, I know you're concerned about her turning on us, maybe doing a search warrant for the hotel room or your car. I can't deny it is a possibility. I gotta say, I don't think she will. We can sell it to her about helping her solve the whole thing. I'd wager she's not well liked or respected in a good-old-boy system, so they aren't going to listen to her unless she has some proof. She needs us like we need her."

Without turning Kenny said, "She did seem a little awestruck with your comment about liking to work with women detectives."

"Glad you agree."

Kenny brought his arm off the rail enough to raise his middle finger.

Chuckling, I said, "You hate admitting Seth or I are ever right." I waited a couple of seconds before adding, "Speaking of Seth ...."

Kenny spun around. "What about him?"

"I kind of thought we might want him to join us. You never know when you need a good sniper, and we both know we aren't going up against amateurs."

"I'll see if Ellie can meet us for breakfast. Then I'll get in touch with Seth while you shower. You stink."

I laughed, not at the comment, although there could be some truth to it. I laughed at Kenny's confirmation I hit the nail on the head...he hated it when Seth or I had him backed into a corner.

WHILE SHOWERING I THOUGHT ABOUT THE POSSIBILITY of the three of us working together again, even if only informally. I reminisced about some of the bigger cases on which we worked together. The good thoughts drifted away when I thought about the jeopardy I could be putting them in with us surreptitiously going after killers, along with the possibilities of how it could end.

When I stepped back on the balcony Kenny said, "Seth has to finish up some negotiations for a couple of police associations. He figures he can be here in three days, and I already emailed him a synopsis of what's happened and some of our thoughts."

I hesitated, almost wishing we had not taken the step to involve Seth. All three of us should not end up dead or in prison. Knowing Seth, there would be no way to get the cat back in the bag and take back the request. Time to accept it and move on.

"What about breakfast and Ellie?"

"I know you. Nothing comes out of your mouth unintended. You think breakfast is more important than meeting with Ellie."

I nodded. "Okay, so what's the big deal? I'm hungry. Let's go eat."

Kenny shook his head. "Whatever. She can't meet us for another forty-five minutes."

"That gives me time to enjoy a couple cups of coffee and read the paper. Like I said, let's go."

He half-snorted, shook his head, then ambled to grab his keys.

WHEN WE WALKED IN THE NOOK, TOM SEEMED MORE relaxed than the last time we visited.

Kenny again made his rounds chatting with various patrons, including a stop at the counter to talk with Luci. I perused the paper and read the article Kenny talked about. He never told me the writer mentioned a witness and what she saw from her upstairs apartment. The hair on the back of my neck stood up.

I continued looking through the paper and noticed two short articles about a couple of men being found dead, the same reporter having written both. One occurred in the Chancellorsville Battlefield, and an unidentified source from the sheriff's office said it appeared to be a man illegally looking for artifacts at night when an illegal bow hunter accidentally shot him. The second appeared to be a robbery considering the unidentified dead man had been stabbed in the neck inside his car and his wallet had not been found...again according to an unidentified source from the sheriff's office.

Same reporter, same night...someone at the sheriff's office likes to feed this reporter information so she can have the initial scoop...or someone in administration is silencing the official media relations deputy.

When I saw Ellie approaching, I folded the paper. She looked tired and I wondered if she ever got to bed.

"Good morning Ellie. Did you get any sleep?"

"Not much. We got called out again, and according to my supervisor, Major Potts told him to assign it to me...so I'm the lead investigator."

"Nothing related to Ric then?"

"No. A man killed in his car in the parking lot of a Fredericksburg shopping center...probably a robbery. No ID and no wallet. Looks like a stab wound to the neck. The car came back a rental from Charlotte, North Carolina. We found a password locked cell phone in the center console. It's no help."

Exactly like the article in the paper. No investigator worth their salt would mention the victim being stabbed in the neck. Something doesn't feel right.

"Did your crime scene techs get his fingerprints for the Automated Fingerprint Identification System?"

"Yes, AJ. Just because this isn't California doesn't mean we don't know what AFIS is or what we are doing."

"I'm sorry. I apologize. One of my bad habits used to be, and apparently still is, not to automatically trust what others should have done. I've been grilled on the stand a few times for being the lead investigator and trusting techs to follow through with my directions. I considered myself

lucky to have a thorough main tech. Some other techs…
not so much."

"Well, some parts are universal. Kind of like driving near
some road workers and seeing one working while three are
leaning on their shovels talking."

I grinned. Some things are easy to visualize.

Kenny and Luci walked up, we ordered and when Luci
walked away, we caught Kenny up on our conversation.

"Don't put your foot in your mouth and ask her if they
got the victim's fingerprints," I said to Kenny.

"AJ questioning every little thing, again?"

They laughed at my expense, as if it would stop me from
questioning details about things being done right.

"Have you seen the article about Ric's attack in the newspaper yet?" I asked to break up the laughter.

"I saw it made the front page is all. I haven't had time to
read it." Ellie raised her left eyebrow at Kenny and grinned,
and then asked, "Anything specific you need to enlighten
me on Detective Conti?"

They continued to have a good time and I enjoyed seeing
a more relaxed side of Ellie.

"Of course, there is. Would you expect anything less?"

Kenny pointed his thumb at me and they both shook
their heads.

"So, what's the deal with Major Potts from your department inferring the cause of the attack has to be Ric's doing
something illegal?"

"You're shittin' me?"

"No, he's not, and I'm not happy about it," Kenny said, a
glare replacing his smile.

"I understand, and I apologize. All the detectives hate
him. We call him Major Putz; he cares about one person,

himself. The rest of us are expendable the way he sees it. The Sheriff hinted he may not go for re-election, so the politics and maneuvering has begun, none moreso than Putz."

"That seems like a plausible culprit considering there are two small articles in the same paper, and one is about your dead guy in the car. Holding back important information to use later in an interview to see if the person really is the suspect is taught in Homicide Investigations 101 across America. You've said the other investigators in your division are pretty good, so I suspect the unidentified source leaking information about how the victim got stabbed in the neck isn't one of the investigators."

Ellie put her elbow on the table and rested her head in her palm, slowly rubbing her forehead back and forth while her eyes remained closed. "Fucking Putz. It makes sense now."

"What makes sense?" Kenny asked.

With her hands at her temples she said, "Like I said earlier, I got assigned the stabbed guy in the car, only my supervisor did not assign me, Major Putz did. The way I see it, administration doesn't want me to put any more time in on Ric's investigation based on two things…the major's comment to the paper and me being assigned lead investigator to another case so quickly."

"It definitely looks that way," I said.

"I'm almost positive the leak about the stab wound didn't come from one of our investigators. A couple might not be considered hard chargers, nonetheless they all have integrity."

Believing Ellie about her administration and her peers came easy. *I wonder if the person skewing information to the press has ulterior motives beyond the obvious political ones.*

"I hate to add insult to injury ...."

"But what?"

"What are your plans for the witness Major Potts so foolishly laid out in the article?"

"I agree," Kenny said. "Ric's attackers acted as a team, fairly well organized. I would not be surprised if they try to take the witness out of the equation."

Within seconds, Ellie had her supervisor on the line. She advocated the victim needed a guard for a minimum of a few days while she tried to get a better grip on who Ric's attackers were. When she went silent and her jaws started clenching, we knew things weren't going her way.

"Putz is an A-1 ass," Ellie said putting her phone on the table. She looked at us with an anger in her eyes we had not seen before from her.

"He had my supervisor call the witness and suggest she go home for a few weeks until things die down. She told him she needs to finish final exams first and requested someone guard her apartment until exams are over."

"Let me guess—"

"Yeah, Putz denied her request."

CHAPTER TWENTY

Ava smiled when she saw Danny's note on the bathroom mirror about going to work early. She did not hate him, yet she increasingly found him harder to be around with his sad face and mopey attitude since Janice Ray died.

She grabbed an energy bar before heading to the Country Club to meet the three women with which she regularly played a round of golf. Ava had long known the ladies pretended to be her friends, the whole time talking about her behind her back, and seldom mentioning her good qualities. If she did not love playing golf and taking their money from the side bets on every hole, she would have distanced herself long ago.

Taking her coffee, Ava glanced to the paper on the counter. The lead article about a Roseville man fighting for his life after being attacked caught her attention. Ava stopped sipping and began reading. When she saw the part about a witness, she thrust her cup on the counter.

Despite agreeing to only text so he could call her back on a burner phone, Ava's anger overrode practicality...she could care less what Colonel Harbaugh thought.

The instant she heard his voice she said, "Are y'all fricking incompetent, are your men incompetent, or is it you're all a bunch of lame asses who can't seem to complete a job without a witness seeing y'all ."

"We agreed never to talk on this phone," Harbaugh said.

Harbaugh's voice leaning on the shaky side instead of strong and confident only fueled Ava's anger.

"You damn well better finish the job on mister high and mighty Afghanistan veteran, and soon. Plus, you're taking care of the witness for free. You aren't receiving another dime of my money until you can prove to me you're capable of completing a task like experts instead of some flunky boy-scout troop."

Harbaugh silently chastised himself for not getting a larger portion of money up front. Instead, he agreed to scheduled payments given she wanted to dispose of so many people.

Before he could respond, Ava said, "You'll meet me at two o'clock on the dot at my Country Club in the restaurant. Before you go whining about being seen I happen to know that's when the least number of customers are in the restaurant. That's called *planning*."

Three beeps followed her getting in her final dig. Harbaugh pulled the phone from his ear and stared for several seconds.

What a bitch, he thought.

He tried sitting a little taller, except the longer he thought about her the more his shoulders sagged from the humiliation of being deemed incompetent. Worse yet, he had little doubt Ava would do everything in her power to spread the word of their incompetence unless they could right the ship.

AVA GATHERED THE OUTFIT SHE WOULD WEAR AFTER she showered at the club. She shuttered at the thought of sitting around for an hour in sweaty golf clothes waiting for the Colonel.

Getting out of her Lexus she thought, *Get a grip. Take their money, deal with them after the round, then deal with Harbaugh. First things first.*

The front nine went better than expected so she decided to deal with the ladies before starting the back nine.

I want all their money, she thought. *I'll scare the hell out of them which will screw up their golf game.*

"I'm tired of y'all talking behind my back. I've put up with your shit for a long time, until you threw me under the bus telling my husband I missed one of our rounds a few weeks ago."

Ava moved forward pointing her driver at them, causing each woman to back up until their carts stopped them.

"If any of you does something like that again, rest assured playing golf, especially at this country club, will become a fleeting memory. And don't forget, I hired a private investigator once you all started regularly talking about me behind my back. We have some interesting video of some of your all's charades."

Ava turned and walked toward the tee box. The three stared, clueless to her not having a PI or video. Over her shoulder, using the best chipper voice she could muster, she said, "All right, let's see if you girls can win some of your money back."

At the end she had profited a little over two hundred more, the most she had won in a round. Ava offered to pay for drinks in the bar...not surprisingly each woman had something important to do.

Ava's tactic had worked in getting her more money and putting the ladies on their heels, it also left her with less time to enjoy a sauna and a shower before she had to meet with Harbaugh. In the sauna room she focused on the girls, trying to recall the looks on their faces on each green and how her staring at them with a smile caused many a bad stroke.

Once in the shower Ava's mind shifted to preparing for Harbaugh.

AT TEN MINUTES BEFORE TWO AVA SAT IN A QUIET CORNER, making sure to put her back to the wall. She figured people passing through or scanning the room would only see the back of Colonel Harbaugh, which should make him somewhat comfortable. Plus, she wanted to be able to look across the room at faces who might stare if she started to lose her temper, a cue for her to take a breath and calm down.

Ava ordered a glass of white wine and enjoyed the taste left behind on her lips. Three of the nine ounces disappeared before Harbaugh walked up. When he put his hand on the back of the chair and scanned the room, she recognized his aversion to not being able to see everything.

"Relax, Colonel. I did it so less people would see your face. You're not the only one who understands tactics."

His head tilted at the same time his cheeks rose.

"Very well."

Harbaugh came knowing he would not take back control without information to show Ava what happened had been a glitch and his team had taken steps to neutralize people. They could move on to the next employee. Although he generally did not like lying to a client, he presumed it would minimize the risk of Ava sticking her nose too far into checking.

He hoped a long swallow of single malt would booster his confidence and held his glass up for a refill. Ava sat erect sipping wine, her silence doing her talking.

"Operations are not an exact science, despite the planning," Harbaugh began, unable to hold his stare in return. He swirled the ice around in his glass and took a deep breath.

"I understand your concerns, I do. Rest assured my contact at the sheriff's office guarantees me the witness saw nothing more than one of our guys carrying another one out to a van. Nothing else. Not even any descriptions." He tried to take another drink only to be met with ice. He looked over his shoulder, saying a silent Amen when he saw the second scotch on its way.

"We will take care of the witness like you requested, totally at our expense. Given the witness did not see a great deal we may wait a few days."

"The hell you will," Ava said through clenched teeth, her eyes darting to confirm she had not been too loud. "You did well at making the first ones look like accidents. Do the same with her. Hell, an overdose of sleeping pills for the poor young thing who couldn't sleep due to fear."

Harbaugh held up his palm. "No problem, we'll handle her right away. Happy?"

Ava glared, then took a sip of wine. "And the soldier?"

Lou had gone to the hospital and overheard some of the nurses talking about the soldier being in critical condition and they would be surprised if he pulled through. Harbaugh relayed the information and before Ava could demand more be done to make it official, he lied and said, "He's not being protected, and my guy knows he can slip in and put another shot of nicotine in his IV. Nobody will be the wiser and it definitely will put him over the top."

Ava leaned back, folded one hand under her elbow while the other held her wine glass in front of her lips. To feign concern, she asked about the health of his injured man, the one the witness saw being carried out.

Clearing his throat and hesitating, Harbaugh said, "He died. Clean punch to the throat, no blood or evidence left behind. We disposed of him on federal property to create confusion. He won't be traced back to the soldier, I promise."

"Hmmm," she groaned. "Now, tell me, who are you targeting next?"

You really are a bitch. You don't even care one of my men died for you.

Harbaugh took two more gulps of his Scotch hoping to balance his ever-increasing dislike of her.

Harbaugh continued, "On the list of major players on the web site there's one guy without a picture, he's a retired cop. We have two reasons to take him out. One is, with their backgrounds and experience he and the soldier are the main contacts for the military and law enforcement. Losing them cripples the owner severely. Secondly, the owner likes the fact he has his own personal protection duo. We predict the owner folds up shop and sells before the month is out if we take him out."

A large smile crossed Ava's face. She raised her hand for the waiter's attention, stating, "Very good, Colonel. I'm pleased…now let's eat. My treat."

CHAPTER TWNETY-ONE

———— ◆ ————

Special Agent Todd Pham of the National Parks Investigative Services had barely made it to work when his boss notified him about being the lead investigator on a dead body discovered in Chancellorsville Battleground. Pham disliked receiving any information beyond the location of the crime believing too many investigators make up their minds early, and spent the entire time trying to prove their theory.

Pham's crime scene technicians arrived almost fifteen minutes after him allowing Pham time to get contact information from the sheriff's deputy. He had secured the scene with crime scene tape, along with carefully getting a look at the body without disturbing anything. An arrow through the guys back would have been enough for some of his peers to label it a hunting accident so they could quickly close the case, despite the illegality of hunting on federal property. Pham would not allow himself to get suckered into such beliefs so early in the investigation.

Hours later the medical examiner from the Central District office in Richmond mirrored Pham's concerns. There had not been any obvious bleeding from the arrow wound, nor from where the man's face scraped against the wall after presumably falling forward. Before leaving, the ME indicated things not adding up already had her uncomfortable, so much so she wanted to get to the autopsy soon.

Beyond the obvious, two other things bothered Pham. The fingerprints on the half-full water bottle beneath the dead man gave him pause. If the man had been alive when the arrow pierced his body the bottle likely would have landed where they found it, explaining the man's fingerprints. If, however, he died prior to being shot, the killer would have had to go to great extent to stage the scene.

Could it have really been staged this perfectly, he thought?

No sign of other people's footsteps on the forest floor prior to law enforcement videotaping and photographing the scene also disquieted him. The forest floor had a brushed look to it, almost too smooth in his mind. His crime scene techs did not hesitate to let him know they disagreed. Even though they thought Pham might be kidding himself they did what he asked and took a few photographs trying their best to show the pristine look of the forest floor before they trampled it.

Once they cleared the scene Pham offered to feed the crew at a diner in Fredericksburg before they headed home. Most of them had finished eating when Pham received a call from the ME.

She meant what she said about wanting to get to the autopsy, he thought.

Pham had no problem with making an extremely long day out of driving to Richmond. He knew it would be close to midnight before the ME completed the autopsy and he got back to the office. He decided to release the techs, offering to photograph and collect any evidence. None of them expected any evidence beyond the arrow and what looked like a phone in his pocket. They appreciated Pham's offer and agreed to get the items they had collected booked into evidence and the victim's fingerprints run through AFIS before they went home.

The drive south to Richmond on I-95 took a little over an hour. During it Pham's mind covered a lot of ground. His desire years earlier to be a Secret Service agent had drifted away. He no longer wanted to leave the Park Service. He enjoyed the work, especially cases like this. Occasionally, he wondered why the Secret Service had passed him over several times, although it did not take long before his mind returned to the investigation at hand.

Pham had never been to the Medical Examiners Central District office after normal hours. Seeing so many people still bustling about when he arrived surprised him. There never seemed to be a lack of bodies needing an autopsy.

Pham grinned, thinking, *Brings a new meaning to a skeleton crew.*

Within a short time, he and the ME went to work. Before Pham left, they exchanged small talk about the case, and he liked the way she thought. They agreed conflicting messages emerged. No ID meant someone did not want the man to be easily identified, yet they left evidence in his pockets, a phone in one and a note in another. The attractiveness of the words *PIs-insurgents-NY* written on the tiny paper in his pocket could have led to much longer conversations, although exhaustion caught up to them. Pham left promising to keep her updated.

By the time Pham left, he had no doubt his victim had not died on the battlefield, instead learning he died of asphyxiation from a crushed larynx hours earlier. Exactly where had yet to be determined, nonetheless knowing the battlefield scene had been staged intrigued him and the ME alike.

COLONEL HARBAUGH TEXTED ROCK AND DINGO, TELLing them he wanted to meet in the bar at The Founder's Hotel at 10 p.m. When they arrived, they found him near the far wall nursing his second Scotch, the best they could tell with another empty SoHo glass on the table. Outwardly he seemed relaxed, even having ditched his suit coat and tie.

Harbaugh raised his arm and the waitress arrived seconds later. Beer on tap seemed to be the choice, except for Harbaugh who ordered a third Scotch. When Harbaugh threw two twenties on the tray and told the waitress to keep the change Dingo's eyes slid toward Rock who raised an eyebrow. They had never seen Harbaugh drink before, much less three, so how he handled his booze seemed foreign.

Once alone with their drinks, Harbaugh said, "You boys see the paper this morning?"

Both nodded, although neither seemed eager to be the first to speak.

"A witness…a goddamn witness," he growled, slamming his fist down on the table.

Rock had his mug in his hand, in contrast Dingo's sat on the table and his beer went everywhere. Many patrons gave a quick glance, although most dismissed it as a belligerent drunk and went back to their own conversations.

The waitress arrived within seconds and began mopping up beer with her towels while Dingo stood and tried brushing the moisture off his clothes. Seconds later the bartender strolled over to the table.

"Problem gentlemen?"

"No, no. We're fine," Rock said.

He stood, setting his mug on the table, then put his left hand on the bartender's shoulder and extended his right hand.

"I hope so. I'd hate to have to ask you to leave." He shook Rock's hand and his eyes shot over to Harbaugh for a brief second and then back to Rock.

Rock nodded and the bartender left.

Dingo went to the bathroom to try to clean up.

Picking up his mug and putting his elbows on the table, Rock leaned forward. Almost whispering Rock said, "You better hope nobody heard what you said, or we have bigger problems than a witness."

Colonel Harbaugh had gone quite a few years without admitting something he did might have been wrong, and he had no plans to do so now.

Leaning forward himself, putting his nose inches away from Rock's, he growled in a low tone, "If you lame ducks hadn't screwed up, we wouldn't be down two men and in the mess we're in. The target isn't dead yet and we have a witness. I'd say we're at strike two...we reach strike three and we all go down."

"Thanks for imparting such wisdom, we could have never figured it out without you," Rock said, standing and taking cash out of his pocket.

Dingo walked up a split second after Rock stood. Rock set a twenty on the counter near the bartender on the way out and mouthed the word *sorry*.

"I've never seen him like this," Dingo said walking through the door.

"Me either. I know at one point he had a problem with overusing opioids for some war injuries. I thought he got past it, I guess maybe not."

"Yeah, he looked, I don't know, buzzed...and drunk."

"Other than acting like a drunken idiot everything he said rang true. We've never underestimated a target like we did."

Dingo chuckled and Rock tilted his head. "What?"

Dingo stood at attention. "Sir, the government of the United States of America regretfully informs you that you're a drunken idiot, Sir."

Rock busted up laughing and they got in the car.

Neither of them noticed the solid black Suburban backed into a slot, the person in charge staring without expression while the driver held the parabolic microphone to the partially rolled down window. Shaking her head in disgust, she wondered how much longer she could be tolerant.

CHAPTER TWENTY-TWO

Once a homicide investigator, always a homicide investigator. I slept well for three hours, until my brain decided to flick the *on* switch. Our conversation with Ellie at the restaurant the morning before came to the forefront.

I put on my running clothes and intentionally chose a dark shirt. I had no problem with foregoing a little safety for some stealth, especially at three in the morning. The light on my phone came on when I unplugged it.

Three percent charge? Dammit, I grabbed the wrong charger cord.

I could feel my anger rising...at my own stupidity. I could not believe I didn't throw the cord away when it first started intermittently charging a month ago.

What the hell are you being frugal for, you cheap ass!

Since I had decided I would be going to check on Ric's witness, I wanted an extra magazine. Knowing I would need the extra space, I put my arm strap on and my phone in it. Unwilling to give in to the stereotype a fanny pack looked stupid, I put my ID, gun and one extra magazine in mine, strapped it on and headed out.

Despite the extra distance I headed toward Ric's apartment complex. Snooping around there for a little bit would provide some rest before starting the run back.

The mention of a witness in the newspaper had been eating at me. Only two apartments existed above Ric's so anyone wanting to go after her already had the odds in their favor. Ellie's agency letting information get out about a witness had me perplexed. I usually despised complacent employees, even though it seemed like a better alternative than someone there being dirty, which I had not yet ruled out.

I had almost passed the Augustine Golf Club when the deputy in the patrol car following me for the past five blocks turned on the emergency lights and lit me up with a spotlight. Before the deputy got out of his car, I turned in time to see the second patrol car racing up Courthouse Road towards us.

Both deputies exited at the same time and stayed behind their doors. I admired the fact they both turned the front of their cars toward each other's providing some cover from their engine blocks. Their tactics appeared spot on.

I decided to do what I did in Albuquerque the last time officers confronted me and verbally give them all the information necessary to run me in any system they desired. Fortunately, the deputies did not think I had tried to be evasive. One of them entered the information in his Mobile Data Terminal and had results in no time.

"What's in the fanny pack?" the primary deputy asked.

"My retired police ID."

"Let me guess, and your gun?"

"Yep, and one extra mag. These are normal working hours for dirtbags across America. Old habits die hard."

"Why don't you unsnap your fanny pack and lay it on the ground, then backup ten paces."

I complied and watched them approach together, with the secondary keeping me square in his gun sights while the primary deputy confirmed my being legit. After the search, he handed me my fanny pack and his partner put his weapon away.

"You know we gotta ask what you're doing out here, right?"

"I get it. I'm a former homicide detective who doesn't sleep well. I find a good run sometimes helps me relax and I can grab another couple hours later. Plus, I'm less likely to be ran over, intentionally or unintentionally, at this hour."

They glanced at each other and I suspected they had been on duty when Laird Spencer got ran over not far from our location, although neither said a word. We did the shop-talk thing for a good ten minutes before their dispatcher gave them a call for service and they left.

The remainder of the run to Ric's apartment went without a hitch. When I got on the road leading into his complex, I slowed to take in any movement. The driveway went in a semicircle around various buildings, so I entered the first drive I came to. Before I started around the backside of the complex I stopped and found a dark area under the covered parking to stand and watch.

After what felt like five minutes of not seeing any movement, I slowly began making my way towards Ric's building while staying close to the wall under the covered parking. I made it past seven cars when Ric's building came into view. The apartment in the upper left had lights on and I could see movement inside. Within minutes the living room curtain opened exposing the silhouette of what looked like a woman with long hair. *She had to be the witness.* Ellie texted us late the day before to say the witness refused to go anywhere until she completed major exams in her college classes.

Most people, regardless of why they would be up at such an early morning hour, would not look out of their apartment window towards the parking lot...unless they're waiting for someone, they're hearing noises, or they're scared like her, I thought.

The instant she stepped away from the window I quietly moved two cars closer so I could have a better advantage of looking straight at the building. I had not heard or seen anything out of place and from my new position I could tell she kept looking to her left. I followed her gaze. One car backed into a space in the covered parking about a half dozen spaces away appeared to be the only thing out of place. Lighting from the streetlights in the parking lot did not reach under the covering where I stood so I could not make out a distinct color.

The woman left the window again and I got ready to move. I stopped when I heard the slight creaking of a car door opening nearby, although I had no way of knowing exactly where. I hugged the wall and hunched over starting to make my way towards the backed in car.

Somewhere around my third step I kicked a can, which in the quietness of the hour sounded like a gunshot. I then heard two distinct voices, one saying, "Shit" and the other saying, "Let's go."

When I heard a car engine revving, I tried to make my way around the side mirrors of parked cars. By the time I made it to the open area the car had already started leaving without lights. I could see it had two doors on the driver's side, no rear license plate, and it appeared to be either gray or light blue.

Pushing the home button on my phone did not produce a screen.

So much for three percent, I thought. *I only have myself to blame.*

Looking to my left I saw her silhouette in the upstairs window and her hands covering her mouth. I pulled out my ID wallet and held it up, hoping she would see the badge. I inched my way toward the building, my arm still extended with the badge.

Stopping fifteen feet from the building and almost directly in front of her, I touched my chest with my other index finger and then pointed to my right hoping she figured I meant the stairs. She paused for several seconds before nodding.

When I got to her door, I lightly tapped while I held my badge close to the peep hole. Given the circumstances I figured she would not see the word retired, instead she would be happy a cop stood on the other side of her door. The door creaked open four inches and the right side of the girl's face looked around the edge.

"I'm AJ Conti. I'm friends with Ellie Svenson, the deputy in charge of the investigation of your downstairs neighbor."

Her eyes remained wide and her face rested against the edge of the door. The movement of her head up and down seemed beyond deliberate, almost the appearance of someone in shock.

"I can see you're scared so all you have to do is shake your head 'yes or no'. You've been watching the car that took off, haven't you?"

She nodded twice.

"Something told you the car did not belong here."

She nodded.

"Now can you see why Ellie, sorry, Deputy Svenson, wanted you to go somewhere else?"

A tear started to run down her cheek, and she nodded.

"I...I wanted to finish exams first. My dad told me...I asked for police protection until I finished...they told me they couldn't." She started crying and covered her face with both hands.

Between her shaking and crying I felt she should not be left alone, much less try to drive.

"Do you have any friends inside the complex I can escort you to? I don't want you to drive away until lots of traffic is coming in and out later this morning."

Her face moved from the door and she looked at the cell phone in her hand. "My friend...she's in the next building," she mumbled at the same time her thumbs texted.

After we heard the ding, she checked the response, grabbed her keys and came into the hallway. Once downstairs she walked so close to me I could feel her body on my left shoulder blade.

Groggy from being woken up, her friend had no panic about her coming over. I ran the whole thing down and explained what they should do later in the morning. I would be calling Ellie and suggested they call her also. I made sure her friend understood the witness needed to go somewhere safe, and not to use her own car.

When I made it back into the parking area no new apartment lights seemed to be on giving me the impression not another soul knew what took place. I went through the lot the direction the car fled, and once I got to the street, I began my run, staying on the side running toward oncoming headlights.

I had about a quarter of a mile of darkness before I would be at the main road in Roseville when the hair on the back of my neck raised, the sound of a car registering a split second later. Looking over my right shoulder I saw it bearing down on me without headlights. A muzzle flash with a somewhat suppressed noise came from the right side of the car. I saw the front of the car jut my way at the beginning of my dive toward the grass and gravel of the sloping shoulder and felt the rush of air hit me in midair from the near miss.

I hit the ground and rolled twice, taking my Glock out. The car had continued moving away from me at a high rate of speed making return fire questionable at best. I bounded up and got behind the cover of the forest trees in case they returned.

"Turnabout is fair play. Hope you're ready," I said in the darkness.

.

CHAPTER TWENTY-THREE

———◦———

Rock remained quiet and Dingo knew not to interrupt him. They rode in silence for several miles before Rock pulled into a parking lot and backed into the open space closest to the driveway.

"I think we both missed him," Rock said. "He didn't react like one of your rounds hit him and I barely missed him when he dove."

"Damn, what do we do now? That witness ain't gonna stay there now."

"No, and we can't be seen over there again."

Rock leaned forward putting both elbows on the steering wheel and his prayer hands up to his lips. He contemplated Dingo's question for several seconds before deciding they needed to take a risk.

"We haven't heard any sirens this whole time. I don't think the cops have been called so we need to see if the guy runs somewhere. The way he reacted...he did not look like Joe Citizen out for a morning run. He moved through the parking lot with stealth, hell we had no clue of him being there. And then the way he didn't freeze up when you shot at him and I drove the car at him, he has to be someone with training."

"You think he's friends with the military guy we put in the hospital?"

"Probably. How do you feel about going back the way we came to see if we can find him again?"

Dingo's head bobbed while he thought about it. "If we find him, I say we go right at him instead of another drive by. We can dump the car at Dutch's for a while, he'll hide it for us."

"Agreed. Better than average chance the guy isn't staying in Roseville, he's most likely going to run back to Stafford unless he had a car stashed. If he runs back, he'll need to come down Mountain View Road. I say we go to the intersection…what's the name of that road?"

"Shelton Shop Road. Good idea. He probably stayed hidden for a little while to see if we would return so if he's running, I wouldn't think he got far yet."

Rock drove the three minutes to the intersection and parked on the gravel shoulder a little south of the intersection so they could see towards Roseville. They agreed to wait fifteen minutes, and if they did not see him, they would start driving around to look for him, including going back toward the witness' apartment building.

HIDING BEHIND THE TREE COULD NOT GO ON FOREVER, so after several minutes I decided their return seemed unlikely.

Great time to have a dead phone, I thought.

I put my Glock back in the holster inside the fanny pack and made my way to the road. I knew I had about seven miles to the hotel and figured Kenny would still be asleep even if I slowed my pace to make sure I didn't get ambushed.

I made it to Mountain View Road and turned left to head back toward Stafford. The signal lights from the intersection a little south of Roseville came into view. Staying on the wrong side of the road I had trees nearby instead of the open field on the other side. A car appeared to be stopped in the right turn lane, and I realized it had no headlights. I barely made it another fifty feet when the car began to move forward and turned right, the headlights still off.

My options seemed limited without any charge in my cell phone and no other traffic on the road at such an early hour. I looked at the street names on the light poles and for the first time I paid attention to the name of the road I needed to turn on, Shelton Shop Road.

They are either going to try and get me on this dark little stretch before I turn toward the golf course, or they're going to follow and see what hotel I'm headed to.

The adrenalin rush cops get from heading to major calls or chasing someone is different from the sixth sense feelings some get knowing something bad is about to happen. I had been in enough critical incidents to realize my unique sixth sense feelings and not to ignore them. When the roller coaster feeling of my stomach climbing into my throat hit, I slowed to a stop. Once my stomach came back down, I took out my Glock and began to jog away from the intersection and into darkness. Strangely, I thought of the deputies who stopped me earlier and how their actions might be in my favor depending on what they tell their superiors about me. I could only hope.

Recalling my run to Roseville I thought I remembered mostly long driveways, with only a few homes close to the road. I recalled only one seemed somewhat well lit, along with a church on the northwest side of the road, the side I ran on to face oncoming traffic. Less than a quarter of a mile away, the driveway leading into the church seemed like the perfect spot, allowing them to be parked fifty feet back from the road making them tough to spot.

Time to find out, I thought.

Sixty yards before the church I passed the last house and spotted what looked like the silhouette of a car close to the main building well away from the road. The ambient light from the church parking lot lights helped me make my last mental preparations. I had an open area of fifty feet to cross where I would be exposed, so I sprinted to the one piece of cover existing, a huge tree next to the driveway into the church.

The front of the car came into view and both doors looked half opened. I heard the suppressed sounds of gunfire a split second before I felt the flesh in my right leg burning. I fired two rounds each in the general vicinity of the car doors hoping to cause a pause in their shooting long enough for me to get to the tree.

Diving, I landed on a slight raised section of root, causing me to expel air like I had been punched.

I heard a voice say, "I think we got him."

A thought jumped into my head and I went with it.

"Help, help, I've been shot," I said with my free hand over my mouth to muffle the cry.

A different voice from the direction of the car said, "Hurry up. You approach to finish him off, I'll cover you."

I rolled into a sniper position on the left side of the tree figuring he would approach from my left since his cover man had a good view of the right side of the tree. The man raced from behind the passenger door to a small tree at his two o'clock. He had all the appearance of a trained gunman, arms extended, head looking down the barrel and upper body turned to minimize exposure.

Seth popped into my mind. Having been one of our SWAT snipers, he grilled me to no end to practice shooting off hand and in varying positions, including from a prone position. I silently thanked him, took a deep calming breath and waited.

The man's first step toward me after he cleared the tree turned out to be his last. One of two shots struck him in the head and the other looked like an upper chest shot. His body jerked backward, and his knees collapsed. I paused for a second to make sure he didn't move and heard the rev of the car engine. I rolled to my right and transferred my gun to my right hand in time to see the back end of the car driving across the lawn next to the end of the church.

The several trees directly across from me appeared to make great backdrop to shoot at the car when it slightly turned toward the road. Something in my head told me not to without knowing what existed on the other side, so I released pressure from the trigger. The car hit the asphalt, fishtailed a second before straightening out and the headlights came on a couple hundred feet down the road.

The pain from my leg kept me from bounding up. Still, the need to make sure the guy left behind could no longer shoot overrode my pain. Instinctively, I made my way toward him.

Within ten feet I could see he had a one-way ticket to the morgue. I thought about kicking his gun away from his hand, ultimately deciding it would make for a perfect evidentiary photo, his finger still in the trigger guard and a suppressor on the end of the gun.

Knowing what would be coming next, I stepped to the driveway and pulled out my wallet with my ID and badge. I laid my gun down on the driveway and held up the wallet.

Seconds later a man came out of the last house I passed. He had a rifle and began making his way across the grass.

"We called 911," the man said with a slight drawl. "You best stay right where you are mister."

"I need to sit down," I said, deciding to play on the man's emotions a little. "I'm out for a run, minding my own business, and he attacked me. Shot me in the leg. I really need to sit down."

The man had moved within fifty feet of me and closer to the dead guy. He looked down at the gun and then back at me. He nodded.

"What's the badge?"

"Police officer, I'm from California," I said as I got settled on the ground.

The man turned and yelled to the woman on the porch, telling her to get an ambulance right away for an injured policeman.

He looked at the dead guy and back at me. He seemed like he knew how to handle a rifle and probably had seen his fair share of dead animals. Still, something about a dead human body draws people's eyes in and he could not keep from looking at it every few seconds.

CHAPTER TWENTY-FOUR

The first deputy on the scene happened to be the primary deputy who stopped me earlier. His recognizing me right away kept him from sprawling me face down on the pavement. Instead, he walked up to me with his gun at a low ready position.

"What the hell happened, Detective?"

"I'm not sure. I kind of think they might have been ready to burglarize the church and saw me. When I saw them, I tried to get to the big tree next to the driveway, except they opened fire on me and one of them hit me. I returned fire and dove behind the tree where I stayed."

We heard a tremendous number of sirens and the deputy's eyes sprang wide open.

"Oh shit," he said, before he started barking out some code on his radio.

"Let me guess, dispatch said officer down?"

The deputy scrunched his eyebrows and tilted his head. "Yeah ..."

"I kind of identified myself as a cop when the man saw my badge. I didn't want him to shoot me, and trying to explain being retired seemed like, I don't know, not the right time to get into details."

The deputy did a half-snort and grinned, his head nodding as he walked away.

Ellie arrived about the same time the paramedics started to load me into the ambulance.

"Can you give us a second," she said, looking at the paramedics. They backed away giving her the space she wanted considering I had a non-life-threatening through and through wound on the outside of my thigh.

"I only have a few seconds before the boss will question why I'm over here."

"Then for now all you need to know is I did not say anything about being over at the apartment earlier and helping the witness find a safer location. I said I interrupted a burglary. Now, get out of here, we'll talk later."

Ellie turned to leave, and I reached out and put my hand on her wrist.

"Can you call Kenny? My phone's dead," I said with the best pretty please face I could muster, and my shoulders hunched up.

"Men," she said, shaking her head and grinning.

When Ellie began to drift away, I said, "Let's go gentlemen, I've got an ER nurse waiting to lavage this wound."

The medics jumped in and we took off to Stafford Hospital. The paramedic in the back called in my injury to the ER and confirmed more than once I had not gone into shock despite my bradycardia. Their bantering over my lack of shock took up most of the drive and I expected I would have a hard time convincing the ER staff my low heart rate had been something I lived with my entire life.

Fortunately, I only had some cheap running clothes on since cutting clothes off seems to be universal in emergency rooms. The ER doctor looked to be close to my age, other than she had some gray hair in her roots and near her temples. She slapped her stethoscope on my chest and listened intently for several seconds. She started to pull away then paused, her eyes floating across my face and upper body.

"This isn't the first time you've visited an emergency room," she said, her open palm pointing out scars.

Figuring her statement had been rhetorical, I only grinned.

"I can tell why the medics remained adamant you did not go into shock. Most people who get shot do, you know."

"I think you'll find I'm not most people, Doc," I said, grinning again.

She smiled, shook her head, and walked away. "Get x-rays and flush the wound out," she said over her shoulder to the nursing staff in the room.

My wound did not warrant a trauma room any longer, so they transferred me to a normal ER room. I returned from X-rays to find Kenny carrying on a conversation with one of the male nurses about the Reno air races like they had been friends forever.

"Don't stop on my account. I've only been shot."

"We won't," Kenny said.

Kenny could feel the staff staring at him and said, "What, this is nothing for him."

For the women in the room his lack of caring went over like a lead balloon, one of them even asking if I wanted him to leave.

"Dude, you've got to go to their air museum," Kenny said, the museum talk with the male nurse continuing the entire time other nurses irrigated my wound.

When they finished they left Kenny and I alone while we waited for the ER doc to release me.

"Ellie texted, said some investigators are on their way to talk with you about what happened. She said the best she could tell, nobody else knows you had been at Ric's apartment building, although the witness contacted her. So, the white elephant in the room is, why did you tell them you thought you interrupted a burglary?"

"They've done in two people, three if Ric doesn't pull through. They went back to finish off the witness and had every intention of killing me. I like the deputies we've met, and I think Ellie is a good investigator, on the other hand you've heard the way she talks about their hierarchy. Do we really want to turn this whole thing over to the sheriff's office when they are in the middle of political positioning for who will be the next sheriff? Besides, a car backed up to a business in the middle of the night…what's your average deputy going to think?"

"You better hope they buy the burglary thing, otherwise you're in a cesspool up to your knees."

"Thanks for the graphic picture. Don't you have air races or something to go discuss with someone."

THE PHONE IN THE HOTEL ROOM RANG FOR QUITE SOME time before Harbaugh woke from his drunken stupor to answer it.

"I don't need to hear any shit from you right now …."

Harbaugh threw back the covers and swung his legs over the edge of the bed. The frustration in Rock's tone told him something had gone wrong and he knew better than to say a word.

"I'm in my car down in the parking lot. What room are you in, I'm coming up?"

The colonel paused, not due to Rock, instead by reason of his alcohol and drug induced lack of recall.

"What the hell's your room number?" Rock growled.

"Uh, I'm not sure, I'm looking for the key card. Uh, here it is," Harbaugh said, pausing a split second, unsure if he really wanted Rock in his room…he had no choice.

The instant Harbaugh read off the number the phone went dead. Rock made his way into the hotel and punched the elevator button with the outside of his hand…no prints.

Harbaugh barely had enough time to throw on pants and a t-shirt, splash some water on his face and hair, and gargle the foul taste out of his mouth before he heard the low rapping on the door.

After he neutralized the locks and the door began to creak open, Rock shoved it pushing Harbaugh up against the wall. Rock took four steps inside and stopped, his head swiveling to find the liquor. In seconds he had the caps off the miniature bottles of whiskey and poured all of them at the same time into a glass.

Having been around battle-tested soldiers Harbaugh knew they needed to vent sometimes, without a ranking officer making foolish comments about their performance, or lack thereof. Harbaugh peeked into the hallway to look for Dingo, becoming nauseous the instant he cleared it and realized the implication.

Despite sensing the worst had happened he knew better than to derail Rock's need to go at his own pace. Harbaugh made his way to the small table across the room and took a seat opposite Rock. He leaned into the back of the chair, crossed one leg over the other, and interlocked his fingers in his lap. He could not do anything about the paleness in his face or the clamminess of his skin, instead he did what he could to feign being in full control and prepared for anything Rock might say.

Rock drained the first glass and proceeded to open three more miniature bottles. When he had those poured in his glass, he took one sip and turned around, yet could not bring himself to look directly at his boss. The full weight of what happened seemed to arrive at once; his feet shuffled across the carpet.

Pulling the chair from the table Rock turned it at a forty-five-degree angle and dropped into it hard. Rock's right elbow landed on the table with a thud and the side of his head fell into his palm.

"Dingo's dead."

The color remaining in Harbaugh's face slid away, while telling himself repeatedly not to vomit. After several deep breaths he thought how swiftly bad news could sober a person up, although he had no desire to be abstinent. He made his way to the room phone, putting the receiver to his ear.

"I'll tip you twenty dollars if you can deliver a half-dozen of your little whiskey bottles to my room in under five minutes. Make it a dozen."

Harbaugh made his way to the bathroom, splashed more cold water on his face and dabbed it dry, hoping to see an unshaken face in the mirror when he pulled the towel away. He didn't.

Neither said a word until after the whiskey delivery and Harbaugh had a chance to put three bottles in a glass for him and three more in Rock's.

Trying to sound in control, Harbaugh asked, "Look, before we go any further, is there anything needing immediate attention or cleaning up?"

Rock shook his head twice and chased it with whiskey.

"Very well, then we—"

"Wait…for safety, we probably need to have Dutch take the car and get it out to a chop shop. I can report it stolen in a couple hours when it's daylight."

If this is it, then we got lucky, Harbaugh thought.

Retrieving his cell phone off the nightstand Harbaugh pulled up Carli's number and sent a text.

MY HOTEL. ASAP. TEXT WHEN PARKED.

CHAPTER TWENTY-FIVE

I could hear two deputies talking with Kenny outside the curtain of my emergency room. One of them said he would stay with Kenny while the other one poked his head in and asked if he could speak with me.

"Sure. AJ Conti," I said, extending my hand.

Shaking hands, he identified himself as Sergeant Carothers and said the interview should be short and sweet. He informed me he already spoke with the two deputies who stopped me earlier, and the crime scene techs had recovered some bullets from the tree.

His own patrol deputies had already somewhat validated me to set the tone, a blessing I did not see coming when I talked with them near the golf course early during my run. Still, no different than testifying in court, I had no intention of giving him any more information than he required.

"Where all did you run to?"

Although I thought the odds seemed extremely low, I knew I had to validate being in Roseville considering I may have been caught on some security camera. "I'm not overly familiar with the area, it seems like I made it to a town called Roseville."

The sergeant's nod appeared to be confirmation rather than simple verification for me to go on, leaving me to wonder exactly how much they knew. I decided to test the waters while accounting for time I spent at the apartment complex without mentioning the complex.

"I turned right on one road and ran a little while until it became apparent I kept getting further out into the country, so I decided to turn around."

"You ended up several miles from the hotel you're staying at…a normal distance for you to run?"

"To be honest, Sarge, I got a second wind when the deputies stopped me. When I started running again, I went further than I realized. When I ended up turning around, I didn't know if I would be able to make it back without walking some. Until I came across the boys at the church."

Without skipping a beat the sergeant went right into asking me about noticing the car backed up next to the building, so I felt pretty certain he had no idea I stopped at Ric's apartment complex or those fools had tried to run me over and shoot me near there. The risk of being discovered not telling the whole truth still existed, in contrast the fact the sergeant never asked about Ric's apartment would be my fall back if ever questioned about it.

"Did you ever see them trying to break into the church?"

"Not really. Why?" I asked, hoping he would fall for my bait and give me information instead of asking more questions of me to figure out what I saw.

"We think you interrupted a drug deal, not a burglary. The guy you killed had no ID and his gun had a suppressor. Not common equipment for a burglar."

They already showed their hand believing I interrupted nefarious criminal activity, so if they wanted to believe I interrupted something other than a burglary I would be happy to oblige them.

"Man, Sarge…I'd focused on a car backed up next to the

building, which is why I tried to run to the tree, so I could watch them. Now, since I'm not trying to dodge bullets, you're probably right, a pair of burglars would have jumped in and drove off."

"Understandable, AJ. Hell, you getting shot at trumps the crime they intended to do there. Right?"

I nodded and tried to look a little sheepish, rubbing the top of my head up and back once.

"Hey, the good news is, you're here instead of going to the morgue like the schmuck you dumped. Great job, AJ. I won't bother you anymore."

The sergeant shook my hand and left. I heard him and Kenny talking, their voices trailing off while Kenny walked with them outside.

The emergency room doctor came in with a slight grin. I tilted my head, unsure if the grin had to do with me or it lingered from something else she saw or heard.

"Gotta say, one of the shortest interviews of a shooting victim I've ever listened to."

"Oh, you eavesdropped, did you?"

"The advantages of curtains being the only separation of emergency room beds. And nobody questions a doctor walking into the next room and pulling the curtains."

I chuckled, realizing no patient existed in the bed next to mine.

"Smooth, Doc. Did you enjoy it?"

"Immensely, thank you. Other than I need to raise the bullshit flag."

"Oh, do you now?"

My thumbs pointing at the curtain on both sides of my bed, I looked in each direction before looking back at her and tilting my head.

"Don't worry, the ER's almost cleared out. No patient even close to you so nobody can hear us."

Nodding, I asked, "So why the BS flag?"

"The deputies did not see any other scar besides the one on your cheek, which could have been from any number of non-police related things, like a car accident for example."

"But …"

"Well, I will admit my seeing all of the other scars helped me to speculate the scar on your cheek probably came from a violent confrontation while working, I'm guessing like most of the other scars I saw. The luxury of seeing them all helped me to formulate the opinion you no more thought those men might be doing a burglary at a church than the man on the moon."

"Oh really?"

"Yes, really. The tone of your voice told me you lacked sincerity in your explanation of not realizing it."

When the corners of my lips went up, she smiled and nodded, likely more in approval of her reading it correctly.

"Good obs, as one of my field training officers used to say. Observant, Doc. So?"

"Don't worry. I won't say anything. Besides, who really cares? They turned out to obviously be bad people up to no good and I'm pretty sure they shot at you first from what I could tell."

"They did. No BS."

"See, so burglary, drug deal, whatever…I kind of figure it's like me doing something as an emergency room doctor based on my gut feeling of having done this for several years and not necessarily putting it in the report I dictate later. Something told you to watch those guys and they opened fire on you. You trusted your gut and it probably saved your life."

"So, I have to ask, what prompted you to go to the bed next to mine and pretend to be seeing a patient?"

"Simple curiosity. Plus, the ER is finally slowing down, so I had the time. I don't have some exciting explanation. Sometimes it's nice to get more than gossip. When everyone else around here is talking about this like they have the real scoop, I can sit back and laugh knowing I'm the only one with the actual answers."

The doctor stood and we shook hands.

"Thank you, AJ, for your service. You've obviously put yourself in harm's way several times for the safety of the public, and I for one appreciate it."

She turned and started to leave. Pulling the curtain back she looked over her shoulder.

"You're right…you're not most people."

I gave her a half smile and shrugged.

Thanks Doc.

A thought started to enter my mind about the doc telling someone about our conversation, then I dismissed it. The crux of what she said centered on her appreciation for someone trusting their gut instincts like she does.

You're not most people either, Doc.

CHAPTER TWENTY-SIX

———— ◆ ————

T he entire drive from her hotel to Harbaugh's, Carli nervously ran possibilities through her head. The overriding thought centered on the note.

If they found it, I'm dead, she thought.

Carli reasoned Harbaugh had never called her in place of Rock and Dingo in an emergency. With it being early morning and still dark, everything seemed to be pointing toward them having found the note.

Carli contemplated driving straight to Dulles airport and catching a flight to some foreign country, deciding instead she would only extend her life for a couple days with death likely following either way. Going to the feds and trading information for the witness protection program crossed her mind, although if her time on the United States Capitol Police force taught her anything, she learned money talks. She could not be sure if the stories she heard about federal officers or prosecutors giving up witness locations in exchange for money had been true. Being fired for taking bribes surely gave others in law enforcement a valid reason to give her up as payback.

What cop or prosecutor would not be okay with a former dirty cop getting whacked?

Pulling into the parking lot Carli spotted Rock's rental car and she parked in the first spot closest to his. She sent a text to Harbaugh letting him know she had arrived. The return text read, my room, then a number followed. In no hurry, Carli made her way to his floor, taking a deep breath before she tapped on the door. Harbaugh opened it and motioned her in. She could see the tension in his face, especially in his monobrow. Four steps in she saw Rock sitting at the table and at a quick glance she counted six small liquor bottles, all empty. Dingo had yet to be seen.

Shit, where's he at?

"Have a seat at the table," Harbaugh said.

Carli wanted to again ask about Dingo's whereabouts, mostly out of fear he might slither in and put a garrote around her neck. According to Rock patience and listening happened to be some of her better qualities, so she remained quiet. She had never seen Rock that distraught and hunched over, so much so he never looked up when she pulled out a chair.

"Rock," she greeted him.

His head came up a couple inches in a slow upward nod, his eyes never leaving the table.

It's the note…or is it something else? Damn! Where's Dingo?

Harbaugh walked to the table and sat directly across from Carli. He had way too much to drink before midnight and really did not want to explain things to her. One more look at Rock told him he would not be so lucky.

Carli put her ankle on her knee and interlocked her fingers around her lifted leg. She didn't want them to see her hands shaking and since she often sat in a similar fashion while waiting for her assignment, she hoped they would not notice.

"There's no way to sugarcoat this…Dingo is dead. He and Rock got in a shootout with some guy, fortunately Rock got out."

Oh my God, thank you, she thought.

Harbaugh could see the shock in Carli's large eyes. He would never know her shock came from the realization of her new lease on life, thankful Dingo died instead of her.

"We can explain everything later, right now we need to get Rock's car to Dutch so he can get rid of it. Rock's not feeling much like talking so you explain to Dutch what we need. Rock will pick you up in your car and then go to his hotel. He's going to report it stolen, have the rental company bring him a new car, and then we will meet at some restaurant. I'll let you know which one after Rock lets us know he has a new car."

Carli tried to keep her distraught appearance, though inside she felt overjoyed her peers had not discovered the note she left in Thumper's pocket in the battlefield. She unclasped her hands and leaned forward, putting her elbows on the table, and crossing her arms, staring straight at Harbaugh, all the while telling herself to *look serious and not smile.*

Harbaugh started to explain he wanted the car chopped right away when his phone dinged.

Rock raised his head surprised Harbaugh would be receiving a text so early in the morning. Harbaugh's monobrow returned, he reached for the phone, looking at Rock and Carli before looking at his phone.

The text read:

YOU'RE LOSING CONTROL. FIX IT OR I WILL.

Harbaugh pushed the side button and the screen went dark. He started to lay the phone on the table, instead he slid it in his back pocket after seeing the inquisitive looks on their faces.

"It's nothing, it's personal," Harbaugh said, his attempt at confidence doing nothing to stop his hands from shaking until he interlocked his fingers and placed them on his lap. "Carli, even though I've already spoken with Dutch, I want you to reiterate how important speed is. Remind Dutch I will pay him handsomely for this."

Hell yeah, you now have three less employees to reimburse so you ought to pay him handsomely, she thought.

Since Dutch had already been called Carli stood and set her keys on the table. Rock looked at Harbaugh who nodded and opened his hand and set his keys near Carli without looking at her.

She grabbed his keys and turned to leave and broke the silence, saying, "Take your time."

Several thoughts ran through Carli's head on the way to Dutch's junkyard, including the possibility they might be done soon in Stafford, Virginia. Something told her she needed to make a move soon if she wanted to break free of Harbaugh and his insurgents.

FORTY-FIVE MINUTES LATER SHE ARRIVED AT DUTCH'S as the sun began peeking over the horizon. She parked in front, popped the trunk and slid her phone out of her pocket. After making sure Rock had not made it to the area yet, she leaned into the trunk to be hidden from any cameras Dutch had in the parking lot. Carli got her phone camera ready and placed the phone in front of her thigh. When she leaned back, she could take several shots, hoping to catch the license plate. She bent over one more time to surreptitiously slide the phone back in her pocket and closed the trunk.

A man Carli did not recognize unlocked the glass door and said, "You work for Harbaugh?"

Never having met him, she nodded, said her first name and walked inside.

"I'm Dutch. Did you get everything out of the trunk? I need it to be clean when I give it to the guys to strip it."

"Yeah, got it all," she lied.

"Shit must have hit the fan for Harbaugh wanting me to get rid of this in such a hurry. Everybody okay?"

"Yes…and no. Dingo is dead. Don't really know the details. I get the impression whoever shot him may have seen the car."

"Is Rock okay? I mean, him and Dingo seemed like two peas in a pod. Never saw one without the other."

"Yeah, me either. He is not hurt, which is good. Although Dingo's death has him pretty stunned."

"Well, let him know I'm sorry about Dingo. I'll go ahead and take the keys. The guys I deal with are sending a runner over. Tell Harbaugh I don't know where their shop is, and neither does the runner. He is a wanna be, still trying to earn their respect. Safety precaution, you know?"

She nodded.

"From what I've been told he drives the car to a location in the country and leaves it. They pick it up from there when they are certain he did not snitch to try and screw 'em. He's supposed to be here any minute and they promised it would be unrecognizable within an hour after they pick it up."

"Perfect. I'll pass the message on. I'll make sure Rock waits at least a couple hours before he reports it stolen."

"That'll work, Young Lady."

Carli headed out the door to text Rock. An old Jeep with no doors and roll bars came to a stop in front of the junkyard, so Carli tapped the camera icon and began taking pictures while she moved her thumbs to make it look like texting. A teenage kid who looked barely old enough to drive jumped out, hesitating a second to pull up his sagging pants. The driver of the Jeep never looked over and punched the gas pedal the instant the kid hit the pavement. The teenager nervously acknowledged her presence with an upward tilt of his head. He started to shuffle towards the door, one hand holding onto his pants.

Unless he's good with a torch, this kid's never going to chop a car, he'll be a runner forever, she thought.

Hoping she got a couple of decent photos she switched over to messages and began to text Rock when he pulled up. She deleted the message and cleared her screen, stuffing her phone in her back pocket.

"Dutch told me to tell you sorry about Dingo," she said once in the car. Getting it over with right away seemed best.

Rock did a slight chin-lift without looking at her, staring at the steering wheel for several seconds before inching away from the junkyard.

In the awkward silence Carli said, "I started to text right before you pulled up." Her comment did nothing to make it any less awkward and the silence remained.

After ten minutes of nothing Carli said, "Dutch said the car would be totally unrecognizable a couple hours after the runner picks it up, and he walked inside shortly before you arrived."

Rock looked at his watch, then remained silent for the rest of the drive to his hotel.

CHAPTER TWENTY-SEVEN

———◆———

Ava awoke to find the covers on the opposite side of the bed undisturbed...Danny had never been to bed, at least not theirs. He had never resorted to sleeping in one of the three spare bedrooms, so she wondered if he slept downstairs in the recliner where she left him. Something told her to check, so she flung the covers back and put on her robe. She had no desire to entice him with her satin pajamas. The need to check on Danny did not outweigh her personal need to clean her teeth and brush her hair.

He can wait, she thought.

As she descended the stairs and toward the kitchen, she saw Danny holding a coffee and wearing the same clothes from the night before.

"Did you get any sleep; you never came to bed."

"No...too much running through my head."

"Are you okay? Is something wrong?"

"Yes, I'm okay."

"You only answered half of my questions." Ava paused, the fifteen seconds of silence enough to get her blood churning. "Well ...."

Danny turned and stared at her, wondering how she had convinced him years before she would be the perfect wife, and more importantly the perfect friend.

"Yes, if you must know something is wrong."

He took a sip of coffee and decided during his sleepless night he would no longer play Ava's games...especially one he despised. She expected him to answer her—immediately.

"What the hell is wrong? You know this irritates the crap out of me."

Danny looked over his shoulder at her, reached for the fridge door and pulled out the creamer.

Ava slapped her hand on the island countertop and yelled, "Answer the question."

"You just did," he said, setting his cup on the end of the island.

Danny saw her squinting eyes of anger. He stirred his coffee, waiting.

Her churning blood turned to boiling. Ava took a deep breath to calm herself and give her more time to think. *I cannot let him think I don't give a damn about him. If he gets to a lawyer, I'm screwed.*

"You're saying I'm the problem?" she asked in the calmest voice she could muster.

Danny took a sip of coffee, nodding to himself about the flavor.

When Ava saw the nod she said, "You do. Oh my God."

Trying to feign being distraught, Ava put her prayer hands to her lips and looked around, without making eye contact with Danny. She reached out and felt through the air to grab a barstool, seating herself in front of the counter. Her elbows rested on the counter and she began rubbing her forehead slowly.

Danny took a step back, watching with curiosity. He had run many scenarios through his head throughout the night, including her throwing things at him. This response surprised him.

"Are you...are you going to leave me?" Ava asked, her voice cracking.

"Isn't it what you want?"

Ava let her hands fall, intentionally opening her eyes wide. "God, no. Is that what you think?"

Danny paused, not due to lacking an answer, instead the sincerity on Ava's face caught him off guard.

"Frankly, yes."

Ava tried to sink deeper into the back of the stool, her hands returned to her lips.

"You have not had any passion toward me for months, ever since you started sleeping with Keith Dignam."

Seeing her posture stiffen and her eyes staring straight ahead Danny knew he managed to shock her.

Unbeknownst to him, her shock had not come from Danny, it came from this being the first time she had misplayed the timing of her magnificent plan, a plan based on her misguided belief Danny would never leave her. She believed no matter what she did he would never initiate a divorce and figured he would bury himself in his work... maybe have a romantic tryst of his own.

Janice Ray, she thought. *This is all due to her death. I...I started with the wrong person.*

"You've known? How? Did you hire a private investigator?" she asked.

"No, of course not. You have gotten so far away from caring about others you've lost sight of the goodness in the people around you. People talk, Ava. And Keith's secretary is not the only one, trust me."

Her mind went to several faces, all women. Her blood pressure rose again. *Stop! Forget about them. Fix this or you're screwed. Deal with them in due time,* she thought.

"You're right," she said, a tear running down her face. The thought of losing everything scared her.

Danny stood taller, his head leaning to one side. Her physical reactions stunned him, and he could hardly believe she admitted to him being right.

Through tears Ava noticed Danny's confusion. Her instincts told her to keep going if she wanted to ever have a chance to turn this around.

"I'm so, so sorry." Ava hid her face in her hands and took the next step. "It all makes sense now."

"Makes sense," Danny said, his eyebrows creating a furrow. "What makes sense?"

"Janice...Janice Ray."

Peeking through her fingers she saw Danny's eyes widen and knew she had to act fast.

"I used to be like her when we first got married. I got caught up in all of this," she said, her hands flailing outward. "Janice didn't. She remained herself, something you admired. I became...I became a bitch."

Ava covered her face to simulate being embarrassed.

Danny moved in front of her. He wanted to reach out and touch her, instead let his hands rest on the edge of the counter. Turning, he grabbed a paper towel extending it to her.

"Thank you," she mumbled.

Ava buried her face in the paper towel and in a deliberate move wiped downward with both hands. When she looked at Danny, she saw the smoothness around his eyes had returned and his thin lips suggested she had scored points.

"I'll do anything you want, go to a marriage counselor, whatever. Danny, right now I know you might not believe I love you. I always have. I'm so sorry I hurt you. We can fix this; I can fix this if you'll let me. I do not want to lose you."

Ava's hand turned over, gradually making its way to the middle of the island, waiting palm up. She leaned her head to the side and looked into Danny's eyes.

Danny looked at her hand waiting for his touch, then back into her eyes. The one scenario he had never imagined now had him confused. He had been so sure of what he planned to do later in the morning. Right then, seeing a lawyer had become a distant thought.

He laid his hand in hers. Divorcing her moved from the forefront of his mind to a play he could make if needed. Danny had done enough negotiating throughout his life to know he needed to pass through the door she had allowed his foot to prop open.

"I had prepared to go see a lawyer this morning…for now, I promise I won't. If you are serious, we need to set some things in motion."

Ava let the corners of her lips raise ever so slightly. Too much smile could indicate joy, instead she knew she needed to act sheepishly. At least temporarily.

"Anything. Anything to show you how serious I am."

"To begin with, we do need counseling. We got here on account of both of us, so we need to work together to fix this."

Ava squeezed Danny's hand, the sheepish look still glued to her face.

"You need to promise to be faithful to me, and only me, as I have been to you."

Ava nodded twice, and feigning embarrassment slowly lowered her chin until she no longer had eye contact and thought, *Keith and I will have to be more discreet.*

"And …."

He paused long enough for her to look up into his eyes. "You will be the one to tell Keith this morning he is fired. In my office, both of us there."

"O…okay," she said, dragging out the word, her eyes wide, the color gone from her cheeks.

"And last, other than golf, no more hanging out with the snobs at the country club or attending any of the fake functions any of them put on. We need to work on our relationship and quit worrying about relationships we will lose if we end up divorced and split our assets."

She gulped, taking three seconds to regain composure before she agreed.

I've got to talk to Harbaugh…and soon.

CHAPTER TWENTY-EIGHT

———————●———————

Harbaugh never called the meeting the day Dingo died like he planned. The extra few days gave Carli time to dig.

Carli's desire not to die at the hands of her peers superseded her constant thoughts of how to quit being Harbaugh's insurgent. She knew her chances remained slim unless she continued to help law enforcement...until she found an ally.

Harbaugh seldom told the insurgents all the details, rarely going beyond target information. Carli's reading the local newspaper and eavesdropping on various conversations helped her realize their targets had to do with A-Ray Corporation. Researching the corporation from the computer of the hotel lobby, she concluded they had taken out the CEO's wife and two other officers. When she saw Kenny Love's name without a picture something told her to dig deeper, finding out he retired from law enforcement before taking the job with A-Ray.

Maintaining a few friendships with former coworkers at the capitol provided Carli an opportunity to sometimes get information she no longer should be privy to. She learned Kenny used his credit card at a car rental business at Dulles Airport, a local hotel, and several times at the same restaurant, The Nook.

Carli drove to The Nook in Stafford. Rather than parking in the rear lot she parked in the residential area where she could keep an eye on the business. Within a few minutes she noticed a woman watching her from her apartment front window prompting Carli to go in the restaurant and see what she could find out.

Once inside Carli could tell the elderly woman and man owned the place. One quick scan and she determined her best chance for information stood with the youngest looking waitress taking care of patrons at the counter. In less than three cups of coffee she learned about Kenny being a regular, even though the waitress downplayed it saying he only came there every now and then. Carli returned to her car with the intention of waiting except the lady looking out her front window again thwarted her plan.

Sliding the key into the ignition Carli glanced to the restaurant parking lot. She saw two men getting out of a black car and start toward the front door. The car fit the description of what her former coworker at the Capitol had provided about the car Kenny rented, so she needed the license plate.

Parking on a different side street, Carli walked back to the restaurant parking lot and recognized the license plate on the black car. Taking her notepad Carli jotted a few words. Despite everything pointing to it being Kenny Love's rental car, Carli wrote in police code. Should her information happen to be wrong, the person likely would not understand the code. If it did belong to Kenny the use of police code would hopefully send a double message about her desire to talk with him and her having law enforcement connection.

We need to 11-98. I'll 10-21 you.

After placing the note on the windshield, she wanted to continue her surveillance to see their responses, except Harbaugh and Rock appeared ready to meet. She got to her car, put in the address of the restaurant Harbaugh suggested in Google maps, and went north on I-95.

KENNY WALKED INTO MY ROOM AT THE SAME TIME THE nurse finished taking out my IV.

"If you're finished getting to know everybody in the hospital, can you take me to breakfast? It's been a long night."

"Sure. After we agree on how much you are going to pay me for bringing you some clothes, so you don't have to escape out of here in a beautiful hospital gown showing everyone the crack of your ass."

The nurse chuckled and said, "I'll leave you two alone to hash this out." She left and pulled the curtain closed.

I smiled, understanding I had no recourse, and Kenny knew it. "Fine, I'll pay for breakfast, assuming you brought my wallet."

He grinned, held up my wallet and tossed the bag of clothes on the end of the bed.

Ten minutes later we stepped into the fresh morning air and walked to Kenny's car. We took off for The Nook and I could already taste Luci's fresh coffee.

"That ER doc sure liked you. I overheard her talking with the nurses at the nurse's station. It almost sounded like she happened to be in the room when the detective interviewed you."

I grinned and shook my head. "She went into the empty room next to mine and pulled the curtain to give the appearance of seeing a patient. She wanted to listen in, then came into my room after the detective left. For some reason, the stories behind my scars, including this new one, intrigue her. Besides, she's married and I'm content with waiting to see what happens with Celia and me."

"Okay, although if it falls through, being the good guy I am, I can drop into the ER every time I come back to Virginia to see if the doc is still married."

"Thanks, I don't need your help."

"Says the man who didn't have to wear a hospital gown out in public, thanks to me."

CHAPTER TWENTY-NINE

———◆———

P ulling into The Nook parking lot I hoped Kenny could focus on Tom and Luci instead of me.

Kenny entered first and Luci surprised me when she did not call him sweetie, although she did hug him and whisper something. She started walking to Kenny's table and he looked back at me and raised his eyebrows...his smile gone.

Luci opened her palm to the table telling us to sit and kept walking behind the counter. We settled in and Kenny seemed to be checking out the restaurant.

"Everything okay?" I asked.

"Not sure. Luci's not her normal self and she said Tom needs to talk to me. Here she comes."

Luci set down our drinks, then she pulled the newspaper from her armpit, dropping it on the table and tapping the face in the picture...twice. She shocked us when she walked away without another word.

When Kenny grabbed the paper to read it, I asked, "Who's face?"

"I guess it's the dead guy found in Chancellorsville Battlefield. Doesn't seem like they have much, pretty superficial article."

Tom walked up and sat with us, then pointed at the paper.

"That's the kid," Tom said.

"The kid?" Kenny asked.

"Yeah, the young one of the three guys I told you about. He's the one who wanted to know the next one after the bicyclist."

Kenny shot a look over to me, unfortunately Tom noticed it, too.

"What? You know something, don't you," Tom asked.

"You sure it's the same guy?" I asked.

"Positive. Not an ounce of doubt."

Tom's body language fully supported his conviction.

"Another of Kenny's workers got attacked, although he fought with the attackers for a while. We have reason to believe he seriously injured one of them, maybe even killed him."

"Not the kid," Tom said, pointing at the paper, "a hunter killed him."

"Really," I said, a statement, not a question. I stared at Tom.

Tom shot a looked to Kenny who held the same stare, causing Tom to slowly sit back in his chair. His eyes drifted to each of us one more time.

"Nobody's been in again since, have they?" Kenny asked.

"No, I've been watching. In fact, I kind of started to doubt myself."

My gut told me the dead guy also happened to be Tom's guy, in addition to being the one Ric hurt. Tom paying close attention and not doubting himself helped solidify the feeling.

"Is there something else?" Kenny asked, picking up on something about Tom I had not noticed.

"Yeah. It's probably nothing. Our waitress told me right after you guys came in some woman had been asking if you come here every day. Apparently, she even knew your full name, Kenny."

"Really?"

"Yeah. She said the lady only had coffee and left probably ten minutes before you showed up. Before you ask, our waitress told the woman no, you only come here every so often."

"Any description of her?" I asked.

"I asked her, and she said the woman's black, looked around thirty, short dark hair, maybe five-foot-five, and she thought the woman looked to be in good shape. She seemed to think she might be able to recognize the woman if she saw her again. Yeah right."

"You don't think she can?"

"I doubt it, she has trouble remembering her own work schedule."

"Okay. Same thing as before, call us if she returns."

"Are you in any danger?" Tom asked Kenny. When Kenny did not respond right away Tom looked at me. "Is he?"

"Tom, I'm not going to lie to you. It's a possibility."

I knew then they had not seen me walking with a bit of a limp, and I said a silent thank you prayer. Had they seen it they would have hounded us to find out what happened and then they may not have let Kenny leave the restaurant.

We assured Tom it seemed unlikely, and we would take every precaution to make sure Kenny remained safe. Although he did not seem totally bought in, he finally took our orders and headed to the kitchen.

After eating, we headed outside before another barrage of questioning, convinced Tom and Luci would worry regardless of what we said. Kenny unlocked the car twenty feet away, slowing his approach the closer we got.

"There's a note on the windshield," Kenny said.

I knew we thought alike, nobody from The Nook would have left it. I walked with him to the driver's side and looked over his shoulder.

We need to 11-98. I'll 10-21 you.

"You thinking it's the woman Tom described?"

"Most likely. Strange she didn't simply say she needed to meet you instead of using police code," I said.

"Cop?"

"Good chance. The question is, current or in a past life?"

"Might be someone from Ellie's department who doesn't mind sharing information yet has no desire to be identified based on the political climate."

"Yeah. Whatever she is, we need to see if the video inside captured her face."

"Oh, it did. I set it up," Kenny said, patting his chest twice.

Sometimes not acknowledging him seemed the best way to stop the flow of information he wanted to impart on me. Unfortunately, ten minutes later staring at the clear shot of the woman's face I had no choice, I had to admit he had done a good job.

Kenny looked at the text on his phone, then at Luci, and said, "Guess we need another cup of tea and coffee. Someone's going to meet us here shortly."

"No problem sweetie. There's no time limit, plus if you're here I know you boys are safe."

Heading back to Kenny's private table, he said, "Ellie wants to meet us. Told me to stay right here. The text almost felt like a directive."

"I hope she's not going to tell me those detectives didn't really believe my story. If so, we might be in a world of hurt."

"That's not it, trust me," Kenny said. "I spoke with those

boys out in the parking lot. They bought in…hook, line and sinker."

"Guess I need a fresh cup of coffee then while we wait."

CHAPTER THIRTY

L ou put on blue slacks, a button up shirt, and a tie, topping it off with the white lab jacket he purchased at Goodwill. On a previous visit to the hospital he overheard a doctor comment about changing before heading to his office. Lou followed him, discovering the otherwise unoccupied doctors lounge, where he stole a name tag. He determined the risk to be low considering he only needed the name tag to get him in the room.

Walking through several areas of the hospital Lou finally had the opportunity on the second floor to lift a patient file without any fanfare. He walked upstairs to the floor with the former soldier he previously injected with nicotine. Instead, Lou found the man's room empty.

Having no desire to speak with a nurse, especially the charge nurse, Lou waited for the young administrative clerk to be alone in the nurse's station.

"Excuse me. Can you tell me where they transferred the patient from room 401?" pointing to the empty room.

"Yes, Doctor...Doctor Porter," the young clerk said, making sure to look at the name tag. "I'm sorry, he passed away sometime last night. I'm fairly sure he's already at the coroner's office in Richmond."

"Thank you, son," Lou said. "I wish somebody had notified me. I feel like a fool. Thanks again." Lou turned and walked away with a faint grin.

Lou removed the name tag, broke it in half and threw it in a biohazard waste container. A dozen steps later he discarded the lab jacket and patient file in a dirty linen container, near the stairs he took to the first floor.

About the time Lou made it to his car and began texting Harbaugh about the man's death, the administrative clerk had finished his text to Ellie.

Seconds later the clerk answered his phone.

"This is Detective Svenson. Did you write down the man's description like in the instructions I left you all?"

"Yeah, I've got it right here. I even made sure to look at his name tag. I gotta say though, he didn't seem like some killer. In fact, I'm not sure he's not really Doctor Porter."

"No problem. There's only a couple of people allowed in my guys room; trust me, Doctor Porter isn't one of them. You made sure the man believes our guy did not get transferred to another floor, he supposedly died, correct?"

"Yep. I even told him the guy's probably at the coroner's office in Richmond."

"Perfect. I will hook up with you later to get the description you wrote down. Thank you."

Staring at her phone Ellie's thoughts drifted to being thankful she trusted AJ's instincts enough to move Ric to another room.

Ellie thought, *Who would have thought putting a stop to a kid being bullied a couple months ago would come full circle and his Nursing Administrator grandmother would help me hide Ric?*

WHEN DANNY TOLD AVA HE WOULD MAKE SURE HE LEFT

work before 5 p.m. and they could meet for dinner, it reinforced her belief about being on the right track. She had to pretend like his choice of a simple family style restaurant would be great when in fact, she would never choose anything so average, nor could she recall the last time she ate in such a place. She did not count her meeting with Harbaugh at Denny's…she did not partake in the food.

While Danny showered, Ava sent a quick text to Keith telling him they would have to take a break for a while. She also told him he would have to trust her and not overreact later when they saw each other. She decided not to tell him Danny wanted him gone, figuring Danny needed to see real shock in his face when she told him.

She deleted the message and set her phone on the bathroom counter. Looking at herself in the mirror she said, "You can do this." She slid out of her pajamas and admired her nakedness, knowing Danny would not be able to resist. She took a deep breath before rounding the corner to the walk-in shower.

She took up a provocative pose while Danny finished rinsing his hair, Ava knew she had to close her mind so she could focus on the task at hand, leading to her stimulating herself in preparation. When Danny turned and wiped the water from his face his wide eyes told her she made the right choice. She glanced down at his growing excitement knowing she needed to do something she had not done in years. She took two steps forward, laying her hands on his chest. She kissed his body several times, then slowly made her way to her knees to finish what she started.

Even though they each achieved orgasm, she decided to let him help himself to another, putting her hands on the shower wall while slowly sliding her feet back to offer him the opportunity. She looked over her shoulder at him and smiled, nodding approval.

While they toweled off, Ava said, "I promise to have made an appointment with a marriage counselor today before we meet for dinner."

"Thank you," he said, intentionally not specifying why he thanked her. Danny did not believe Ava would be able to make a complete turnaround, still for now he planned to enjoy her efforts at trying.

CHAPTER THIRTY-ONE

D anny arrived at the office a few minutes before Ava, waiting in the parking lot so they could make their way inside together. During the drive he had time to think about sending a message throughout his workplace. He would never intentionally seek enjoyment out of making his wife uncomfortable, although he wanted the gossip in the office to stop. He hoped to accomplish his goal when people saw them enter together, and he immediately called Keith Dignam to his office. He knew of the rumors about him not having the moxie to put a stop to his CFO meeting Ava. His actions in the next half hour would suggest otherwise.

The instant Ava arrived she looked at Danny and said, "Let's get this over with."

Putting his hand on her shoulder walking from the door to his office, Danny wore a thin grin. Passing his secretary, he asked her to have Keith Dignam come to his office.

When Keith arrived, he stopped a few feet inside the door, his eyes growing wide. With minimal head movement, his eyes darted back and forth between Danny and Ava. Danny looked at Ava, waiting patiently for her to speak, causing Keith to do the same.

"Danny knows about our affair. There is no easy way to say this, so I'll be blunt. You're fired."

Ava looked at Danny, fighting hard not to let him see the disdain she had for him at that moment. She turned, walking past Keith without looking into his eyes. She made her way through the employees' evil stares to the exit. She had accomplished what Danny wanted yet she had no intention of accepting any more humiliation on his behalf. Driving away she decided she needed to meet with Harbaugh to plan the next phase.

Having already researched marriage counselors in the Fredericksburg area before she left the house, Ava called to make an appointment. Knowing the majority of people she socialized with would seek counseling in one of many major cities to the north, Ava chose to go south. If she had her way the counseling would be for a short period, only long enough for her to bring about the end of Danny's reign. She could not bear the thought of her country club friends knowing about, much less seeing her going into a counselor's office.

Twenty minutes after Ava left security escorted Keith out with IT personnel changing passwords to ensure he could not sabotage the company.

———

Harbaugh decided to meet at a diner in Springfield. He knew the insurgents would be coming from the Stafford area, and decided not to have them drive back to DC.

Carli arrived last finding her peers well away from other customers at a back table of the diner. She needed coffee more than anything.

Harbaugh looked over the top of his menu to nod at Carli and Lou greeted her with a smile. Rock appeared to be zoning, his back slouched, his eyes never looking up to acknowledge Carli when she sat across from him.

Despite being after 11 a.m., they ordered breakfast at Harbaugh's suggestion, except for Rock who only wanted coffee. After the waitress left Harbaugh cleared his throat, more out of nervousness about mentioning Dingo's death. Having played it all out in his head he believed they could make it through without mentioning Dingo, unless Lou or Carli brought him up. Harbaugh had no idea how Rock would react, and he feared them making a scene like he had at the hotel bar.

"I wanted to bring us together to let you all know I have decided on the last person we will go after. His name is—"

Harbaugh's phone rang halting his speech to look at the caller ID. He pushed the green talk button and then the speaker button.

"Mrs. Lloyd, I'm having a meeting with my employees as we speak," Harbaugh answered.

"I hope you have some good news for me, I need some right about now," Ava said.

"As a matter of fact, I do. The man taken to Stafford Hospital died, they transported him to the coroner's facility in Richmond. He never recovered enough to provide any statement," Harbaugh said, shrugging his shoulders and rolling his eyes to his crew.

"What about the witness?"

"Took care of her, too," he lied, holding up his finger to the others. "She's been taken to an area where nobody will find her."

Rock quit staring at his coffee cup long enough to lift an eyebrow at Harbaugh, shaking his head. He knew Harbaugh would not normally lie to a client, although truthfully, he did not care enough to question his tactics.

"Very good, Colonel. I have a development here we need to discuss. Can we meet when you are done with your current meeting?"

"Sure. I'll text you the address and the time when we wrap things up here."

"Fine." She disconnected.

Shaking his head Harbaugh looked at his phone.

"Wow, glad you have to deal with her," Lou said. "She kind of sounds like a bitch."

"Yeah, most of these rich clients are. Ones like her is why I run interference for you all, so you can focus on the task at hand. Which brings me back to our next target."

Harbaugh reached in his satchel pulling out three pieces of paper, each containing the same picture and background information.

"His name is Kenny Love. He is a former cop from California. From what I have calculated, I believe if we take him out now that the soldier is dead the CEO of A-Ray Corporation will fold up his tent and drift away. I genuinely believe this Love guy is the last potential threat we face to finishing this job."

"What about the witness?" Lou asked.

"I know she's still alive, you know she's still alive…Ava Lloyd has no idea. It's not like the newspaper is going to print she is, despite whatever dumb ass cop told them in the first place a witness lived in the same building. We can catch up to her anytime to put a bullet in her head. Hell, she's probably scared enough from last night, she may run back to her parent's home in South Carolina…if need be we can take care of her there."

"I can start trying to track down this guy," Carli said, hoping her voice did not sound shaky to them like it did to her. "Your paper says he's a west coast rep for the company so he's probably staying in a hotel in the area."

"I'll start getting background information on the witness. If we can find out she did leave the area you can assign the other group to take care of her," Lou said.

When Harbaugh saw the server approaching with their food, he raised his hand to stop all conversation.

The instant the server left Rock wadded up the paper Harbaugh had given him.

"That's not the son of a bitch who killed Dingo. I'm going after him, not some former high-tech cop." Rock stood, causing his chair to slide back across the floor. He stormed off before anyone could say a word, not that any of them really wanted to try stopping him.

Carli sensed the guy with Kenny Love at The Nook earlier might be who Rock wanted, especially since she noticed he had a little limp. She did not want Rock finding the two together without her seeming like a team player, so she said, "Hey, maybe he's a friend of this Kenny Love guy," waiving Kenny's picture. "Who knows, if we find one, we might find both."

Harbaugh nodded, his wheels turning on all the possibilities. "Good point. You both go ahead, do what you suggested…it's a good start. I'll talk to Rock once he's had a little time to calm down. He and Dingo were close, hell they've worked together for me for ten years. I'll let you both know if what Ava Lloyd wants is important enough to change our plans. For now, start doing the work-up on each of those targets."

Thankfully, Lou changed the topic to how good the food smelled. Carli tried to listen to them talk about places they enjoyed eating at in various cities while she ate, except her mind kept drifting.

I've got to be careful if I want to play both ends against the middle...and not die trying, Carli thought.

CHAPTER THIRTY-TWO

———•———

A lthough we had been waiting for Ellie at The Nook longer than I expected, I knew she would have let us know if something came up. I trusted the length of time had to do with bringing information we needed.

A large lunch crowd still wanting breakfast began filling up tables. People chattering would help keep our conversation private.

I saw Ellie trudging along the sidewalk closest to Kenny's table. Despite fatigue, when she walked through the door the closeness of her brows and the hint of tightness in her jaws expressed her being all business.

"You look like a woman on a mission," I said, as she pulled out the chair across from me.

"It's been a long morning and I've yet to have a good cup of coffee," she said, her cheeks rising in a slight smile.

I looked to see Kenny putting clean cups away to help Luci. When he looked over, I held up two fingers and my coffee cup. He nodded, grabbing the freshest pot off the warmer.

"Miss Ellie, you look like you could use this coffee," Kenny said with his best southern accent while filling her cup.

"Geez, do I look that bad? You're both giving me a weird look."

Topping off my cup Kenny said, "I'm not saying another word." He smiled walking away with the coffee pot.

"You look like a normal detective running on little sleep. You look fine, seriously."

Thankfully she relaxed.

"You must have something for us, otherwise you wouldn't have asked us to wait here. Unless, of course, you didn't want to eat alone."

Ellie half-smiled. "Despite the last part being true, maybe I wanted to check on you…I mean you did get shot you know."

I grinned. "Sorry, I believe you. It's one of many, shall we say close calls, so I've kind of gotten immune to others concerns about me. Thank you for checking on me."

Ellie took a sip of coffee, then almost said something when Kenny and Luci walked up. The two women chatted for a minute before Ellie ordered.

When Luci walked away Ellie said, "You're right, I do have some information for you, but I really did want to see how you're doing."

I could see her sincerity, so I thanked her with a smile.

"We have a woman in our department who has an uncanny ability of tracking down information. No surprise, she is nothing more than a records clerk to most of our male-dominated department, yet to the few of us who have taken the time to get to know her she is willing to put her mad skills to work."

Kenny looked at me with raised eyebrows confirming he thought the same way I did, *where is she going with this*?

Ellie grinned seeing our confusion. "I wanted you to know she's the one who found out my dead guy in the car is an ex-cop from Abington PD, near Philadelphia. Ex-cop for insubordination. My gal contacted her informant at his agency who did research for her—found out he has no reason to be down here according to the informant's contacts. Here's the kicker…she told my gal several people commented on him coming into money over the last six months, plus he's leaving town unexpectedly for days at a time, all the while telling people he's not working. Clearly, they may not know everything about him, on the other hand him literally having nothing on him is fishy. We had to ID him with his fingerprint through AFIS."

The silence lasted thirty seconds while we took in the gravity of her information.

"It brings more questions to the forefront than answers," I said.

"Like?" Ellie asked.

"The first one, what's a fired cop doing down here without any ID, in a rented car, where he ends up getting stabbed in the neck, which incidentally begs more questions although we won't go there right now. The second question I have, is the guy Ric most likely killed who ended up in the battlefield an ex-cop, too?"

"What makes you ask?"

Kenny cleared his throat, drawing Ellie's eyes to him. "My guess is he's thinking it's a quick way to link the two together, or completely separate them until such time we find a different reason to link them together."

"What makes either of you think they're linked?"

"I told you, AJ gets these gut feelings, most of which are pretty accurate."

"I think we can all agree Andy Ray isn't doing all of this to sabotage his own company," I said.

They both nodded.

"Add in the fact there have been several murders or attempted murders in this county in a relatively short period of time, leading the average detective to deduce there must be a connection to some, if not all of them. The most probable possibility in my mind is there is a group of somewhat highly trained people working together, armed with weapons and suppressors similar to my two thugs. So, when you said a fired ex-cop who's been coming into money without supposedly working, it made me wonder if the rest of the people in the group are ex-cops."

Luci brought Ellie's pancakes, filling our cups while Ellie covered her pancakes in syrup.

"Kind of a stretch, don't you think?" Ellie asked.

"Mercs makes sense," Kenny said.

"Aren't mercenaries former military?"

"That's only one possibility," I said. "The most important factor is they are trained to kill for profit. Could be training from any number of sources. Do me a favor, call your source and have her do a quick check on the guy I killed to see if he's an ex-cop, too."

Ellie made the call, then went after her pancakes like she had not eaten in some time. After inhaling the stack Ellie sat back into her chair, both hands around her cup.

"I guess it's a possibility, I'm not there yet is all. Let's shift gears...you said my guy stabbed in the neck begs more questions. What did you mean?"

"What's an ex-cop doing letting his guard down enough to be stabbed in the neck? Most one stab neck wound shots are pure luck...or from?" I paused, hoping she would fill in the blank.

After several seconds of silence Kenny said, "A highly trained killer. Hello."

Ellie's eyes narrowed with the glare she shot him. We chuckled, making her glare more intense.

"Either way, you have to wonder who got the drop on him. It could be a simple robbery…or more likely someone taking care of him, then intentionally cleaning up the scene to make it look like a robbery."

"Shall we tell her?" Kenny asked with his Cheshire cat grin.

"Tell me what?"

"Tom recognized the picture in the paper of the dead guy at the battlefield. We believe the guy might have had something to do with Laird Spencer's murder," I said.

"We also had some woman asking the waitress here about me this morning before we got here, then we find a note on my car," Kenny said. "The note says we need to meet so she'll call me, except…drum roll please."

Neither of us obliged him.

"Whatever. It's in police radio code."

"So, with my guy being an ex-cop…I see where you're headed."

"Good," I said. "Now we can move on. Can you contact whoever investigates dead bodies on a federal battlefield?"

"The National Park Police. Sure."

"Okay, don't give Tom up yet. If the investigator is one of those stiff feds who doesn't want to share information, then we go about it on our own. We can always share Tom's info later."

Before Ellie could say anything, Kenny asked, "Didn't you tell AJ you found a phone in the console of your dead guy's car?"

"Yeah, why?"

"I'm going to give you a way to find out if we have

another link between the two dead guys, now three counting AJ's, once you determine who the Parks investigator is."

Kenny explained what he wanted Ellie to do. She voiced some concern about chain of evidence given her administrators did not want her looking into Laird Spencer's case or getting too deeply involved with Ric's assault. With a little convincing she appeared bought in, agreeing she could find a way to work around it.

"Oh, speaking of Ric, I followed your gut instinct and secretly moved him to another floor. Good thing, too. Some guy posing as a doctor went into his old room early this morning, then wanted to know where he had been transferred. The staff told him since the man died, they sent the body to Richmond for an autopsy."

"They had no intention of letting Ric live, he killed one of their own," I said. "You need to get him transferred to another hospital right away on the q.t., in case they have contacts at the coroner's facility."

"Or worse yet, my own agency."

"That too."

"Should keep him safe. Thank you," Kenny said to Ellie. She smiled.

The ding from her phone put a halt to the smile. The text read: DEAD MAN AT THE CHURCH FORMER MIAMI COP; FIRED FOR STEALING SERVICES FROM PROSTITUTES.

"The guy you killed is an ex-cop," Ellie said. "You do have a sixth sense about this stuff, don't you?"

I shrugged.

CHAPTER THIRTY-THREE

———◦———

Since the guys wanted Ellie to connect with the lead investigator of the dead man at the Chancellorsville Battlefield, she needed to meet with Special Agent Pham. She wondered what she might be in for after a contact at the National Park Services office told her good luck when she met with him. Ellie scheduled a meeting, resolving any information he provided would be better than speculating.

Kenny wanting Ellie to get the phone recovered from her stabbing victim's car created apprehension for her. She did not want to justify to her supervisor why she signed the phone out of evidence while not telling him the whole truth about a possible link. Ultimately, she decided to fall back on what worked for her in the past. She met the evidence clerk when she arrived for work at 6:30 a.m., handing her a fresh bear claw with warm glaze icing, and a hot latte.

"What is it you want now?" the clerk said, her eyes locked on the bear claw.

"Just need to borrow something out of evidence for a few hours to run a private test."

"I suppose you think a single bear claw and latte will be enough for me to risk my career?"

"That, plus the knowledge the asshole Major who most likely will be the next sheriff can't stop us women from doing good work, despite telling me directly my case needs to be suspended." Ellie fibbed a little about the direct order knowing the clerk hated Potts for always covering things up.

Ellie left without signing out the phone, heading to her office before meeting with Agent Pham. She despised the department for her being the token woman investigator when several other qualified candidates existed, only to have Major Potts' be the final decision on who got in. Despite hating the idea of hanging out at the office with evidence hidden in her satchel, Ellie wanted everyone in the unit to see her while she acted like one of the team, hanging out drinking coffee before 8 a.m.

Hours later Ellie arrived at the National Park Services Investigations building. After locking her gun in one of their lock boxes a guard escorted Ellie to Agent Pham's office.

"You can call me Ellie," she said while shaking hands. "What should I call you?"

"Agent Pham," he replied coldly. "Have a seat Detective, unless this isn't going to take long. What can I do for you?"

Ellie stared into his eyes for two seconds, looked at the seat before looking back at him. "Thank you," she said while sitting.

Pham's head shook ever so slightly, then he moved to his chair.

Having done her homework Ellie knew Pham had a reputation of being cold until he liked you. Several people had told her his desire to get in the Secret Service when he started with the National Park Services made him easy to get along with knowing people would be contacted on a background check. After nearly a decade of being put on hold for any number of reasons his attitude became one of cynicism. She needed him, more specifically his information, so getting him to like her seemed paramount.

"Agent Pham, you have quite the reputation for being a thorough investigator." Ellie paused hoping to see something in his posture saying she made a good first impression. It never happened.

"I have to tell you, Agent Pham, I appreciate good investigators, regardless of the agency. There are too many investigators willing to close a case or suspend it given the alternative means they might have to dig deeper to find the truth."

Pham nodded, his shoulders relaxing into the back of his chair.

That's a start. I'll take it, she thought.

"I don't know about your agency but mine has some administrators who don't care about the right conclusion, all they care about is a quick resolution."

"We have a few of those, too," Pham said in a much softer tone.

Keep going, you're on the right track, she thought.

"Well, I have to be honest with you. I hope you don't mind?"

"I prefer it actually."

"Agent Pham, I think your dead body in the battlefield and my dead body in the parking lot in Fredericksburg, both discovered the same day, might be connected. Here's the dilemma," Ellie said, taking a deep breath before continuing. "My agency…ah hell, my major who wants to be the sheriff someday doesn't want to hear anything about a connection, all he cares about is me putting someone in jail. Truth be told, he would prefer it be someone who would not check the White Anglo-Saxon box on an application, if you get my drift."

Ellie could see Pham's tight jaw when he cocked his head to the side, the major's preference not sitting well with him.

"You?" Pham asked.

"Ah, I'm kind of like the black sheep. First, I'm the token woman investigator in a good-old-boy system. There's only one female administrator in the whole agency so they don't really care what I think. I'm not a good-old-boy. More importantly, they hate the length of time I put into my investigations. I'm into finding the right suspect, they're not. Any suspect will do. They are on me, mostly the major, to arrest someone soon so I can close my case or suspend it. If they knew I came here to see if something linked our cases together, they would be pissed."

After a deep breath he said, "My name is Todd Pham, call me Pham. Everyone here does."

The corners of her mouth went up slightly. "If you're comfortable with using it, I'd prefer you call me Ellie."

He nodded. "Back to my original question, Ellie. What can I do for you?"

"I don't have a lot to go on, what I do have is my dead guy's phone. I kind of hoped I could get your guys phone released to me so I can have our techs do an extraction of both to compare messages, look for common numbers, see who sent info, who replied. If not, maybe your techs could do an extraction of messages, common numbers, etcetera, minus pictures, on your guys phone within dates I provide, putting it on a flash drive I brought with me."

"It doesn't work that way. I have an open case, so our crime scene evidence stays here, period. The information from my guy's phone on a flash drive, it would be like waiting for an Act of Congress before I could get approval, if at all."

"Ah."

"But…if you turn over your evidence, I can easily get approval for our techs do the extraction. We will give you back your evidence with a hard copy of the commonalities. I know, crazy right. You get the same information you wanted while God forbid no federal evidence is handed over to local law enforcement. Semantics, right."

Ellie smiled. *Wow, exactly like Kenny said it would happen.*

She pulled out a clear plastic evidence bag with the cell phone. She started to extend her arm toward his open hand, pulling back at the last second.

"This may sound strange…we need you to skip the part where you sign for chain of custody."

Pham's arm slowly drifted to his side. After several seconds he said, "Let me guess, those good old-boy administrators wouldn't authorize you doing this follow-up on a go-nowhere case."

"Pretty much," she said, hoping he did not want a more in-depth explanation.

When Pham finally extended his hand, Ellie handed him the bag.

"You anticipated we wouldn't hand over ours?"

"I had no way of knowing, so I wanted to be prepared for multiple options."

Pham grinned his approval. "Follow me."

"Gladly," she said bouncing out of the seat.

"Geez, relax," the grin still on his face. "We're only taking it over to our techies."

"Sorry, I'm a little excited. I didn't expect this."

"Let me guess, you did a background check on me, heard I'm cold, callous, hard to talk to, not a team player."

Ellie's eyes got big, her torso drifting back unintentionally.

"It's okay, I know what people say behind my back. I can be cold, no doubt…I usually reserve it for lazy people getting a paycheck without earning it. When I work with people like you who care about doing things right, about finding the truth, I'm a different person."

"Thank you," she said, She remained quiet throughout their walk down the sterile hallway. "I don't have a great deal to share with you. My dead guy is a former cop from Abington P.D., outside of Philly. He got canned about a year ago for insubordination, at least that's all they would tell me. I've dug deep into his background and cannot find any reason for him to be in Fredericksburg. No drugs in his system or prostitutes around there so him trying to score either doesn't seem likely. He has no ID, so our info came from a hit in AFIS with the red flag he had been a cop."

Pham stopped and looked down the hallway while Ellie waited for him to say something.

"Wait here. You aren't authorized to go in. Have a seat over there, I'll go see if our guys will do this for us sooner than later."

Ellie stood in the hallway looking at the door. *I hope AJ and Kenny didn't talk me into something I'm going to regret.*

Pulling out her cell Ellie made her way to the chairs on the far wall and pulled up AJ's cell.

SPECIAL AGENT PHAM WOULD NOT HAND OVER HIS PHONE - TOOK OURS - SEEING IF TECHS WILL DO EXTRACTION. HASN'T SHARED A THING – YET.

She no sooner hit send when she saw Pham standing over her. She had no idea exactly how much he saw although his scrunched eyebrows suggested he probably questioned who and what exactly she texted. Despite being shorter than average height, him standing over her still intimidated her. *Christ, now what do I say?*

Ellie stood, sliding her phone in her pocket. She wanted to appear confident, act like she had done nothing wrong, so she looked him straight in the eyes. She held the stare, hoping he could not see her knees shaking.

"Are they going to do the extradition, I mean extraction?" she asked, embarrassed.

Pham nodded, turning to make his way back toward his office.

"I hope whoever you're texting is another investigator?"

"Not exactly."

Pham spun towards her.

Ellie flinched, then looked both ways in the hallway before she quietly asked, "Are we safe to talk here?"

Pham's expression went from dead serious to quizzical. He did one slight head shake then turned, continuing the trip toward his office. When inside, he closed the door despite the internal policy preventing him from being alone with a female in the office behind closed doors without a witness.

"I know you want some information about my case," Pham began. "If I share information with you, I'm going to want something in return. Your case doesn't really have jack, so it's not like you could say you already shared much with me."

"Go on, I'm listening."

"You need to share who you texted, exactly what you said, and what agency the person works for. I sense you are going a little rogue, for all the right reasons I might add, still rogue, nonetheless. I want to know what you know."

"We talk this time, nothing more. No note taking, no recording devices. If all goes well, we can explore other options later. If it doesn't, we split and do our own separate investigations."

"Agreed." He paused for a few seconds before saying, "They found my dead guy in Chancellorsville Battleground, although I don't think it's where he died."

Ellie relaxed into her chair, crossing her legs, ready to hear what already sounded like the makings of a good story.

"The ME says the guy died from a crushed larynx. The weird part, someone shot him in the back with an arrow to make it look like a hunting accident. Whoever killed him staged his body, so it looked like when he fell after being shot his larynx hit a small wall, which supposedly is what crushed it. The thing is, there is no blood associated with the scratches from the wall or the arrow, so he had to have been dead already. It's your turn."

Pham did not have a problem with the possibility of giving more information, he merely needed to see what Ellie provided before he let her know the rest.

Ellie explained Ric's attack along with the previous two deaths of Janice Ray and Laird Spencer. When she told him of the three being connected to A-Ray Corporation, Pham leaned forward resting his arms against the edge of his desk. He wanted more and she could see it.

"The text you saw went to two former California detectives, one of whom works for A-Ray Corporation. Between the first death being ruled an accidental drowning in a different jurisdiction, and the suits in our agency unwilling to connect the dots, I decided to work with them. Being pragmatic, they've worked a hell of a lot more major investigations than I have, not to mention they planned to keep digging with or without me, so I figured maybe working together we could help each other."

Ellie paused, assessing Pham's body language. She had piqued his interest, his large eyes staring at her told her he wanted more.

"Here's the real reason I'm here...bottom line. Ric used to be a highly trained soldier with lots of battle experience. He fought back before they got him, dropping one of the attackers. Not with a weapon though, there's no blood. An independent witness saw the attackers carrying one of their own to a van."

"You're wondering if my dead guy is your dead attacker."

"Pretty much."

"I need some tea. There's a trendy little shop a couple blocks away."

Ellie stood, sensing Pham had a reason he wanted to leave the building, and it most likely had nothing to do with tea.

Although, a cup of coffee sounds good right about now, she thought.

"Coffee?"

He grinned, then nodded.

CHAPTER THIRTY-FOUR

———◆———

L ou went to the apartment complex in Roseville where they had attacked the former soldier.

No sense in presuming our witness tucked tail and ran home when I can check here first to make sure she left, he thought.

He parked his car several buildings away and walked toward her apartment, fishing out a couple of fake private investigator business cards he always kept with him. He used the cards before believing if you act like you belong, people will trust you do.

Walking onto the lawn of her building Lou spotted a young man with a backpack coming out of an apartment caddy-corner to the witness's apartment. He waited for the young man to come his direction.

When the young man said hello Lou greeted him back, then went back to looking up at the witness's apartment window hoping to appear lost.

"Excuse me sir, is there something I can help you with?" the young man asked.

You gotta love the South. People are so friendly, Lou thought.

"Why yes," he said, turning toward the young man, extending a business card. "The parents of the girl who lives up in that apartment hired me, I'm a private investigator. Here's my business card."

The young man took a quick look at his phone before looking down at the card. "I'm going to be late for class," he said, without taking the card.

Lou smiled, mostly at the business card ruse working again. "All's I'm wondering is if you've seen the girl lately. Her parents want me to locate her and bring her home after what happened here the other day. They're scared, you understand."

"Yeah, I do. I saw her yesterday, but to be honest we're in finals week at school so I've been studying. Look, I gotta go. I can't be late, or the professor won't let me take the exam."

"Thank you, Son, and good luck." Lou smiled and turned.

Two seconds later the young man said, "Oh, hey, she's pulling in now." His left hand pointing to a small four door red car coming to a stop in a parking space facing away from the building. He did not wait for Lou to respond and took off in a sprint toward a waiting car on the road.

Lou heard the car leave at a high rate of speed as he walked toward the red car with brake lights still on. He scanned the area, picked up his gait, and not seeing anyone he pulled out his 9mm, went to the passenger side, pulled on the rear door handle and the door opened. In one swift move Lou slid in, thrust the gun toward the girl's wide eyes and gaping mouth, frozen in a pre-scream position.

"If you want to live, you'll do exactly like I say."

She nodded, her mouth closed slightly, her eyes remained large and stared at the gun.

Lou slid to the middle of the back seat, partially laying over to his right, keeping the gun pointed at the girl.

"Go to the road, turn right, then at the stop sign turn right. The road snakes over to route 643. Take a right there."

With tears forming in her eyes she nodded and turned forward, started the car, wiped her eyes with the backs of her fingers, then backed out.

"You still got your seatbelt on?"

She nodded.

He knew undoing her belt to escape would be hard if she kept both hands on the wheel, which he instructed her to do. She nodded again.

Once on the route, Lou said, "This road runs into Garrison Road. Turn left, head towards Shiloh."

She barely looks eighteen. What the hell am I going to do? I'm a tactician, not a cold-blooded killer.

Before long they passed the towns of Shiloh and then Ruby. Lou spotted a dirt road leading into what looked like a wooded area not far past Ruby and told the girl to take the dirt road. Far enough in not to be seen he directed her to stop and turn the car off.

"You have two choices," Lou said. He sat up, putting the gun close to the girl's neck. "You listening closely?"

She nodded, trying not to break into a sob.

"One choice is for you to drive out of here heading toward your parent's house. Never ever go to your apartment again, do not go to the college, instead transfer to one closer to home. If the cops want to talk with you again you refuse, tell them you didn't see anything you could really testify to and you simply want to get on with your life. The most important thing though, you tell no one, not a single soul, about me."

The girl looked in the mirror making eye contact with Lou, then spoke for the first time. "What's the second choice?" she nearly whispered.

"I put two bullets in the back of your head and bury you out amongst these trees."

"The first one…please. I promise I'll do exactly what you said."

"Give me your purse."

She hesitated, then grabbed it off the front seat and handed it to him. He took her driver's license out of her wallet, asking her where she lived. She rattled off the address on her license in Florence, South Carolina. Lou set his gun on his lap while he took a picture of her license with his cell phone. He put everything back and handed her the purse.

"Why are you doing this…for me?"

"Why do you think?"

"I…I don't know. I mean, I know several of you ran to the van. I …."

"Go ahead, what is it?" Lou asked in the softest tone he had used thus far.

"I've seen enough stuff on TV…don't get me wrong, I don't want to die, it's just I would think your partners would not have all agreed for you to let me go."

"You're sharp, young lady. You're exactly right, in fact they will kill you, torture me and then kill me if you do anything other than what I told you." Lou paused and she waited, her eyes locked onto him through her rearview mirror.

"Look, there's been enough death. I'm sorry your neighbor had to die, I'm even more sorry you had to be a witness. Still, you don't have to end up like him, your whole life is in front of you. Be smart, do what I said, get out of here, and don't look back. If the rest of them think I killed you and you stay the hell away from here then you can go on to *live long and prosper* as Spock would say."

He saw the girl tilt her head, noticing in the mirror she had scrunched her eyebrows together.

"Dr. Spock? Star Trek?"

When her confusion did not change, he said, "Forget about it. It's an old show and you helped prove I am, too."

Lou smiled and for the first time he saw the girl's tension fade some when her cheeks raised slightly.

"You turn right when you leave, snake through back roads until you get over to Route 17. Take 17 to Fredericksburg then head south on I95. Got it?"

She nodded, her eyes still fixed on him. "What about you?"

"I need to have one of them come pick me up here, so they think I killed you. For your sake, you better hope I'm a good actor."

Lou opened the back door and stepped out.

"Thank you," she said, looking back over her shoulder.

"You're welcome young lady. Now, get out of here, go do something with your second chance at life."

They each smiled…he closed the door and watched her leave, following his directions to turn right. Something told him she would follow his instructions to the tee.

You did the right thing. Now, let's hope you can BS the rest of them.

Walking deeper into the large trees, Lou stopped and shot two rounds into the ground. He stuffed his brass into his pocket, turned and walked toward the road.

Pulling out his phone Lou tapped Rock's number.

"Yeah."

"Hey, I need you to pick me up. I found the witness and took care of her. I'm walking out of the woods now. I've got a couple miles to go, so if you can head this way, I'll meet you near the Rockhill Volunteer Fire Department."

"What did you do?"

"Two to the back of her head, not close enough to get

any blowback, exactly like you taught me. Covered her with limbs and vegetation out there. Hid her car in a different spot in the woods. Wiped it all down before I walked away."

"Did you police your brass?"

"Yep, got both in my pocket." Lou tried elevating his tone to sound excited. "I'm pretty proud of myself actually. All you guys ever want me to do is be a tactician, this time I got to get my hands dirty."

God, I hope they don't want me to start killing all the time now.

The silence seemed to last forever; long enough Lou began to perspire fearing Rock did not believe him.

"Alright, proud of you. We're going to need more from you since our numbers are down. I'll head your way…text you when I get closer."

Rock did not wait for a response before disconnecting, which Lou appreciated. He could hardly believe Rock bought it, although Rock could not even say Dingo's name when he commented on their low numbers so this seemed like the perfect time to pull the ruse. Lou stood tall and smiled, a bounce to his gait when he resumed his departure.

CHAPTER THIRTY-FIVE

———◆———

P ham walked at a smooth pace, the relaxed look of
someone on his way to a break outside of the office.
Despite the façade, Ellie could almost feel the questions
formulating in Pham's mind.

"Do you trust those two guys?" Pham asked.

"They used to be detectives, one high tech, the other
homicide. Something tells me to go along for the ride. Wish
I could give you a better reason beyond a gut feeling, except
it is what it is."

"Why do you think they are so into it? I mean, for them
to be digging like they are ...."

"Truthfully, they have never said this, nevertheless I
believe they think Kenny, the guy who works for A-Ray
Corporation, might be a target given his detective background. Guess they want to take the fight to the bad guys
before the fight gets to them."

"If there's any truth to someone targeting A-Ray, their
wanting to take action first kind of makes sense."

"What do you mean?"

"Kill the CEO's wife, cause a disruption outside. Kill
the CFO, cause a disruption inside. Kill the only two guys
with tactical training, who's the CEO going to lean on for
answers if law enforcement isn't connecting the dots. Hell,
he probably closes shop then—I would. Logic says they

already know Kenny is an ex-cop, so he's next on their list."

Neither said anything for the last block. After they ordered drinks, they sat at a two-chair table next to the window towards the back.

Ellie felt a little out of place given all the dark suits of the various federal agents. She could easily tell the feds conducting business, leaning across tables to whisper instead of sitting deep in their chairs and talking normally.

Pham took out a notepad…wrote two things down then slid it to Ellie before he took a sip of tea. He watched the expression on Ellie's face turn from wondering why the notepad to almost making a fool of herself, her head ticking from spot to spot looking around the room. Pham laid his hand on hers to bring her back to focusing on him, removing it once he felt her relax some.

Ellie wanted to lean forward and whisper her question, although she did not want to look like the feds.

"What agency?" she asked softly without leaning forward.

"Bridgeport…Connecticut."

"Fired?"

Pham nodded then took a sip. "Excessive force."

Ellie tried to lift her cup, steadied it with both hands and took a small sip, more for a show of normalcy than for the caffeine.

"And the second thing?"

"The exact words handwritten on a note in his pocket."

"Any idea of the meaning?"

"Not yet. Fairly sure it's a women's handwriting although so far nothing else."

"Mind if I text AJ and Kenny?"

"No, except for I need you to do this. When you pull out your phone act like you got a text, pretend something is funny and laugh, then show it to me and I'll laugh. Finish with acting like you're responding to the text."

"Okay," she said, dragging out the *y* to emphasize her unsurity.

Both felt pleased at making it look almost natural. AJ responded asking if they could meet Pham, so Ellie chuckled showing him the phone again to keep the ruse going. He smiled and nodded. She told AJ they would discuss a time and let him know.

"I know you're wondering why the drama," said Pham.

"Yeah, actually."

"I'm not sure if we are being followed. Do not look but two guys sat on the bench across the street to your left. One took photos using an actual camera with a telephoto lens. Hell, around here, it could be an FBI or DEA agent taking pictures on a dirty federal employee. Better to be cautious since their camera looked pointed in this general direction."

Prior to leaving Pham put on his sunglasses. When they stepped onto the sidewalk they tried to look at the men without making it obvious. The cameraman turned enough to get a frontal shot of them which confirmed their suspicions.

CARLI PUT ON A SUIT TO MIMIC ONE OF THE MANY PRO-fessionals in that portion of the east coast. She parked in the A-Ray Corporation lot at 4:30 p.m., in time to watch several employees leave while she waited to enter five minutes before closing.

With her phone next to her ear Carli feigned being in the middle of a conversation when she entered the lobby. Her eyes focused forward on the reception desk as she pulled back her jacket to expose a police officer badge attached to her waistband, one she stole working a previous case. When the receptionist saw it, her head fell forward. Carli could not have asked for any better reaction.

Putting her phone in her pocket, Carli said, "Sorry, I know you want to get out of here. I'm Special Agent Miller," she lied. "I need to see Kenny Love right away, please."

"I'm sorry, he's not here right now."

"Can you call him, tell him to meet me here? It's urgent," Carli said, making her way to the counter.

The receptionist closed her eyes and her head drifted back, another show of frustration.

"You look like you have someplace to be."

"I do. I promised my daughter I would take her shopping before she had her dance class tonight."

Carli smiled, hoping to relax the woman. "I'll tell you what," she said, pulling her cell phone out. "Give me his phone number and I'll 10-21 him."

The receptionist leaned her head to the side, squinting in confusion.

"Oh, sorry. In police code it means I'll call him directly." Carli shrugged and grinned.

The receptionist nodded grinning. She glanced at her watch, then at Carli. Ten seconds later she read off the number, thanking Carli profusely for letting her get out of there on time. She followed Carli to the door locking it behind her and turned off the interior lights.

Carli walked to the car pretending to dial the number in case the receptionist kept an eye on her and drove away before the woman walked to her own car.

CHAPTER THIRTY-SIX

———◆———

Harbaugh let Ava decide where to meet since they never met the day before and she chose Smith Lake. They both parked in the lot near the empty softball fields then walked together down the narrow road towards the lake's edge.

"I've decided on the fourth person from A-Ray to go after. I've already briefed my personnel who are out doing recon at this very moment."

Ava abruptly stopped, turning to face him. "Whatever, that's fine. I'll pay you for it if you complete it, alternatively I need you to take care of something…immediately if possible. If you have enough people to do both great. If not, do this one first."

"Do who first, Mrs. Lloyd?"

She glared at him for a second for using her last name again despite having told him before not to.

He knew it frustrated her, nevertheless he did not break eye contact.

"I need you to kill my husband."

Harbaugh leaned his head to one side, intentionally widening his eyes trying to act surprised. He had suspected from day one the additional person she said she would tell him about after four A-Ray employees had been eliminated would likely be her husband.

"Don't give me that look. I know you think I am a bitch, besides you don't feign surprise well."

"Fair enough, Bitch." Harbaugh grinned, feeling good about clearing the air and using the name he called her outside of her presence.

Ava had no desire to banter; it had already been a long couple of days. She continued walking.

"I have a lover, Keith Dignam, my husband's CFO—until yesterday. He made me fire him after he threatened to file for divorce. Of course, I told him I would do anything to keep our marriage together."

Harbaugh chuckled, no longer feeling like he had to proceed on pins and needles for her. He had already lost three men in this assignment so appeasing her personality no longer seemed a priority.

"Smart move on your husband's part, making you do the dirty work."

"Yeah, well, he's going to pay for it."

"Let me guess, you want us to kill both; make it look like they kill each other when the lover goes postal on the boss."

Ava froze. She slowly turned toward him, the corners of her lips curling in unison with her rising cheeks.

"I hadn't thought…that's brilliant. I can easily get another lover."

"Really?" Harbaugh said sarcastically.

"Screw you. I'm an exceptional lay, if I do say so myself. What's more, since I'll even be richer than I currently am, I can have any number of lovers."

I feel sorry for them, Harbaugh thought.

Her nasty disposition made him forget about her well-above average good looks. One part of her last statement jumped out though…her wealth.

"It will cost you one hundred fifty thousand, plus you are still paying us for the last one from A-Ray. He's a former cop who has to go, for all of our sakes."

"What the hell! You're gouging me."

Ava almost said more until she saw the anger in Harbaugh's eyes. The tables had turned. She needed him and he knew it.

"Fine, fine. Still…you're going postal idea only works if it happens right away."

"No problem. Does your husband, or soon to be ex-husband …" he paused, waiting for her to smile. "Does he have a gun?"

"Yes, two. One in his nightstand drawer, one in his office desk drawer. Don't ask me what kinds though."

"I won't, though do you know if he keeps them loaded?"

"Yes. He's always said what good is an unloaded gun."

"Perfect. Now all you have to do is follow the instructions my guys give you. If you fail to follow them to the letter we back out and you're on your own."

"I understand."

Heading back to the parking lot they discussed the transfer of half the money before Harbaugh would get his people working on it.

Sitting in his car after Ava left to go to the bank Harbaugh texted Rock.

HAVE A LITTLE SIDE JOB TONIGHT. LUCRATIVE. MIGHT HELP YOU TAKE YOUR MIND OFF DINGO FOR A COUPLE HOURS.

Harbaugh smiled when Rock's return text said he agreed. Harbaugh decided to bring what team he had left to the parking lot near the softball fields, so they could plan the assault there. He believed Ava seemed motivated enough to get the transfer completed before his team made it to the parking lot. He thought about putting it off for a few days until the three replacements for his dead men arrived from Nashville, except for taking care of business right away had previously proven to be the most appropriate time to make a former disgruntled employee appear to have acted out of pure revenge.

Rock and Lou showed up quicker than Harbaugh expected, both pulling into the lot at the same time.

"Where you guys coming from? I'm surprised you got here so quick."

"Not far from here. I had to pick Lou up and take him back to his car near the apartment complex the witness lived in."

"Wait, did I hear you say lived? Like past tense."

"He found her and finished her off. Two to the back of the head like I trained him."

Lou had a huge grin on his face when Harbaugh looked at him. Harbaugh's face lit up and he walked over to shake Lou's hand. Lou fully enjoyed the positive attention, to the extent his pride in himself centered on being so convincing. His peers had no idea he could not bring himself to kill such a young innocent girl whose being in the wrong place at the wrong time appeared to be her only downfall.

After waiting thirty minutes they decided to start without Carli since people began showing up for evening games. She seldom said anything during the planning phase anyway, and Rock knew he could count on her to complete any assignment he gave her.

By the time Carli arrived Harbaugh had received confirmation fifty percent of the money had been transferred to his account and Ava confirmed the guns remained in place.

"Sorry I'm late. I checked out A-Ray's to see if the former cop showed up. He didn't, although I found a perfect spot to watch from with my nocks. He'll show, then we got him once I know his car and his hotel."

"Good job," Rock said. "We have a little task to pull tonight. Double homicide, justifiable on the part of our client's husband, revenge from her lover. Make it look like they killed each other."

"Sounds straightforward. What do I do?"

"First, we are going to have the lover go to an open area across from Green Aquia Community Gardens on Potomac Drive, tonight around 9:30 p.m. You are going to come walking around the corner then approach his car like you had car trouble and need a ride. When he opens his door or rolls down his window I'll come up and take him. Then you'll drive us to the client's house. Lou will follow so we will have a car to leave the area."

Harbaugh listened as Rock finished the instructions. His dislike of Ava Lloyd prompted a thought…then a smile. They would help her get away with murder, although not without paying a price. Harbaugh had a contact who could use some of her money, too.

He pulled out his phone to send the first text.

YOU MIGHT WANT TO SHOW UP SOMEPLACE TONIGHT.

CHAPTER THIRTY-SEVEN

At nine o'clock they heard a knock on the hotel room door. Ellie answered knowing Pham would only recognize her. After introductions and handshakes, they took the stairs to the main floor and into the smallest conference room close to the stairwell. Between Seth's good looks, Kenny's gift of gab, and the forty dollars they gave the desk clerk, she had no problem unlocking the room for them to use after hours.

"Okay, I'm a little confused," Pham said. "Ellie told me about you two, however, who is he?" he asked pointing at Seth.

"Seth worked with us in the detective bureau and arrived earlier today," I said. "Considering the potential threat level to Kenny, we figured we could use an extra …."

"Gun," Pham said.

I shrugged.

"Whatever, I'm not sure I want to know any more. Before I show you the extraction results, I need to know there is no doubt in your minds this whole thing is connected."

"None, zero, nada," Kenny said with a stern look to back it up. We lacked solid proof, except Pham only asked about doubt, not evidence.

Pham looked at each of us one last time, took a deep breath and pulled papers from his leather folder.

"The top one is a Connecticut DMV picture of my guy in the battlefield. I don't know what to call these phone map things, nonetheless my tech guys tell me it's got the extraction information you requested."

All eyes went to Kenny who took the remaining papers while we passed the DMV picture around. He analyzed them for a few minutes and walked to the table in the front corner containing the previous group's leftover items. Tearing off several pieces of clear tape he began posting papers on the white board so everyone could look at them together.

"The first thing jumping out at me is Pham's dead guy receives a text from a phone at 5:02 a.m. the same morning Janice died. At first glance I don't see that sender's number used again so probably a burner phone. Then, within thirty minutes, give or take, of when Laird died, Pham's dead guy received a text from what I surmise is another burner phone. Both of those texts are one word: Ready."

"Tom," I said.

Three faces had the look of *Who the hell is he*, while Kenny grinned.

"Tom owns a small restaurant close to here. A few days ago, he tells AJ and me he overheard some guys. He said the youngest commented about the dead bicyclist being gone before asking the other two who they thought the boss would want to go after next. They shushed him up."

"You're thinking he's the driver," Seth said.

"Most likely," I said. "Tom confirmed the picture of the guy in this morning's paper is the same person, which also turns out to be Pham's dead guy. Anything else come out of the extraction?"

"Oh yeah. You are going to like this. Two days before Ric's attack—"

Kenny's phone dinged and the room went silent. He looked at the phone then at AJ, the corners of his lips raising slightly.

"To catch you two up," Kenny said, pointing at Pham and Seth, "a woman left a note on my windshield this morning at Tom's restaurant. It said we need to meet, and she would call me, all in police radio code. I think this text is from her. It says,

'YOU ARE THE NEXT ONE THEY ARE TARGET-ING. EXCEPT FOR ONE GUY WHO WANTS YOUR PARTNER FOR KILLING HIS. BE CARE-FUL!'

Guess we're on the right track boys and girls."

Kenny thanked the unknown woman for the heads up.

"Hell, we already figured that," Ellie griped, rolling her index finger towards Kenny. "You said two days before Ric's attack ...."

"A little anxious," Kenny said, grinning.

"Hell yeah. We're getting to my investigation now."

"I thought we had several fronts to work on together, not just *your* investigation," Seth said with a plain face.

Ellie flashed him her middle finger and the rest of us chuckled.

"Two days before Ric got attacked, we get the first link between both dead guy's phones. The same text message at the same time from someone they both have listed as Rock in their contacts. It tells them CH, whoever that is, wants a meeting. It gives them the address and time, so it appears the meeting took place the same day."

Using her cell Ellie made a call to her dispatch center, asking for the business name attached to the address she provided in Washington, DC. She thanked the person then disconnected.

"The Founders Hotel."

"I know I'm playing catch up here," Seth began, "still, I don't get Ellie's dead guy. I mean, I think we all agree there's a better than average chance Ric took out Pham's dead guy. In contrast Ellie's does not make sense to me. At least not yet."

I said, "Tie up loose ends would be a good reason. Maybe he started to panic after one of them got killed and they had to try to cover it up?"

"Or …" Ellie interrupted, "he had been let go from the PD he worked at for insubordination, so maybe he tried pulling that crap on these guys and they 86'd him."

"Definitely plausible. Hell, I wanted to hurt some young detectives who didn't listen on my cases, so I certainly understand."

Ellie and Pham grinned when my guys confirmed I had to be held back a few times.

"Pham tell us about the note again, Seth hasn't heard this," I said.

"Stuffed in the guy's pocket is a handwritten note, black ink on a small piece of paper, like someone tore it off something. We think maybe the corner of a newspaper based on the texture. The writing is in print, not cursive. Our expert says it is written with the left hand, and a better than average chance a woman wrote it. It simply says, PIs-insurgents-NY."

"Thoughts anyone, beyond the obvious the woman who left our note is probably the one who left Pham's," I said.

"The two guys are former cops. She probably is too, based on printing instead of cursive, plus the police code on Kenny's note," Ellie said.

"Maybe she's telling us something about them, like she chose her words carefully since she only had a small paper to write it on," Pham said.

"And you, Mr. Union Negotiator," I said to Seth.

"First of all, I like what they said. Second, knowing you have a negotiator background like mine, the terminology quite possibly had dual meaning...and you are probably thinking what I'm thinking, she's the one we can negotiate with if we can find her. She wants to get caught. Based on Ellie's dead guy, she figures death is her only other option."

"You got that from four words?" Ellie said. "Holy shit."

"He's a good mentor," Seth said, pointing at me.

I shrugged.

"You're not going to believe this," Kenny said, without looking up from his laptop. "Holy shit is right, Ellie."

"We're not mind readers," Seth said, sarcasm in his tone and a broad grin on his face.

"Whatever," Kenny said, holding up his open palm to Seth.

Kenny looked to make sure everyone had their eyes on him.

"I found a private investigations company out of New York whose business name is PIs. Obviously, there is no mention of doing insurgent dirty work, except...the owner is Rich Harbaugh, a retired Army Colonel."

The quiet lasted a split second before Pham said, "Around here anyone with serious military rank still uses it even after they retire. Here at least, nobody would say Rich Harbaugh, they would call him Colonel Harbaugh. The retired part would only be thrown in if warranted."

"Here's another thing," Kenny said, pausing to make sure he still had everyone's attention. "I love it...all of you needing me."

Ellie slung a pen nailing Kenny in the chest leading to a bunch of smiles.

"Get on with it unless you want the rest of us to hit you, too," I said.

"Fine. The number from the text I got a few minutes ago received the same texts the other two did about the meeting at The Founders Hotel."

I looked at Ellie and Pham. "You two might not want to hear the rest."

"What? Why not?" Pham asked.

"Plausible denial," Ellie said. She stood looking at Pham. "Let's go. You can buy me a burger."

When she looked at me, I nodded my appreciation.

"Oh, I almost forgot," Ellie said. "The witness, the college student who lived above Ric, she texted me right before we got here to let me know she made it to her parent's house. She said she's not coming back here; she's looking for a college closer to home."

CHAPTER THIRTY-EIGHT

Ava sent the text telling Keith Dignam where to meet her so she could share her plan on how they could keep seeing each other. His return text within seconds told her he would be there. She texted Rock to let him know Keith would be there.

Rock discovered the open area across from the community garden a few weeks earlier. Trees lined the eastern and western edges of the field with a river bordering the north edge. Rock had seen cars parked in the lot during daylight hours though never at night.

Thirty minutes before the supposed rendezvous Lou dropped Rock off at the field. He hid in the tree line on the east border while Lou and Carli drove around waiting for Rock's text to signal Carli to journey in.

Rock hunkered down when a dark Lexus like Ava described turned into the small asphalt driveway then made a U-turn in the open field. He sent the pre-typed text to Carli once the headlights went off.

Carli got out of Lou's car thirty feet before the road turned north to go past the Lexus. Carli rounded the corner on foot and when she turned to make her way down the driveway toward the driver's side of the Lexus, Rock moved from the cover of the trees to the rear of the Lexus and squatted. She executed the plan exactly like Rock instructed, the driver of the Lexus listening to her plight of car trouble with his driver side window rolled completely down.

Rock hugged the side of the car and stuck his Glock 22 with a suppressor in the driver's ear. The shock of talking with a nice lady one second to a gun in his ear the next had the driver frozen, unable to hear or process Rock's initial directions to move over into the front passenger seat. Carli leaned in nearly face-to-face with the man, grabbing his chin with her hand. His eyes gradually moved, looking into hers.

"We are not going to kill you, unless you don't start doing what he's telling you to do. Do you understand?"

The man's eyes shifted far left trying to see Rock before coming back to Carli. He nodded affirmatively.

The man began climbing over the console to the passenger side. When he cleared it, Carli hopped in while Rock got in the back seat. Rock had gone after enough people and knew in an instant the man would not be a fighter, although Rock could only hope he would not be the type whose legs gave out from complete fear when they needed him to proceed up to the house.

The man tightened up when Rock touched his neck with the suppressor, somewhat relaxing once Rock pulled it away. Carli directed him to put his seatbelt on and the instant he clicked it into place Rock slapped a piece of duct tape across the man's mouth.

"You try to take the seatbelt off or pull off the tape your brains will be on the dashboard," Rock said, touching the man's neck one more time. "Interlock your fingers across your lap."

Carli started the car and before long they drove towards Ava's home. Turning onto Ava's cul-de-sac road made the man tense and look over at Carli. Rock put the suppressor behind the man's left ear and pushed his head back to facing forward. He put the gun on the backseat then slapped a piece of tape over the man's eyes, touching the man one more time with the tip of the cold metal behind his ear.

Carli parked in the driveway next to the silver BMW while Lou positioned their car for the getaway. Carli punched in the garage door code while Lou approached. Both kept their guns close in the event someone checked on the garage door noise. Feeling secure Carli nodded, and Rock stepped out of the back of the car.

Rock whispered instructions in the man's ear, undid the seatbelt, grabbed his shirt, and pulled. Once on his feet the two escorted him into the garage. The instant Carli saw all three men clear the red sensor she pushed the button and the garage door descended.

Waiting for Rock to give the signal to execute the next portion of the plan, Carli wished she had been able to text Kenny Love a warning about their impending actions, except for Lou picked her up ten minutes earlier than she expected.

I screwed up, Carli thought. *This would have been the perfect time for them to come through the door to take out Rock and Lou. I really blew it.*

CHAPTER THIRTY-NINE

When Kenny finished putting away all the extraction paperwork Pham brought, he cleared his throat to get our attention.

"I've waited long enough to make sure Ellie and Pham had time to leave the hotel. Now it's time for us to go see if we can start tracking the phone belonging to our girl who's leaving us notes so we can locate her."

"How do you propose we do that?" Seth asked.

"I've never really told you guys everything about the equipment this company makes. My vehicle back home is set up to do what we are about to do, which is only part of the capability. Ric's does the same thing for various agencies out here, so we need Ric's vehicle to try to find her."

"Not a problem, except I need to grab one of Ric's guns. The sheriff's department took mine as evidence, remember?" I said.

"Who could forget hop-a-long. You're whining every five minutes about the pain," Kenny said.

Seth grinned along with Kenny, and I fake-smiled shaking my head.

"Whatever," I said, doing everything I could to stride normally toward the door.

Their laughter behind me told me I failed.

THIRTY MINUTES LATER WE PARKED IN FRONT OF A-RAY Corporation and Kenny went inside. He said it would be at least fifteen minutes, so we waited in the car while he talked to security guards without having to explain who we were. He drove through the gate in Ric's black Tahoe in eleven minutes.

Kenny got out and told Seth to drive so he could work the equipment while I hopped in the cramped back seat behind Seth. Kenny fired up his computer and entered the girl's phone number. We drove around waiting for the screen to go live with a hit to find her phone.

Kenny gave a quick lesson on how it worked and entered Ellie's phone number. When we got close to a twenty-four-hour diner Kenny had activity on his computer, including verbal commands.

TARGET IN AREA
REDIRECT ATTEMPTED
TARGET IN CHANNEL
DIRECTIONAL FINDING

Even without Kenny, we would have easily been able to follow the verbal comments and the directional beacon to the location of her phone.

"I see what you mean now," I said. "This really is like the movie *Zero Dark Thirty*, when they had tried to locate the phone, exactly like you said."

"Suffice it to say, the technology is much more advanced now, capable of things I cannot even show you guys without you having the right security clearances," Kenny said, in his all-business face.

When we approached the intersection of Garrison Road Kenny stopped in mid-sentence, the computer showing indications to the northwest for our unidentified girl's phone. Seth turned left on Garrison Road and passed the Stafford Plaza heading due west.

"We have a strong signal," Kenny said. "It looks like it's going to be in our twelve or one o'clock position. We're getting strong signals from her phone and the one who sent out earlier messages to the dead guys. I have directional beacons and we have a green circle which is the target area."

As we passed Vinny's Italian Grill things changed in an instant…we lost the signal.

Target Out of Channel, a new command we had not heard before.

"What the hell?" Kenny said.

"Does that mean what I think it means?" Seth asked.

"Yeah. They turned their phones off, put them in airplane mode, or the batteries went dead, which is not likely with more than one phone. My bet is on they turned them off."

"I went running this way one morning," I said. "There's not much out here besides homes and schools."

"So, we don't have anything to go on," Seth asked.

"We still have the large green circle giving us a general subdivision. On the other hand we won't have any idea of exactly what house. Another thirty seconds and the green circle would have narrowed. Still, she is somewhere in the subdivision, I'm certain of it."

"How close would you estimate?" Seth asked.

"Definitely less than a mile or we would not have gotten the Target in Channel command or the green circle."

AVA TEXTED ROCK TELLING HIM SHE UNLOCKED THE door leading into the house from the garage and they would find her husband in his study with the door closed. Looking at the other two, Rock said, "Time to go dark." Lou had his phone out shutting it off. Carli had hoped to be able to text Kenny once she had some separation inside the house. Instead she shut it off while Rock watched. She had no doubt if Rock caught her turning her phone on during the op, he would kill her, no questions asked. Getting a text out now seemed unlikely.

Rock took a small Maglite and shined it on all team members feet and hands, including his own; his last check to make sure they all had on latex gloves and disposable shoe covers. He took a hunting knife out of his pants pocket and wiped down the handle and the blade on Keith's shirt, then handed the blade to Lou. Rock slid the sheath into Keith's pocket. Rock nodded and Carli touched Keith's left temple with her handgun while Rock grabbed Keith's right hand and made sure he left prints on the handle and blade of the hunting knife Lou held.

Rock entered the house first, propping the door with his foot while he visually cleared the rooms in front of him. He saw Ava in front of him twenty feet away, standing in the middle of the great room with her hands covering her mouth. Rock motioned for the rest to follow while he held the door.

"Two steps in front of you," Carli whispered. "Go."

Keith took the steps slowly, his right hand reaching out for the door frame. Carli made sure her gun maintained contact, ready to pull the trigger if his hand went anywhere else.

Once inside Carli closed the door behind her. All eyes, except for Keith's tape covered ones, focused on Ava. She made a half-loop motion to her left with her index finger. Rock and Lou moved forward around the corner toward a set of closed double doors with light coming from underneath. Lou set the hunting knife on a small table, then lightly grasped the door handle. Rock stood to the outer edge of the door waiting for Lou to open it.

Rock burst in the room catching the middle-aged man off guard. Danny instinctively looked to his right near the desk drawer, contemplating whether to reach for the gun inside.

"I wouldn't, unless you want to die," Rock said.

Danny's eyes shifted to the man in front of him, down to the desk drawer, then back up to the man. He slowly raised his hands and leaned into the back of his chair.

Rock nodded. Lou put his gun in his holster and got the duct tape from his cargo pants pocket. He made his way behind Danny, ripping off two pieces of tape.

"Where's my wife?" Danny asked.

"In the front room, duct taped. Can't have her screaming or running, now can we? Do what we tell you, you both live. Don't, and you know the alternative," Rock said.

Lou covered Danny's mouth before he could say anything else. He then covered Danny's eyes, who kept his hands raised, palms toward Rock.

Danny did not show fear like Keith, so Rock motioned for Lou to tape Danny's wrists together.

When finished Lou drew his gun again, putting it against Danny's neck. Lou pulled Danny's shirt so he would stand and with verbal directions he walked Danny toward the doors. Lou picked the knife up off the table, then gently slid it inside his pocket.

When Ava saw both men duct taped tears ran down her cheeks. She could not believe she had gone this far although backing out now would mean her death. Her legs became weak, her knees shook, and she shuffled to the couch and collapsed, covering her face with a pillow.

Lou guided Danny up the stairs, stopping him on the landing near the master bedroom door. Rock went in and retrieved the .38 from the nightstand drawer and slid it into his pocket before he returned to the landing.

Lou holstered his gun, cut the tape freeing Danny's hands, then handed Rock the knife. Lou placed Danny's arms into a position in front of him roughly how they would be if he pointed a gun.

Before Danny could move Rock thrust the hunting knife through Danny's heart, twisting once and yanking it out.

Danny's hands instinctively went to his chest. Seconds later his knees gave way, dropping him to the carpet.

Rock nodded at Carli, who directed Keith up the stairs like Lou had done and stopped him within a foot of Danny. She then got his right arm bent, his fist closed, with his arm roughly chest high. She stepped to his side helping his hand remain in the set position.

Rock had taken out the .38 and the instant Keith's hand got in position he shot two times, hitting Keith in the heart. The former CFO mirrored Danny with his hands going to his chest, stumbling backward two steps before he fell to the carpet.

The gunshot surprised Ava who screamed into the pillow still covering her face. Lowering it, she looked up toward the landing. When she saw them lying still on the carpet, she began sobbing.

Carli pulled the tape off Danny's wrists then took the tape off both men's faces while Lou placed the knife in Keith's right hand, making sure some of the blood covered parts of his fingers. Rock wiped his gloved hand over Danny's right hand to smear gunshot residue on it before placing the gun in Danny's hand, his finger through the trigger guard. Between the two looking like they killed each other, Ava's statement, blood transfer and gunshot residue, he believed the cops would close the case.

They took one look around to make sure nothing got left behind, went downstairs and out through the garage, leaving Ava sobbing on the couch. Carli punched the door code to close the garage door behind her. They got in Lou's car and pulled away before a single light from a neighbor's house went on.

CHAPTER FORTY

A va's crying and stuttering breaths seemed real when
she spoke with the 9-1-1 operator. In contrast her ease
of giving the information caught the operator's attention,
specifically the home address and what took place. Not once
did Ava plead with the operator to "hurry up."

The patrol sergeant who arrived first called the Major
Crimes Unit supervisor who notified Major Potts. When
Ellie received a call, her supervisor told her she would be
in a supportive role.

Ellie paid for her meal, told Pham she would be in touch
when she got some free time, then made her way to her car.
Before driving off she sent AJ a text to let him know of the
homicide and she had no idea when she would be able to
meet up again.

DID IT JUST COME IN?

YES???

CAN YOU TELL ME WHERE? WON'T CAUSE
ANY PROBLEMS; EXPLAIN LATER.

18269 SAWYER COURT – PER DISPATCH POSS
2 DEAD – HOME INVASION?

STAY ALERT – WE LEFT THAT AREA LESS
THAN 10 AGO – WE LOST THE INSURGENTS
IN THE VICINITY. POSSIBLY DID A DOUBLE

HIT. TRUST NO ONE AND BE CAREFUL.
GOES WITHOUT SAYING – THANKS.

I shook my head, a sickening feeling in my stomach knowing we had been so close to preventing it.

"You guys aren't going to believe this. Ellie got called out to a double homicide on Sawyer Court, very near the phone signals we had been tracking."

Seth made a U-turn heading back towards Garrison Road. We all knew we would not be allowed into the crime scene, yet collectively we needed to see the exact house to know how close we had been. Seth parked around the corner and we walked in on the opposite side of the road.

We noticed scene control seemed somewhat lenient given none of the patrol officers on the perimeter had a sign in log. We saw what we believed to be two detectives go inside then come out to their cars before going back in, neither wore shoe covers though they did put on latex gloves. We had been there ten minutes when a pricey Chrysler pulled up to the crime scene tape and an older man got out. We overheard the patrol officer call him "Major" and held the crime scene tape up for him.

Within ten minutes television news trucks and local reporters started to arrive. The sidewalks filled with neighbors and people from nearby streets. In eavesdropping on the conversations, we found the house belonged to Danny and Ava Lloyd, the same Danny Lloyd we had spoken to about Janice Ray's death.

A detective holding a notebook approached the crowd and asked for anyone who might have heard or seen anything suspicious to step forward. Nobody moved. Somewhat discouraged, the detective took off to start knocking on neighbor's doors.

We had no reason to stay and headed back to the hotel.

ELLIE'S SUPERVISOR GAVE HER THE TASK OF TAKING AVA Lloyd to the station for a video interview. Before she could get Ava out of the house Ellie received another order to do the interview in another part of the house. When she questioned why, her sergeant shrugged his shoulders saying Major Potts made the decision.

Major Putz, she thought, shaking her head.

Ellie introduced herself, asking Ava to accompany her to a private room, which turned out to be Danny's office.

"Can you tell me what happened?"

"My husband recently fired Keith, his CFO. Keith and I had an affair." Ava flipped the business card Ellie gave her in her fingers several times, breaking eye contact, looking at the ground. "Danny found out, and we agreed to try to save our marriage. I had even contacted a marriage counselor, only we had not had a chance to meet her yet. Danny insisted Keith had to go, so he fired him."

"What happened in the house tonight…between them?"

"Keith came over pounding on the door. He barged right past me when I opened it and then Danny came out of his office and they started yelling. I knew I caused all of it, except for I couldn't take sides…I love them both. I didn't know what to do. I ended up on the couch somehow, my face buried in a pillow. I kept trying to cover my ears during all the yelling, then the next thing I knew I heard a gunshot. That's when I called 9-1-1."

"How exactly did they end up on the landing outside the master bedroom?"

"I don't—"

"You're done in here, Detective," Major Potts said. "I'm sure Mrs. Lloyd has been through enough; we can always interview her another time."

"But we need to determine—"

"I said you're done, Detective Svenson," Potts said, raising his voice. "Why don't you go see if your sergeant has anything else for you?"

Ellie squinted, unsure about Potts being there in the first place, much less why he wanted her to go no further in her questioning. She looked at Ava who had the hint of a smile on the ends of her lips. Ellie walked away, although not before she made eye contact with Potts and shook her head. He held her stare, his jaw beginning to tighten, although he held his tongue knowing he could take care of Ellie later. He made sure the door closed behind her.

"Do you mind if I sit?" Potts asked, not waiting for Ava's approval.

"Thank you," Ava said, an uncertainty in her tone. She had no desire to answer the female detective's questions, at the same time the feeling she got from Major Potts told her the detective might be the lesser of two evils. "I sense you have something on your mind …?"

"Major Potts."

"Very well, Major. Am I correct, you have something on your mind?"

"Perceptive, Mrs. Lloyd. I do indeed. I suspect you might even have a clue what I am thinking."

Ava stared for several seconds, disliking his air of cockiness. He wanted what all men wanted in her opinion… control. She sensed he had a purpose for backing off the detective and keeping her away…for what in return though?

She had no intention of making it easy on him, regardless of what he wanted.

"No, actually I don't, Major. Something traumatic happened a short time ago, I must say I am not thinking clearly. Please, do us both a favor and cut to the chase."

"Alright Mrs. Lloyd, if that's how you would prefer it. We have a mutual friend. Colonel Harbaugh."

Ava gasped and sat back. With huge eyes she began looking around the room, almost expecting Harbaugh to appear.

"Perfect, Mrs. Lloyd."

"Ex...excuse me? Perfect...what's perfect?"

"Your response. You had the perfect shocked look I would expect to see when you realized I know what happened here. The shock of 'What is he going to want in exchange for my freedom?' Classic response," he finished, nodding.

Ava tried to take a deep breath without looking obvious, trying to formulate her thoughts while she looked around for Harbaugh.

"I'm starting to think I might need an attorney," Ava said, trying hard to stare directly into the Major's eyes.

"You might, Mrs. Lloyd. Unless, of course, you would rather me keep the wolves off your back so we can, I don't know, maybe come to some simple financial agreement."

He paused to let it sink in for Ava.

"You see, I have the power to make this investigation look like a straightforward double homicide between a homeowner and a vengeful former employee, closing it without much actual investigation at all. On the other hand, I can unleash those same wolves with the full fury of the legal community, creating serious doubt at a minimum in the insurance company's view about you receiving a payout or not. Your bringing in an attorney tells me you would rather roll the dice. I have to say, should you do so, I for one would be quite impressed with your backbone and resolve not to share your proceeds from your husband's untimely death. It would be a foolish mistake, still I would be impressed none the less."

"The only thing you haven't said Major is how much you are looking for. You must know I cannot make a decision on whether I should contact an attorney without at least having an idea, and in addition a guarantee it would only be a one-time payout."

Major Potts smiled reaching into his suit jacket pocket. Handing the business card to her, he said, "I thought you might say that."

Ava took the card and looked at it. She recognized the Stafford County Sheriff's Department business card, except it did not have Major Potts's name. The name on the front read…Cpl. Ellie Svenson. When she turned it over it read: *A payout of $100,000 in exchange for a closed case on your husband's and lover's homicides.*

"Major, you obviously did not write this, it looks like a woman's handwriting. What's more, it is not your business card."

"Very astute, Mrs. Lloyd. It's a woman who works for an associate of mine. You see, the Sheriff is retiring, the Chief Deputy is only fourteen days away from his last day on the job, and I plan on being the next sheriff. I need a little financial help to make it happen, which is where you come in."

Ava leaned her head to one side staring through squinted eyes, trying not to let her anger over his greed show.

"I have no problem ruining Detective Svenson's career or putting you in prison for a long time if you want to make waves. Blackmailing you again and again would be a risk to my career, and quite frankly my personal freedom. I make sheriff and I'm pretty much guaranteed the position for the next twelve years until I retire. It's pretty straightforward, Mrs. Lloyd, you help me make sheriff, I help you maintain freedom."

Why is it I can't believe he will only want to dip into the well one time?

CHAPTER FORTY-ONE

———◦———

The text from Ellie read...NEED TO TALK...COMING TO HOTEL.

Curiosity filled the room once I showed it to Kenny and Seth. At most, thirty minutes had transpired from the time we left the crime scene.

"Besides obviously being upset, something's wrong," Seth said. "Nobody capitalizes an entire text unless there's something wrong."

We agreed. I headed for the door.

"Where you going?" Kenny asked.

"Lobby. I'm going to need some fresh coffee."

"Good. If they have any more of those chocolate chip cookies bring me some." Kenny smiled.

"I'll go with you," Seth said.

I flipped the metal lock to keep the door from closing all the way then started down the hall. Neither of us said anything until we got in the elevator.

"What's the deal with Ellie?"

Seth and I had worked together on major investigations for several years, so I knew he did not question my trust in Ellie. Still, he deserved to know the background on her while we continued to figure out where to go and how to get there.

"From the sounds of it, I get the impression her administration is holding her back, although I believe she's a conscientious investigator. She seems to trust her sergeant, otherwise above him she doesn't seem to have much positive to say. Like a lot of law enforcement agencies across the nation, my guess is the top echelon is built on the good-ole-boy system. Suffice it to say, she is not one of them."

"Plus, she's a woman."

"Yeah, which makes it worse. There's something about her…I think she's a good detective. She has a nose for it. Still, I would not at all be surprised to find out her administration wanted to put one of their cronies in her slot, except for they felt they needed a woman in the position so they would look good to the public."

"I would guess the major we saw pull up might have something to do with her being upset based on what you're saying."

"Pretty good odds. I think he's the same jerk who leaked info out to the press about a witness in Ric's attack."

Seth went to the front desk to check on cookies while I followed the odor of fresh coffee in the breakfast room. I filled three Styrofoam cups, two for me and one for Ellie.

Seth reached for the elevator button and stopped when we heard Ellie's voice saying, "Wait for me!"

Seth handed her a cup of coffee which led to a deep sigh as we stepped into the elevator.

"Thank you. I needed this," she said.

During the ride up we held off asking questions so Ellie could relax.

"When you went downstairs, I started digging a little about PIs, the company in New York," Kenny said once the door closed behind us. "I'll take those."

Seth shook his head and held out the plate.

"What? They're good."

Ellie chuckled when Seth rolled his eyes.

"I guess since he's stuffing his face ..." she nodded towards Kenny.

"Wait, what the hell are those?" she asked, a hint of anger in her tone, pointing at the pile of guns in the corner. "Whose are they?"

Kenny did a sweeping motion from me to Ellie.

"Thanks," I said, looking at Kenny who grinned.

"Those are Ric's," I said. "He had a safe in his spare bedroom in the closet your people totally missed. We figured we might need them so we took them, then locked the safe so nobody would know. Before you go getting all pissy, think of it this way, we saved you from heartache. If Major Potts found out your crime scene had not been thoroughly searched, he would probably fire you."

"Without knowing the whole story, it sounds like they did you a favor," Seth said.

Ellie pursed her lips. "We'll discuss this later," she said, shaking her head and sitting on one of the beds.

"We had two dead guys in the upstairs portion of the house I came from...Danny Lloyd, and his CFO. My sergeant told me to take Ava Lloyd to the station to interview her, so I did not go upstairs. Before I could get her out of the house, Sarge came over telling me I had to interview her there. I barely got started when Major Potts came in putting a halt to the interview, told me to leave and get another assignment from my sergeant."

"Did you learn anything before Potts came in?" Seth asked.

"I learned she had an affair with the CFO and her husband found out. He fired the CFO a couple days ago. She says she let the CFO in when he banged on the door. The two men argued, so she sat on the couch and buried her head in a pillow. She said she heard a gunshot, so she called 9-1-1."

"What about her demeanor?" Kenny asked.

Ellie shook her head. "We really needed her on video. I'd describe her demeanor as…sad, yes…except something felt off. She did not look distraught with either of them being dead. I mean, you'd think one of their deaths would make her break down, right?"

"Generally, I would say yes," I said. "Anything else bother you?"

"I checked with the dispatcher who took her call. She said despite Ava's crying sounding real, she never seemed panicked or told the dispatcher to hurry. In her opinion Ava seemed too in control for a double homicide inside her home. Plus, Ava almost smirked when Potts told me to stop the interview and leave. Who does that?"

Malefactors, I thought.

"Did you hear any of the conversation between Major Potts and her?" Seth asked.

"Not really. He followed behind me and closed the study door, which incidentally is against policy. He should not be in a room with a distraught woman behind closed doors without a witness…like me. I tried to listen for a second, only I thought someone might see me and tell Potts. I'd swear I heard her ask him what he had on his mind. I did hear him say he believed she had a clue what he wanted. I could not risk getting caught so I left. The strange thing though, her tone sounded nothing like a distraught woman."

"I can see your wheels turning, AJ. What's on your mind?" Seth asked.

"The interview did not last long, granted. The thing is though, even if she buries her face in the pillow, she would have heard them race upstairs at some point. I can't believe she kept her face buried the entire time, never saw any physical confrontation, never heard them go upstairs, and never looked when they killed each other.

"Ellie, fifty percent of what people who committed crimes say in an interview is usually true. The rest of what they say is fabricated, to varying extents. What part do you believe rings true about what she told you?"

The pause only lasted ten seconds.

"She probably did bury her head and lift it when she heard the gunshot. I mean, if I buy into the evidence of the insurgents being in the area, they could have done the killings while Ava could not bring herself to watch. The gunshot probably surprised her, so she looked up."

I looked at Seth, my lips having a hint of a smile, then nodded towards Ellie.

With raised eyebrows his head leaned toward her and he nodded.

Ellie's whole body stiffened. "What? Am I being evaluated?"

"Calm down. I told Seth you have the makings of a good detective, you confirmed it is all."

Her posture relaxed. I could almost read her thought of, *Oh, okay.*

"So, you're pretty sure the insurgents did this?"

"Yes. Kenny has some top of the line equipment and we know at least two of their phones had been in the subdivision at about the time the murders took place. We think they went dark, shutting them off when they got in the general area; the serious perps as you call them know phones are a quick way for them to be locked in at a specific location.

"The timing is right. Early on we wondered about Danny Lloyd wanting his competition killed off, since then we've changed our minds. One time during our conversation he called his wife a bitch, so now we have to seriously consider she's behind this whole thing."

"Major Potts," Ellie whispered, her eyes locked on the vision in her head.

We appreciated Ellie realizing why he probably closed the door behind her.

I asked Kenny, "You mentioned finding something out about PIs?"

"Right. Remember earlier I found an investigations company in New York with the name PIs? I only had time for a superficial first look, never finding any mention of doing insurgent dirty work, until I decided to do more digging. I found an article written about some private investigations' companies being a little dirty. Halfway through the article the writer mentions PIs, and Colonel Harbaugh having a possible connection to a covert ops group in Afghanistan. Now, I would classify it a general article about the possibilities of those kinds of companies being dirty, yet there's nothing in this article indicating the writer had something concrete, plus his omission of being sure covered his ass."

Kenny sat back with a smirk on his face.

"Oh my God," Seth said, disgust in his tone staring at Kenny.

"What? What am I missing?" Ellie asked.

"He needs a drumroll or a pat on the back every time he thinks he's done something good. C'mon jerk, spit it out."

"Well, you did feed me." Kenny smiled, not in a hurry to ease Seth's tension.

Looking at Kenny I rolled my index finger to get him going.

"Whatever," Kenny said. "So, I thought about the writer of the article, wondering if he might be someone we should talk with. I started to do a little research on him and then I ran into a brick wall. An informative brick wall, yet a brick wall nonetheless."

"Just get to it before Seth shoots you, would you?"

Kenny smiled. "The good news is I found another article, this time about the reporter. The bad news is, the article is about the reporter being killed in, and I quote, *a freak Metro accident at the Pentagon Station.* The icing on this bad cake is he died twenty-eight days after his article on PIs came out."

CHAPTER FORTY-TWO

Carli did not want to go to prison, though she had resigned herself to the realization she could not continue to kill innocent people simply based on someone's willingness to pay for it. Killing serious dirt bags who inflicted misery yet slid through the justice system unscathed did not create any issue with her. Killing a businessman like Danny Lloyd with no criminal background, and his CFO, Keith Dignam who seemed even cleaner than Danny, no longer sat well with her. Even though Carli knew her presence in The Nook might cause a stir, she had to do something. It seemed a good place to start.

The instant Carli walked in she saw the fire in the female owner's eyes. When she saw the woman's husband put his hand on her shoulder and whisper in her ear, Carli anticipated he wanted his wife to call Kenny Love. On Carli's previous visit the waitress confirmed the close relationship between the owners and Kenny. When the female owner disappeared into the kitchen Carli knew her presence had the desired effect.

Tom approached saying, "Good morning miss. One?"

Carli nodded.

Grabbing one menu Tom started to turn to his left. "Follow—"

"No, over there...at that corner table."

Tom saw her pointing at Kenny's table. He almost said something, except he saw she had the air of someone in control. He knew she had figured them out...she wanted them to call Kenny.

"Fair enough, except for you cannot sit at the chair closest to the wall."

She glanced over, saying, "The one reserved for Kenny Love."

Tom looked into her eyes. No sense in trying to bluff a woman who had reconned his restaurant enough to know the details.

"Correct. I'm sure you're aware my wife is calling him now."

Carli nodded.

"I hope there won't be any trouble. We can't afford to lose this place or any of our regular customers."

"There won't be any. You have my word."

Something about the woman told Tom to trust her.

"Thank you. Please, follow me."

IT TOOK US TWENTY MINUTES TO GET TO THE NOOK. Even though the woman sitting at Kenny's table had her back to the front door, we felt certain she had been the one who left the note days before.

When we entered, Tom tilted his head toward the woman and Luci held up her phone, mouthing the words, *9-1-1, I'm ready.*

"I'm not sure why, but they definitely like you," Seth whispered over Kenny's shoulder.

Nodding, Kenny said, "Everyone does, Seth. Haven't you figured that out yet?"

Seth shook his head, a thin smile attached.

I assumed the woman at the table heard Kenny when she slowly brought her hands out in plain view, setting them on the table palms down.

We walked over and sat, her eyes moving to make direct contact with each one of us…one at a time. Her hands remained on the table.

"Do you have a gun on you?" I asked.

"Of course, so do all three of you. I promised the owner I would not cause a disturbance in his restaurant. I would like to honor my promise—unless, of course …."

I caught the tell, her right hand sliding back ever so slightly toward the edge of the table, at the same time a quick scan to know her possible movements. Her nearly palpable tension led me to say, "I plan on eating breakfast, so the way I see it, you're good."

She looked at Seth and Kenny, waiting until they both agreed.

With a deep cleansing breath, she said, "My name is Carli. I know you are AJ, you're Kenny, I don't know your name though."

"Seth. I worked with these guys in the detective bureau."

Once we had ordered, I said, "This is bold, Carli. It's not like I would expect any less from you though. Still, kind of ballsy."

"Maybe." She paused looking past Kenny, her eyes focused on the wall. "I'm hoping there is still honor amongst you; there surely is none with the people I work for…and with."

Kenny pushed his chair back so hard when he stood the legs screeched across the tile. He stared down at Carli. To her credit she looked at her coffee keeping both hands on the cup until Kenny stormed off to the kitchen.

Looking at me Carli did a slight head jab in Kenny's direction, her eyes asking, *What's up with him?*

"He'll be okay. He wants to choke the shit out of you for trying to kill his friend is all."

"Fair enough."

I waited for the puzzled look on her face to show. I had zero concern over her knowing the truth about Ric since she would either convince us she could be trusted to help us, or she would be leaving in cuffs or a body bag. Her choice.

"Yeah, you figured it out. Ric is still alive."

Her eyebrow raised, then a slight nod followed. "They think he's dead, so at least nobody will be going after him. Besides, they want Kenny...and you, AJ."

"Neither of those are going to happen," Seth said.

"Oh?"

"Look, we've been doing this a long time," I said. "You're here to cut a deal, plain and simple. We will get them before they get us. Period. If it includes you, so be it. We'd rather you be with us instead of against us, nonetheless the choice is yours. Incidentally, so you will quit staring at the scar on my face wondering what happened, some homeboy tried to avenge me sending his cousin to prison for a senseless murder. He brought a knife to a gun fight...he lost."

Tilting her head, she looked into my eyes, then at Seth. He shrugged, bringing a grin to her face.

"What agency did you work for?" Seth asked.

"United States Capitol Police. Six years. I got fired for stealing, except I didn't do it—I got set up. When things started heating up from Internal Affairs my sergeant threw me under the bus after he planted some things in my unlocked car in the gated and locked employee parking lot. When they offered no prosecution if I resigned, I took it.

"Right after is when Colonel Harbaugh approached me. He offered to take care of the sergeant for free if I would come work for him. I sat in a crowded bar a hundred miles away when the bastard died. In the beginning, we only did things to get justice where none could be had. Then it started to change. Harbaugh saw a chance for serious money."

"Why not make a break for it?" Seth asked.

"I heard of one guy trying before I arrived, supposedly they killed him. I witnessed one...he became fish food in the Atlantic. They also killed a guy recently in Fredericksburg supposedly for mouthing off to Harbaugh, mostly it came down to him being a dick. I had been dropping off the van we rented when they did it," she lied, "nonetheless I saw him in his car in the parking lot where we met up. Some shopping center."

Kenny returned having regained some composure.

"I'm sorry about your friend," Carli said to Kenny. "I'm here to help fix this, really."

Kenny didn't say anything, a rarity for him.

"You know none of the three of us are current law enforcement, so there's nothing we can do to get you a deal," I said.

"I know. I'm hoping you will vouch for me helping you try to put a stop to this whole thing. Despite what has taken place locally, PIs have done jobs all over, even taking people across state lines making it federal. I'm prepared to sit down with the prosecutors, and my desire is maybe I end up in WITSEC."

I looked at the others for buy in. Kenny giving the go ahead took longer than Seth, to no one's surprise.

"It looks like we are willing to work with you. Like any informant though, any failure or unwillingness to do what we tell you to puts you directly in the crosshairs. In this situation, I mean Seth's crosshairs. You won't have to worry about the criminal justice system crosshairs."

"I understand."

"Now, before we go any further, tell us about the double murder at Danny Lloyd's house."

A confession means someone admits to committing a crime. Thanks to television most people believe it means the whole story, whereas seasoned homicide investigators know it seldom includes the entire truth. Right away Carli established credibility with the complete details she laid out. Her thoroughness did not go unnoticed.

Ava Lloyd had not become enemy number one…yet. In due time she would, though first we had some insurgents to take care of.

CHAPTER FORTY-THREE

———◆———

Harbaugh decided to treat himself to a nice dinner close to the hotel. The concierge had recommended an upscale restaurant in Pentagon City, even offering one of the hotel limousines, for a price, of course. Harbaugh didn't care, he had verified Ava's wire transfer had been completed. He would share some with Rock, Carli, and Lou, though he had no intention of making it much. He never shared with them the exact number of kills the contract required so they would be happy with a little bonus bump, leaving him the biggest bulk of supplemental Ava money.

Or did I tell them? Too many pills, too much alcohol. I've got to get control of myself again. I need tonight to unwind.

Harbaugh stepped out of the elevator in his nicest dark blue suit, complete with his Ferragamo dress shoes and his Rubinacci silk tie. The concierge offered to set Harbaugh up with female companionship when he returned, so Harbaugh tipped the man handsomely for his assistance. First though, he looked forward to the peace of an elegant dinner alone, complete with fine wine and upscale ambiance.

Standing tall, the concierge had a broad grin on his face, proud of his accomplishments for the likes of what he believed to be an Army hero. Harbaugh sensed the man had no idea what an M-16 was, much less what took place on foreign soil. The more the concierge got caught up, the more Harbaugh embellished the stories.

Standing erect as if in his Army dress blues, Harbaugh gave a slight nod to the concierge then headed for the door. He could see the limousine parked directly in front. The doorman opened the floor to ceiling glass door, acknowledging Harbaugh with a professional greeting. He nodded again and saw the driver of the limo exit to begin his jaunt around, his timing looking like it would line up perfectly with Harbaughs'. The movement and sound of brakes startled both men.

The black Suburban stopped less than ten feet from the back of the limo. The front seat passenger dressed in a black suit, white shirt and thin black tie stopped the limo driver before he cleared the back of the car. He handed the driver cash and an address where the driver should go to and wait. Looking confused yet knowing well enough not to question the order he had been given from what appeared to be a government agent, the driver returned to his seat, driving off seconds later.

"Colonel," the man extended his arm directing Harbaugh where he would go.

Harbaugh's shoulders sank a half inch and he sighed, shaking his head at the poor timing. He walked to the right rear seat next to the opened door and sat, the agent closing it behind him. Driving away Harbaugh could see the doorman and the concierge trying to look in the blacked-out windows, total surprise on their faces.

Three others sat in the Suburban with him. The two male agents in the front seats dressed exactly alike except for being complete opposites in height, shoulder width, hair. The large bald one drove and seemed to be in charge...of the front seat. The redhead in her own dark suit sitting behind the driver outranked them all.

After thirty seconds of silence, she said, "I told you to fix it or I would."

Harbaugh learned in the Army not to speak unless what you had to say added to the conversation. Nothing he could say would be a good response.

They drove around for the better part of ten minutes without him saying a word, sensing her dissatisfaction in what she deemed going off the reservation with the killing of Danny Lloyd and his CFO.

"You got paid handsomely to take care of covert ops in Afghanistan. Then your abuse of chemicals led to you blowing one too many ops. Still, for the ones you had done well we helped set you up your PI business. I told you we would keep an eye on you. I also told you if we had to reel you in what the consequences would be."

By the time the SUV pulled over he felt the perspiration in his dress shirt clinging to his skin. He silently thanked God for being alive, her tone having led him to believe his time on Earth had come to an end.

The car stopped and his door opened. He turned to get out, stopping when she said, "Colonel." He did not plan to look at her, until it became clear she would wait until he did. He slowly swiveled, looking at her thin stoic yet beautiful face.

"There won't be another time." Her chin dropped a millimeter and Harbaugh felt the pull on his right elbow.

"Your limousine is thirty yards behind us, sir," the smaller agent said. Before Harbaugh had time to locate it the Suburban drove off.

HARBAUGH TOLD THE LIMO DRIVER TO TAKE HIM TO THE restaurant, trying to appear unshaken by the recent threat he received. The driver never bought it although saying nothing always seemed the best way to deal with people in Washington. He broke into a slight grin when he recalled his grandfather's monkey figurine, See No Evil, Hear No Evil, Speak No Evil. Good words to heed his grandfather used to say, especially in DC with the number of black SUVs running around.

The concierge had sent him to a nice restaurant, one Harbaugh felt certain he would enjoy under different circumstances. He tried to enjoy his meal yet ate less than a quarter, bypassing dessert, choosing to stick with the wine. After some reflection he pulled out his phone and sent Rock a text. They needed to drop back, to call this mission complete. Harbaugh couldn't risk another screw up, not after the ride he had in the SUV.

The return text from Rock had a thumbs up emoji and talk tomorrow.

He had worried about how Rock would react so the response seemed satisfying. With Rock on board the others would follow suit…no questions asked.

Harbaugh felt a little better after finishing the bottle of wine, although really wanted a Scotch. He asked the driver to let the concierge know he did not want any company for the evening. Then he had the limo driver stop at a liquor store on the way back to the hotel. The Johnnie Walker Blue would hopefully help him to stop thinking of her final words, *there won't be another time.*

Exiting the limo in front of the hotel Harbaugh put a

hundred-dollar bill in the driver's hand, his index finger to his mouth. The driver never looked at the amount, his eyes locked on his clients. He dipped his head to acknowledge the message.

Speak No Evil, the driver thought.

Nodding to the doorman Harbaugh hoped the concierge had left for the evening, having no desire to talk about a restaurant he hardly remembered, his mind having been elsewhere.

Perfect, it's me and Johnnie now, he thought once the elevator door closed.

Stepping into his room Harbaugh began loosening his tie and looking for the Johnnie Walker. The light on over the table went unnoticed. Rock's voice did not.

"How the hell did you get in here?"

"You of all people should know money talks, especially to a pretty young thing trying to get through Georgetown in the day and having to work the desk at night."

Between the slackened posture and the easy tone, Harbaugh sensed Rock appeared relaxed. He walked to the table setting the Johnnie Walker bottle down.

"You want some?" Harbaugh asked, heading to the small sink with the drinking glasses tucked in the corner.

"Hell yeah. Why else would I be here? We need to toast the completion of another mission, toast our fallen brothers."

"Excellent."

He picked up the glasses and began to turn around.

The two stood roughly the same height, although Rock had him in muscle and youth. Not to mention anger.

The force of the pillow pushing into Harbaugh's face drove his head back, striking the cabinet door above the sink. He never felt the muzzle of the gun being jammed into the pillow, or the hollow point bullet that went through his right eye.

Rock took a step back watching the body slide down, falling into the carpet the last few feet. Standing over Harbaugh he looked for any sign of life, ready to put another round in the head. Feeling for a pulse would be quick confirmation, instead he preferred waiting. He patted Harbaugh's pockets, reaching into his inner jacket when he felt the phone and used it to text the others.

> I'VE GOT URGENT BUSINESS BACK IN NEW YORK. ROCK'S IN CHARGE. HE KNOWS WHAT I EXPECT TO BE DONE TO CONSIDER THIS MISSION COMPLETE. STAY SAFE.

Send!

Rock's phone dinged in his pocket telling him they had all received the message. The confirmation texts with the appropriate password, GI, meaning they got it, began coming in. Rock used his phone to respond like the others. Sliding both phones in his pocket he took out a pair of gloves.

Using one of the wash clothes from the bathroom Rock began wiping off anything he touched along with some he hadn't. He put one of the glasses Harbaugh dropped back on the counter, clean of all prints. Opening the Johnnie Walker, Rock poured the other glass half-full and dropped it back onto the carpet from hand height. The majority flew out onto the carpet while a small amount remained in the glass lying on its side. He then poured the remainder of the bottle into the sink before returning it to the table.

Picking up Harbaugh's hand he wiped the gun on it to pass gunshot residue then laid it on the carpet near where he might expect it to have fallen. Rock stood with his back to the counter near where Harbaugh had stood, grabbed the pillow and dropped it to give a natural appearance.

Rock made his way to the phone next to the bed, dialed zero, then told the desk clerk to pass on to housekeeping he did not need his room cleaned for several days since he would be working from his room. Replacing the receiver, he stood and surveyed the room.

"Dingo's death will be avenged, asshole," he said, looking at Harbaugh.

He slid the gloves and wash cloth into his cargo pants heading toward the door, subconsciously patting his gun in the small of his back.

CHAPTER FORTY-FOUR

———◆———

I called early enough to catch Brooke before she left for school. She seemed distracted, not her normal jovial self. I could easily dismiss the distraction based on her having to get ready for school, yet I sensed something more. After she gave the phone to her mom, I realized Brooke progressively seemed less talkative about things throughout the previous two phone calls, though I had not paid much attention until now.

Celia did not wait for me to ask about Brooke, she told me she would call me back in fifteen minutes once she made sure Brooke got to the bus stop. At thirty minutes I began to get a little concerned. When my phone rang another eighteen minutes later, I breathed a sigh of relief seeing Celia's name.

"I worried something happened. I'm relieved to hear your voice."

The pause felt like fifteen seconds, despite being five.

"Brooke is struggling with some things…I ended up driving her to school so we could talk. Sorry it took so long."

"Don't be sorry. I feel like a heel now, not picking up on her struggling. I wish I was there."

With a heavy tone, Celia replied, "I do, too."

Celia laid on the couch, pulling the thick wool blanket over her. "I have to get ready to go to my interior decorating class," she lied, having withdrawn from the class earlier in the week. "I wish we could talk longer."

"I do, too. Celia, are you okay? You sound like something is wrong."

"I'm fine, I've been super busy is all. I'm a little tired. I'll be alright."

"You would tell me if something happened…wouldn't you?"

"Mm-hmm."

In spite of not being convinced I had little recourse from two thousand miles away. I told her I hoped she got some rest and I would call her over the weekend.

"How much longer do you think you'll be there?" Celia asked, hoping not for an extended period.

"I think I might be able to be back there within a week."

"That's great," she said, her voice cracking some. "I've got to go. AJ, I…I love you."

I hesitated, the shock of the first time she said it taking my breath away. I smiled and started to answer when she disconnected. I pulled the phone away staring at the screen, not wanting to believe it ended. When I rang Celia's number back she did not answer.

As I walked around the parking lot waiting for the guys, I kept thinking about Celia and Brooke. I played the conversations over in my head and called Celia two more times, still no answer.

We need to finish this up here. Somethings not right. I need to get back to Celia.

Before I walked inside a thought hit me bringing instant fear. When I went to Albuquerque many months ago to help Mac and ultimately stop a band of rogue cops, I learned about them killing Celia's husband, Brooke's father. A good cop trying to do the right thing to stop the corruption, and for his efforts they killed him. Even though things appeared to be running smooth for the city and the police department once they removed some corrupt members, the possibility of another band of evil could not be ignored. I pulled out my phone to send a text knowing she would not answer a call.

> I KNOW SOMETHING IS WRONG, I CAN TELL. PLEASE ANSWER THIS AT LEAST. DOES IT HAVE ANYTHING TO DO WITH THE PD OR YOU BEING HARRASSED, FOLLOWED, WHAT-EVER?

The forty-five-minute wait before I got her one-word answer, no, seemed like an eternity. A mixture of feelings swirled, happy she got back to me for one. I felt relief the police no longer caused them grief. The way the new police administration had stepped up to support Celia financially I would have been surprised to hear they harassed her again. Still, I had to check.

The good feelings did not last, soon replaced with wondering why she and Brooke seemed down, yet Celia would not take my calls. The feeling of needing to get back to Albuquerque loomed larger.

CARLI HAD PROVIDED US THE BASIC INFORMATION SHE had on her peers. She used the words *think-tank cop* to describe Lou Jenson, not one who liked to kick doors and point guns. She had never heard what law enforcement agency he had been fired from or why, yet she had no doubt it could not have been for excessive force. He seemed useful, always willing to do all the associated things with a contract killing...except for killing. She presumed his not creating problems when arrested would be helpful to us, feeling certain his cooperation on an interview could be quite useful.

She identified the second person as Ben Rockford, Rock to the group. She had heard Harbaugh recruited Rockford first dubbing him Rock early on, saying he would be the foundation to the future. Chicago P.D fired Rock for exercising what he determined to be street justice on criminals he believed the system would kick out. Hence the reason Harbaugh liked him.

She had no background on the three Harbaugh had coming from Nashville. She speculated one of them had to be the decision maker on their mission. The specific information on the Nashville group mission had not been shared with her group, although she felt it would have been an assassination. Carli said she knew Harbaugh originally had three teams of three, before losing three on this mission.

Harbaugh never lacked for fired cops willing to take on the role of seeking justice, especially in the current society where Chiefs and Sheriffs often caved, willing to sacrifice a cop's career to keep social order. Even so, it took a special breed willing to do murders for hire, essentially mercenaries on American soil, beyond taking out a serious criminal the justice system could not, or even worse, would not deal with.

We decided to let Carli take information about me to Rock, knowing he wanted to come after me for killing his friend. Carli assured us Rock would not do a surprise attack with the group without first putting together a plan and a briefing, on the contrary she could not guarantee Rock might not go out on his own to seek justice for Dingo. From everything she told us about him, we believed Rock would do his own recon to validate Carli's information, then put together his plan to get me.

Kenny had asked Carli if they turned off their phones during recon like they did during missions…she said they remained on silent. We formulated a plan to have Seth driving Ric's vehicle, Kenny ready with the phone tracking equipment, while I would go into the hotel parking lot at 7:30 a.m. the next morning. Carli would sell it to Rock she had seen the guy he wanted two mornings in a row making a phone call at the same time.

We factored the risk to me would be low. A trained killer like Rock would not jeopardize himself or Harbaugh's company with a broad daylight shooting, in a high traffic area, when roads would be jammed with morning traffic. Carli's info would be validated when he saw my limp, identifying me as the killer of his friend. He most likely would then plan an attack making sure he stacked the odds in his favor. In the meantime, we would be prepared to follow him to lock down his lair.

CHAPTER FORTY-FIVE

C arli surprised us showing up at The Nook the next morning indicating her uncomfortableness using her phone unless necessary.

"I met with Rock this morning. We all received a text from Harbaugh telling us Rock would be in charge. He had to return to New York for business. It worked out perfectly. I made it sound like I had seen AJ out making his call again this morning before I went to meet Rock."

"Do you think you sold him on it?" Seth asked.

"Not a hundred percent positive but I think so. He's been different since Dingo died, more stoic, harder to read. Still, he nodded, and I thought I saw a grin. He did tell me I had done well."

"This should work out then," I said. "Where do you think he will let you all know the final operation plans...his hotel?"

"No. He never uses an open place with a lot of people who might see us. Harbaugh recently had a meeting at a restaurant and Rock let him know he thought it inappropriate."

Her phone dinged. She looked at the text and put it on the table.

"Rock," she said, flashing the screen at us. "The three guys coming from Nashville asked for one more day and he granted it. Said we would meet tomorrow evening, giving them enough time to get to the area and prepare for an op.

Back to your question, AJ, I'm not certain. He did mention this morning he had gotten an empty industrial type shop nearby from a junkyard owner named Dutch. He's the one who helped us get rid of Rock's first rental after your shoot out. The shop owner owed Dutch a favor. Rock said it's quasi-empty except for some machine shop equipment."

"You didn't ask the location?" Seth asked, his tone bordering on harsh.

"Look, Rock's a hard-ass, and since AJ killed his best friend, he's scarier than ever. So no, I didn't ask where. Rock will tell us when he is damned good and ready."

Carli stood, saying she could not stay and needed to check out where Kenny worked to get layout information for Rock.

She took two steps before turning to look at me. "I hope you remember all of this when it comes time to talk to the prosecutors and judge."

I started to nod, except she walked away.

"Well, somebody has to ask the question so I guess I will. Do we all believe she is helping us out and not setting us up?"

"I do," Kenny said. "Something about her I trust. I plan on watching my back in case, although I think she's tired of killing *contract*s instead of dirtbags."

"Yeah, I agree," Seth said. "Truthfully, most cops dream of having a justified shooting of some dirtbag. I get the impression she bought in early on, killing the sleaze who got away with some major crime. Killing the ordinary people from A-Ray Corporation…I don't think she's going to do it anymore."

"She had us pegged long before we had exact knowledge of who they were, so if she wanted to take us out, she could have passed it on to Harbaugh," I said. "It's going to be hard convincing some prosecutor we don't know to cut her a deal, on the other hand if this ends like we want it to she's the main reason. I'm prepared to go to bat for her so she can have a life after serving ten to twenty."

Kenny raised his hand getting Tom's attention. He and Luci walked over, her with a fresh pot of coffee.

"I'm glad you're both here. We might need a favor from you."

"Always Kenny, you know that."

"I'm not sure exactly when, nevertheless we are going to need to make it look like we came to your house for dinner and stayed for some time. If questioned, all you two would have to say is we had dinner and you really enjoyed getting to know my friends."

"Doesn't sound too difficult. Sunday night would work best, since we could say we stayed up later knowing our restaurant is closed on Mondays."

We all agreed about Tom's suggestion, still Rock wanted Kenny and I dead. Waiting too long increased the chances Rock might get his way.

"We'll try, no guarantees," I said.

"Not a problem," Tom replied, knowing not to ask questions.

"Thanks Tom. We'll finalize it later, right now we need to find an older model car we can use or buy. Don't want to be seen in ours."

"Would an old Chevelle do? It's stick shift, needs some body work, otherwise it runs like a top."

A wide-eyed Seth leaned forward to make sure he didn't miss a thing. He left no doubt he wanted to be the driver, assuming Tom didn't mandate it be Kenny.

"Is it yours?"

"Sort of. Bought it off the widow next door after her husband passed about six weeks ago. She gave me the keys, only we haven't done official paperwork yet. She went to Texas to spend time with her kids after the funeral and we are watching the house for her. I can get it out of her garage anytime. I've driven it around a couple times, you know, to blow out any old carbon build up."

"Yeah, I'm sure there's no other reason, Tom."

Tom chuckled.

"Do we get to know what it is you are going to do or what happens?" Luci asked.

We shook our heads. "I know you trust Kenny, and I hope you trust Seth and me, too. Believe me when I say the less you know the easier it will be for you to stick to the story, so some detective or attorney does not grill you later. I will say what we are doing is appropriate, maybe even virtuous."

Tom held Luci's hand, looking into her eyes. "That's good enough for us," he said. "We'll be ready."

I left and went to find a quiet outdoor spot to have a conversation. Opening my favorites in my phone I tapped Celia's number.

Something felt wrong and I had a nagging feeling it went beyond she and Brooke being in danger. Even though her return text the day before had been short, Celia assured me they had not been stalked or harassed. Still, I could not shake the nagging feeling.

As had happened on all my recent calls, it went to voicemail after five rings. I wondered if she had decided we could not have a relationship if I kept putting my life in danger. I assured her before I left I would not be coming to Virginia to do anything risky, which is exactly the opposite of what I did.

Putting away my phone I walked toward the front of the restaurant. At the corner I looked to my right and saw a black SUV parked on the opposite side of the road maybe fifty yards away. I began walking toward the SUV, except the instant I crossed the intersection it backed up onto a side street and took off.

Being in an area saturated with federal agencies, many of which utilized all black SUV's, I began calculating the possible reasons for the SUV we had seen. I believed I had seen one twice before, along with Ellie and Pham believing they had been surveilled when they went to the tea shop near his office.

I headed back to discuss it with Kenny and Seth. If the feds had eyes on us, following through with our plans might put all of us at risk of being indicted for federal crimes. They had families to think about.

Neither of them expressed a desire to bow out, black SUVs or not.

"Do you have the combination for Ric's safe?" I asked Kenny.

"I know it is the day he separated from the military. I remember where he told me to look for it if I ever needed it."

"Let's go, we need to get to his apartment."

"We don't have a key."

"We'll see about that."

When we got to Ric's apartment in Roseville they stayed near the car while I met the manager. Fortunately, he recalled seeing me the night Ellie took us there. I explained our need to get into Ric's place to gather some things, though not identifying what. He seemed hesitant at first considering Ric's hospital stay put him behind in rent and he had concerns about Ric being able to pay over the next several months.

I pulled out a credit card, offering to pay Ric's back rent along with six months in advance.

"Are you serious?" the manager asked.

"Dead serious. He's a war hero. It's the least I can do."

"Wow. I had no idea."

I told him we might need to be in there several times throughout Ric's recovery, so he offered me a spare key.

Kenny located the combination, opening the safe in under two minutes.

"There you go Seth," I said. "You have your choice of rifles."

Seth peered in, then looked over his shoulder with a huge grin.

"A snipers paradise," Seth said.

After thirty minutes of Seth drooling, we left with the rifle of his choice in a standard metal rifle carrying case.

CHAPTER FORTY-SIX

The time had come for us to be proactive. I didn't like being labeled a mercenary, although Major Potts would freely use the term to define me if we got caught. I had never been a professional soldier for hire and making money at the expense of ethics did not identify my reasoning for acting.

Right is right, wrong is wrong, a tenet I tried hard to live by. Still, I had discovered the unfortunate gray area in-between months before in Albuquerque helping my good friend Mac not become a death statistic at the hands of corrupt police officers. Now, thousands of miles from Albuquerque, good people had once again been killed. A greedy major in the sheriff's department let them down, opting instead to pad statistics and close cases rather than aggressively going after their killers... all for political gain. The gray area had once again beckoned for someone like me to do the wrong thing...yet for the right reason.

The message Ellie received made it clear...Kenny would be the next target. Targeting my friend made becoming proactive a no brainer.

Moreover, Rock wanted me dead for killing his friend. If we had to clash, I planned to do all I could to ensure we did it on our terms.

Back at our hotel room Kenny held up a little black device half the size of his cell phone, asking, "What do you guys think this is?".

"Looks like a spare battery," Seth said.

Having no clue, I shrugged.

"This my friends, a term I use loosely," Kenny began with a grin, "is what will allow us to do what is termed mesh networking."

Kenny stumped us and he knew it.

"It's like a long-range link without needing cell towers. We can put our burner phones in airplane mode, and we can connect provided we are within ten miles of each other. If we want to separate, we can double the distance. I could transmit something and if Seth is within ten miles of me, my transmission will hop through Seth's phone to AJ's, who is another ten miles away."

The enthusiasm on Kenny's face spoke of his being in his element, helping us to learn something new while educating us on the value of companies helping first responders, search and rescue teams, law enforcement, soldiers in foreign lands.

"Now for the best part," Kenny said, displaying his infamous Cheshire cat grin.

Antsy, Seth rolled his hand to get him moving.

"The best part is…there is no footprint in the zone we are working in since we are not utilizing cell towers, or our personal cell phones. We need to leave them at Tom and Luci's so if Major Potts wants to have his technicians check on our whereabouts the records from the cell towers will validate us being there for hours."

"Gotta love innovation," Seth said.

"This is a game changer," I said.

The smile on Kenny's face and the light in his eyes told me he appreciated our instant recognition in the value of his gadget, along with his efforts to keep us safe, and hopefully out of prison.

"When we put the plan into action, I think being seen in the lobby and their video cameras backing us up right before we go to Tom and Luci's will help alleviate any discrepancies," I said. "The phones at their house for the evening will lock us in."

"Using the older model Chevelle without all the computer chips will keep any technician from extracting information, too," Seth said.

"Ah, look at you two paying attention," Kenny said.

"The information is easy to listen to. The speaker on the other hand," Seth said, shrugging his shoulders while holding up his palms.

I smiled, appreciating the way my friends bantered, all the while knowing either would drop everything to help the other.

Kenny shook his head, yet he could not stop the corners of his lips from turning up in appreciation of the bantering. Kenny grabbed his bag of burner phones. He removed one, got it running, punched in a phone number and put it on speaker.

"Hey Tom, it's Kenny. We're going to need that favor from you. Sorry to spring it on you but right now it looks like tomorrow night."

"We understand Kenny, tomorrow night's fine. We'll be ready. I'll take the car out tonight to make sure it runs well, then when we get home tomorrow, I'll have the garage unlocked."

"Do you have an alley behind your house," Seth asked, something we frequently saw in California.

"No, something better. Lots of trees with no fence between our properties. I figured we would have the lights off in both back yards, you could go straight out into the woods out our back door. Work your way over to our neighbors, then when you feel comfortable zip out from the woods straight to her garage."

"Perfect. Thanks Tom," Kenny said, disconnecting.

"Should be easy enough," Seth said. "When the evening visit is over, we exit out the front door to our car, so we're caught on their security camera validating our departure. We need to make sure we have the same clothes on when we leave."

A KNOCK ON OUR DOOR STARTLED US AND WE HURRIEDLY put the phones and Kenny's black device in the suitcases. Seeing Ellie and Pham in the peephole I opened it.

"We've been talking," Ellie began. "We think I should let a story slip to a different newspaper, other than Major Potts' mouthpiece, bring light to the connection of all the attacks. We figure a good reporter will read between the lines, maybe start looking into Potts covering things up."

"Do you both like your jobs?" I asked.

They looked quizzically at each other before nodding.

"Then you need to trust me and not do anything foolish. This whole thing will play itself out, one way or the other, in the next twenty-four to forty-eight hours. You two are going to need plausible denial."

"You're up to something," Pham said. "What is it? Why can't we help?"

"When in Rome, do as the Romans do."

"What the hell's that supposed to mean?" Pham asked.

"It means you're in the world of law enforcement, a world full of rules. You're in a no-win scenario. Without administrative support, trying to stop the insurgents could cost you your careers, if not your lives. They are trained killers, you know. And, not following the rules means losing your careers even faster. Trust me…plausible denial."

"What happened to all the guns you had?" Ellie asked.

"What guns?" Seth asked.

"Ric's guns sitting right there last time," Ellie said, pointing toward the floor next to the bed.

"You must be mistaken, we never had any guns over there," Kenny said, a deadpan look on his face.

"Holy shit. You guys are up to something."

We spent the next ten minutes convincing them to trust us; distance from our operation would be their friend.

"If you really want to help, I think I might have something you can do for us after I text you tomorrow night."

Once I laid out the request Ellie smiled, and her eyes lit up. "It will be my pleasure."

CHAPTER FORTY-SEVEN

None of us slept well and The Nook did not open for a few hours, so we went to a Denny's and began reprocessing our information from beginning to end. We all felt justified in the necessity to take the steps we outlined.

Each of us admitted to being a bit unnerved by the SUVs we had seen. The mission we planned to embark on appeared dangerous, risky on many levels. Still, we needed to go forward, black SUVs or not.

I drove to our hotel in Kenny's rental. Seth drove Ric's work SUV while Kenny got his tracking equipment running. They went to a predetermined location we hoped would be out of Rock's view within one mile of the hotel.

If Rock spotted them our entire plan would have to be ditched, leaving us with plan B, which seemed little more than a hope and a prayer. If Rock fled trying to track him during morning commute traffic would be next to impossible. Worse yet, he would know all about us.

I stepped into the hotel parking lot at 7:25 a.m. Carli told us Rock did not have a rifle, so we figured he would have me in a pair of binoculars. I called Seth's phone solely for them to have an open line to me in case things went bad.

Better to fake it from the start, I thought.

It didn't take long before I heard Kenny's program verbalizing like it did the night Danny died.

TARGET IN AREA
REDIRECT ATTEMPTED
TARGET IN CHANNEL
DIRECTIONAL FINDING

"He's on the move AJ," Seth said, tension in his voice.
"It looks like he's south of the hotel and moving north,"
Kenny said.

"It's passing us right now. It's the blue Camry, AJ," Seth
barked.

I put the phone in my left hand, pivoting like I planned
to drift the other direction, my right hand sliding to my
hip area. I half expected Rock to jump out and start firing.
Instead the Camry only slowed, then kept rolling northbound past the hotel.

I ran to Kenny's rental the instant the Camry got out of
sight. I knew they would start following him using Kenny's
equipment, and I wanted to be close enough in case all hell
broke loose. We kept the phone line open with Seth calling
off streets and directions for me.

We had a stroke of good fortune when Rock started
heading out of the congestion into areas where homeown-
ers clearly had acreage. Maintaining distance while keeping
him within the mile radius improved once out of the city.
Before long he had stopped, so they pulled to the shoulder
and directed me in.

Turning onto Decatur Road I passed their vehicle.
Within a quarter of a mile a huge home came into view to
my left and a narrow gravel road went up to a metal shop
nestled in the trees on my right. In front sat a blue car,
which looked like the Camry. I gave Seth the information
and drove to the parking lot of the Potomac Point Winery

and Vineyard to wait.

Kenny used another computer to pull up the area on Google Earth. Once they had a general idea, they did a quick drive by, Kenny's equipment pinpointing the blue car I had seen.

Seconds later we met in the Potomac parking lot and expanded the view on the computer enabling us to see the building perpendicular to Decatur Road. Though preferable the insurgents give up peacefully, we had no expectation for that to happen. We decided to set up facing the building so if a firefight took place stray rounds would not endanger innocent people. Except for the house across Decatur Road we could not have asked for a better place to take them down.

It's only a matter of time Rock. We're coming for you, too.

CARLI TEXTED...

ANSWER THE INCOMING CALL.

"Where you calling from?" I asked.

"I'm using the business phone in the lobby of my hotel. Rock's called an op meeting tonight at 8:30 p.m. He's amped up. I've seen the same look in his eye before; he's going to try to make a move tonight."

"Let me guess, you're meeting on Decatur Road."

"Yeah, how'd you know?"

"Rock drove past the hotel this morning during my fake phone call from the parking lot. With Kenny's hi-tech equipment we tracked him to a metal shop, hidden in the trees. I'm not surprised he's amped up...I killed his best friend."

Carli said, "The three guys from Nashville got here and

seem raring to go, too. One black guy, two whites. All three look like mid-thirties and in shape. None are over six feet. They came together in a white Forerunner."

"Are you comfortable Rock does not know you've spoken with us?"

"Yeah. He has no idea."

"We will be in place when everyone gets there. How are you going to get out of there to stay safe?"

"Already told them I'll bring pizzas. I plan to carry them in, then say I need to go out to my car to get something. Once I am back outside, I'll take a position of cover. Them stuffing pizza in their mouths should help provide a distraction for you."

"Okay. If you feel uncomfortable at all stay inside. We'll know, so we won't hit the place. We'll wait until they exit to get started on the op. Watch your back."

"I will. I'm ready for this. I've wanted to get away from these guys for a while now."

Carli hung up, relaxing back into the chair, wondering what it would be like to be free from the group for the first time in years. Lost in her thoughts, she never noticed the door to the office ajar or the person in the hallway listening to her conversation.

CHAPTER FORTY-EIGHT

———◆———

Before leaving the hotel I intentionally struck up a conversation with the manager, commenting on being excited for a home cooked meal at the home of the owners of The Nook.

We arrived at their house before six, leaving equipment in the car until after the sun had set.

Luci made sure to let us know she mentioned to a neighbor she would be cooking for three visitors, followed with a wink.

Smiling, I said, "Look at you, tightening up our alibi."

She grinned, patting my cheek.

I told Tom, "Leave the porch lights off. In about an hour we'll go out to get our gear."

Luci may not have known exactly what we planned on doing, nonetheless she made sure we had a good pot roast with mashed potatoes before we could even think about getting ready.

Kenny parked the car in the long driveway with the trunk near the side door off the kitchen. We got our gear, donning our solid black fatigues we purchased in DC, along with stopping at a range to allow Seth to get comfortable with Ric's rifle.

We made sure our personal cell phones remained in the living room, using Kenny's burner phones. Tom's idea of sneaking in from the trees in back worked perfectly. He had backed the Chevelle into the detached garage earlier so we could slip out easily.

Seth drove the speed limit making sure to stop at every yellow light possible. He loved the Chevelle, wanting to take advantage of every available second of driving time. Given he would likely be shot at soon, I figured a few minutes of enjoyment seemed warranted.

Earlier when we had tracked Rock, I noticed a T-intersection where Hoot Owl Road ran south. When I reconned the road I decided parking on the shoulder would work.

We passed the metal shop and Seth pulled onto Hoot Owl. After he U-turned, we waited to see if we had any curious onlookers. Nothing moved so we exited with our weapons, sliding into the woods next to the road. We went to Decatur Road, and made sure we crossed in different locations with a five-minute separation.

Using Kenny's equipment, we had constant communications with each other, always knowing positions while we moved tactically one at a time to prevent giving ourselves away. Seth would have the best position once there, so we made sure we got him in position first to provide our final cover.

Seth took up a position forty yards straight out from the one standard door on the southwest corner. He had Ric's Remington 700 rifle with a Sightmark Photon XT night vision scope, ready to put a hole between somebody's eyebrows.

Kenny getting set would prove the hardest of the three of us. He stayed closest to Decatur Road, so he constantly had to be vigilant of car headlights. Once Seth got fully set Kenny crossed the gravel road leading to the building where the best option for cover existed. From his position he would prevent anyone from driving away once inside the trap. He had one of Ric's .40 caliber Glock 22's, with Trijicon HD Night Sights and four extra magazines.

I went further north to the left of Seth to cover the large rollup door on the north end, making sure the angle of my shots to the front, if needed, would not put Kenny at risk. I had Ric's .9mm Glock with the same Trijicon HD Night Sights, along with three extra magazines.

We reached our final positions at 7:50 p.m.

At 8:15 p.m. Kenny let us know about two cars pulling in…a white Forerunner with three occupants and a dark Ford Focus with two occupants. The cars backed up close to the building a few feet north of the single door. The three from the Forerunner and the driver of the Focus started unloading bags from the back of the Forerunner. The passenger from the Focus went straight to the door, opened it, and turned the lights on inside.

In the stillness I could hear the distinct slides on semi-automatic handguns being released, slamming forward, along with magazines being seated in weapons. Although everyone had weapons, each side had an advantage. They outnumbered us, yet we had the element of surprise, along with them being trapped in a cocoon of a building.

Shortly after 8:30 p.m. Kenny said Carli arrived. She pulled in next to the Focus, parking close to the building. She got out with two large pizza boxes, walking around the front of the other two cars, then headed towards the door. She nearly came to a stop when she looked over her shoulder in my direction, slightly raising the boxes before she made her way into the shop. Carli stopped two feet inside the door, locked in Seth's scope.

"Something's wrong," Seth said. "She's stopped, right inside the door. I hear a male voice almost yelling. He's saying…wait a second, she's backing up…oh shit, he's calling her a traitor."

The rollup door no longer held immediate importance, Carli's safety did. I left my position moving to the closest tree straight out from Carli's car. The second I stopped, gun fire erupted inside the building. I saw Carli make it to the doorway, her body jerking from rounds hitting her. She stumbled outside, collapsing in front of the Forerunner.

"I'm going to Carli. Cover me."

I heard Seth's voice say, "AJ," but nothing else. Tactically they still outnumbered us even without Carli, likely with more firepower. I knew Seth wanted me to remain safely behind cover, although he knew me well enough to grasp I could not leave her there alone.

I started my sprint across the open gravel drive. A man emerged, silhouetted in the doorway, his arms extended with his body in a forty-five-degree angle, working to draw a bead on me. Seth fired one 168 grain .308 round, passing through the man's head with the ease of a melon, before the man could fire a single round. The near headless body dropped like a sack of potatoes, half inside the doorway half outside.

My mind registered Seth's shot and the man in the doorway flopping to the ground. I stumbled causing me to slide into Carli's side on my knees, my left forearm hitting the front bumper of the Forerunner.

I pushed away then gently touched her face.

"Carli, stay with me."

"Somehow Rock knew you followed…that we talked."

A handgun came around the door frame shooting several rounds in Seth's direction. Two men jumped over their dead partner firing randomly straight out from the door. Kenny shot twice at the one closest to him, certain he hit the man's torso. The hit's caused the man to nearly fall before he turned toward Kenny's direction preparing to fire. From a closer distance Kenny would have shot two to the chest and one to the head. Registering the man must have on an armored vest, plus the added distance, Kenny lowered his aim. His next two rounds hit low abdomen a couple inches above the groin, with the third one exploding the man's left knee. He no sooner hit the ground on his side when Seth put a round through the man's throat...terminating his ability to breathe.

The one closest to the car ducked down behind the Forerunner, then slid behind the Focus trying to get a flanking position. From the right rear quarter panel, he would pop up and fire at either Seth or Kenny, never getting off more than two shots before receiving returned fire. He had no idea I even existed on the ground with Carli in front of his car. I laid flat, took aim in front of the right rear tire, waiting for his next shot at Kenny where he exposed his right lower leg. The instant he planted his shoe I fired two rounds, hitting him in the foot. I heard his scream, then I saw him drop to one knee exposing his good leg. I shot two more rounds, the second of which took out his calf. Another scream led to another movement, this time him falling prone.

With all lower leg hits, he had to have known where the shots came from. When he went prone his eyes tried to locate a target at the same time he began to extend his gun arm my direction. I could see his eyes had recognition a split second before he got his arm fully extended, allowing me a clear shot. His head snapped back when my round entered his eye socket, passing through his brain and exiting on the opposite side.

I turned back to Carli.

She forced a grin, saying, "Better than prison, I guess." She took her last breath with her eyes staring into mine.

I reached over, gently closing her lids. She had done so many wrong things, terrible things, yet in the end, she died trying to do the right thing to atone for her wrongs. I admired her for her effort.

"Carli is dead. Two left. We have to do something quick; I can hear sirens."

I thought I heard squeaking metal at the same time a man began to speak.

"I'm coming out, don't shoot," said a voice from inside. "I'm coming—"

Five shots rang out from inside the building.

In his sights, Seth saw a man, no gun in his raised hands, fall to his left against the side of the building, sliding down the metal siding leaving a swath of blood.

I jumped up, sprinting to the doorway, my left shoulder against the siding. Kenny arrived taking the other side while Seth covered us making entry.

The roll up door on the far end no longer sat on the ground. A quick scan validated my worst fear—Rock had made it out.

"Rock killed him. That's Lou. He couldn't have anyone left alive to talk to the cops. I'm going after him."

"We've got to get to the car, we need to get out of here," Seth said. "I'll start moving in that direction. If I can get to the car, I can at least pick you guys up somewhere." He turned, jogging off into pure darkness.

"You need to go with him. If something happens you two need to be able to provide cover for one another."

Kenny hesitated, looking me in the eyes.

"It's okay, really. Now go."

We both knew Rock had the advantage of being behind cover and waiting, and with me being alone his advantage increased. Still, I felt better knowing Kenny and Seth had a good chance of getting out of there if they could make it to the car.

Kenny leapt up, sprinting across the gravel drive passing into the darkness of the trees.

I heard the two of them talking, working together to make sure they would get out of the forest. I sprinted to the north end of the building, did a quick peek to make sure Rock had not been waiting to ambush me, then began working my way east.

I got fifty yards from the building then stopped behind a tree, closing my eyes to recall the area we saw on Google Earth. Rock knew he would kill Carli, most likely figuring they would kill us. Something told me Rock hid his car like we had, in case we killed the rest of his team. According to Carli, Lou would not have questioned Rock on why he wanted a car nearby, he would have simply followed directions and picked Rock up.

I continued moving east keeping Decatur Road within earshot. I felt relieved when I heard Kenny say they had made it to the car. My relief got interrupted when I heard a small branch snap at my three o'clock position. Without hesitation I dropped to one knee, scanning while in a firing position, waiting to see muzzle flash.

Taking a chance, I said, "Rock, you won't get away."

"You can't stop me, AJ."

I heard movement along with more twigs breaking, so I moved forward a half dozen trees.

His car must be close, he's moving toward the road.

"We know who you are. Your name will be plastered on every law enforcement BOLO across America."

"You can't bullshit a bullshitter. None of you are exactly acting under color of authority. Now, if you'll excuse me, I have business to attend to."

Two shots rang out, the bullets hitting trees within a few feet of me. I did a quick peek then sprinted to the next tree. I heard the distinct sound of car tires locked in a skid coming from the same general direction as the gun shots.

Another shot rang out, so I left my position hoping to make it to the road in time. I heard Rock yelling orders, and then the squeal of tires burning. I knew who had the car, I only hoped Rock did not kill innocent people to take it.

I moved toward the sound of the squealing tires. I saw a man and a woman hugging on the far side of the road who I presumed owned the vehicle Rock carjacked.

They don't know how lucky they are.

I moved deeper into the woods knowing I would come across Widewater Road sooner or later. I contacted Kenny to advise of Rock's carjacking along with my intent to keep moving east. He told me I had roughly ten more minutes before I would break out of the forest and they would pick me up at the intersection of Widewater and Flippo Roads.

CHAPTER FORTY-NINE

⟞⟞•⟝⟝

As Seth pulled the Chevelle into the garage around 9:40 p.m. I sent the preplanned text to Ellie. She would tell Potts about the possibility the California detective might have wanted to even the score with the criminals with which he had a run-in. Along with the ruse, Ellie appearing to distrust me like Potts did could score points with him. We had to move quickly in case Major Potts sent somebody to check on us right away.

By ten o'clock we had changed back into the clothes we came in, equipment bags in the trunk, sitting at the table.

"Are you boys okay?" Luci asked. "You all look like you could use something to drink."

"Beer," Kenny said, the other two raising their hands in agreement.

"Any red wine?" I asked.

Luci scurried off to the kitchen. "Heineken okay?"

"Great," Kenny said without checking with the other two.

She brought everyone their drinks to include wine for me and a beer for her.

The silence became uncomfortable after a few minutes.

"Go ahead," I said, looking at Luci.

"What?" Luci asked.

"I know you want to ask about what happened."

"This has been eating me up inside. You could tell, huh?"

She did not wait for a response. "All I want to know is, whatever you did tonight, did you…I don't know…do the right thing for the good people around here?"

Both of my partners nodded, making me feel good inside. I had asked my friends to do something outside the norms of society believing we would be doing the morally right thing, stopping killers from continuing to kill innocent people like Janice and Laird. Now I knew we all believed the same, we helped people tonight.

"We aren't done," I said, taking a sip of wine. "We won't need guns, what we will need is to play chess to finish this."

The rap on the door caught Tom and Luci off guard…not us. We recognized the knock of a police officer, hard, loud, far from the ease of using the doorbell. They went to answer it while the three of us stayed at the table, the perfect guests.

"AJ, sorry to bother you."

I turned in my chair, feigning surprise at hearing my name. I stood.

"Sergeant Carothers, to what do I owe this visit?" I asked, extending my hand. "Did you catch the other guy who shot at me?"

"No, I wish we had. I'm here for a different investigation. I'm actually kind of embarrassed to have to be here."

Wanting to appear calm, I said, "I'm sorry, I didn't introduce you to everyone." Introductions took place with his fellow detective standing in the background, hands crossed in front of him not saying a word.

"I'm sorry I interrupted you, Sergeant. Please continue."

"Look, our major is making me do this…can I ask you and your two buddies if you'll each take a gunshot residue test?"

"I don't know about my friends, but sure, I'll do it. Can I ask why? I mean, we've been here all evening."

"What's a gunshot residue test?" Luci asked.

"It's a way to see if someone fired a gun recently is all," Carothers said.

"Now that seems foolish. These boys came for dinner, we've had a lovely evening. We had pot roast, mashed potatoes, gravy—"

"I'm sure they don't want to know all the details, dear," Tom said.

Carothers smiled…Luci hit her mark. He appeared even more embarrassed to have to follow through with Major Potts's order.

"We had a shooting earlier. Several guys, one chick, like the guy you dumped the other day. None of them have ID, and except for one guy they all have guns, a couple with suppressors. The shooting took place at an abandoned metal shop. Somebody from our agency wondered out loud if maybe you wanted retaliation for the guy who shot you, AJ. I tried telling them these guys looked like drug dealers or runners like the guy you shot. Somebody probably stole their merchandise."

"Somewhat of a regular occurrence in their line of work," I said.

"Exactly. But, Major Potts, he's a pain in the …" Carothers looked at Luci. "Sorry, Ma'am. Well, you know what I mean. He ordered me to follow up on this right away. We went to your hotel, the manager there said you had been invited to dinner, so she gave you directions. Everything she said is backed up on video. She did not remember the address though recalled these folks owned The Nook. We pinged your phone, which of course lined up with the information about where you went to dinner. Besides the gun shot residue test, Potts wants a search warrant to verify the location of your phones for the last couple of hours."

I chuckled, "Not a problem, Sergeant. We've been right here since we arrived at, I don't know, close to six." I looked over my shoulder where four heads nodded. Like I had told Ellie, fifty percent of a statement is true.

The younger silent detective did the actual GSR's on the three of us. Having thoroughly washed our hands, wiped down our arms, face and heads with damp wash clothes, along with completely changing back to our original clothes, the GSR's came back negative.

While the young detective did the GSR tests, Luci talked with Carothers the entire time, even giving him a piece of apple pie, not taking no for an answer. She spelled out everything we had supposedly done all night in an unforced easy manner. Right before the detectives left Carothers told the younger detective Potts sent them on another wild goose chase so they did not need to waste time doing a search warrant on the phones. The younger detective had softened up, even apologizing along with Carothers one last time before they walked outside.

"Luci, I had no idea you could role play so well," Kenny said, his arm around her shoulder on the walk back to the dining table.

"She's been in a number of plays, at least a couple dozen," Tom said proudly. "She's an exceptional actress."

"Good actress, good cook, she's a star in my book," Seth said.

Luci beamed, the reason she had to role play in the first place seemingly already shelved away in her mind. She had been convincing, and the praise from her three guests made her evening.

CHAPTER FIFTY

——◆——

Forty-eight hours passed, and the smoke had blown over from the shootings at the abandoned metal shop, enough that we felt we would not be questioned again. We had surveilled Ava Lloyd believing she could be instrumental in bringing down Harbaugh, plus depending on what she and Major Potts had discussed privately, maybe him, too. From what we could tell she had left her home three times, once for a meeting with an attorney, a separate time to meet with someone at a financial advisors' office, and the mortuary.

We left Ava's neighborhood at 9 p.m. after we saw all the lights go out. A few short minutes later we sat down at the Italian restaurant near her home. My phone dinged.

> YOU ARE GOING TO WANT TO ANSWER THE CALL YOU WILL RECEIVE IN A COUPLE MINUTES.
> WHO IS THIS?
> THAT'S NOT SIGNIFICANT RIGHT NOW-THE CALL IS.

I grabbed a napkin, hastily writing a note, handing it to Kenny. When he got up to go outside I showed the text to Seth.

Kenny returned, nodding. "I had to make my way

around the side of the building, then I spotted the black SUV in the parking lot of the shopping center behind us. What's this about?"

I showed him the text, only before we could discuss it my phone rang. I answered and tapped the speaker button.

"AJ Conti."

"Mr. Conti, you don't know me, my name is Greta Meier. I am the Commonwealth Attorney for Stafford County."

"Well, Ms. Meier, if that really is who you are, how did you get my phone number and what is it you want to talk about?"

"This is not a conversation for the phone. Do you mind if I come into the restaurant?"

Seth looked out the window to scour the parking lot. Not seeing anything out of the ordinary, he shook his head.

"Sure, assuming you will feel comfortable talking in here."

"They will move us to a private corner, trust me."

Car headlights flashed past the window, a black Lincoln Town Car stopping near the front door. The driver opened the back door, helping a woman in a dark pantsuit step out. She looked at us, pushed a button on her phone to end our call, then walked inside the restaurant.

The way the owner of the restaurant greeted the woman we could tell they knew each other well. Our waiter asked us to follow him while the women spoke.

Exactly like Greta had said, they moved us to a private corner close to the kitchen with the nearest customers sitting thirty feet away. I got the impression we would be taking the managers worktable since the waiter cleared off a stack of paperwork. My friends took the chairs closest to the wall giving me the chance to sit directly across from Greta.

She came up to the table, looking at each of us. "Mr. Conti?"

I stood, extending my hand.

"Please, call me AJ."

She had a strong grip, presumably letting me know she had no intention of playing games. I introduced Seth and Kenny, she acknowledged each with a smile and repeated their name.

Greta Meier looked to be fifty, stress lines in her face making her look a couple of years older. Her black hair had lost some of its bounce after a long day, yet the tinge of gray in the roots added a touch of strength. She had a confident air about her. Something about her smile seemed genuine, giving me the feeling she felt comfortable around law enforcement, current or retired.

"Please, call me Greta," she said as she sat. She looked over her shoulder toward the front door, then back at us. "I trust you'll cover my six."

We chuckled at her using cop lingo to make sure we had her back.

"I don't like my back to the door any more than you do, except I drew the short straw," Seth said.

"Any association with law enforcement brings out the haters," I said.

"True. Death threats come with the territory," she replied.

Greta pulled out her identification, along with credentials validating her being the Commonwealth Attorney for the county. While we looked at them, she said she had some basic information about us, saying she felt comfortable we might be able to help her solve a problem.

"Who directed you to us?" I asked.

"No different than you, I won't reveal my sources. I will

tell you I spent a number of years being a federal prosecutor before I got elected the Commonwealth Attorney."

"That's a nice way of saying the feds without saying it."

She did a closed lip half-smile.

"No surprise, really, considering we've seen a black SUV hanging out near us half a dozen times now, including in the parking lot right before your Town Car pulled up."

The waiter came over, and we ordered meals while Greta only wanted red wine. She mentioned they had a Sangiovese red wine she thought might be the best on the east coast, so I decided to have a glass with her. When it arrived, we touched glasses and I said, "Cin, cin."

"Ah, Italian. I like it."

No different than interviewing a criminal, I spent the first fifteen minutes breaking down barriers while trying to get to know Greta, and truthfully, she did the same…except she had three people to figure out in the same time frame.

Greta first took a sip of wine, then a deep inhale.

She asked, "Are you familiar with Colonel Harbaugh and Major Potts? I call them H&P."

I kept a steady head, my eyes locked on her. Being a prosecutor she knew not to ask a question to which she did not have the answer. We waited.

Greta grinned. "You boys have been around the block. You've probably spent more time in actual trials than I have. Foolish of me, I apologize. From this point on I will lay out what I have, asking only questions I sincerely don't have the answers to. Fair enough?"

After looking at each other we nodded.

"We have had a number of suspicious deaths, murders, attacks…more than we normally have in a six-week period. My source tells me H&P are at the center of it all. We, my office, has little information on Harbaugh, only what my source supplied us. We have long believed Potts to be dirty except catching him at anything has been difficult. With him running for Sheriff, we could be in for a corrupt agency before he is done two or three terms from now. My source says they are connected."

"If Potts is dirty, why hasn't he been fired? Good old boy system?"

"Possibly, although we don't think so. The Sheriff and Undersheriff are reputedly good people, and they have made it clear neither of them cares for Potts. The three of them worked patrol together years ago, and we are half-convinced something might have happened back then he's used against them."

I ran my hand through my hair, contemplating what exactly she wanted.

"I think I speak for all of us when I say we would be willing to help you, although we need to make sure you agree not to ask any questions about things we say are off limits. Additionally, you need to agree not to expose us in any manner to the public or press. Instead, you agree to put Investigator Ellie Svenson with the Sheriff's Office and Agent Pham with National Parks Investigative Services out front. Their careers are budding, ours are over."

Greta sat sipping her wine for a couple of minutes. Her eyes had not focused on anything directly, although she had the look of someone running possibilities through their mind.

"I'm not a hundred percent comfortable with it, nevertheless I think I understand. I can agree to your terms. So, where do we start?"

"We believe Ava Lloyd will be the key."

"Ava Lloyd? Isn't she the wife of the CEO who died when the CFO he fired attacked him? I'm lost, how is she the key to H&P?"

We smiled.

"Since your office is paying for this, I'm going to need another glass of wine to be able to get you caught up."

"Go for it. Something tells me this is going to be an interesting trip."

"Trust me, Walt Disney would call it an E-ticket ride."

I held up my wine glass drawing a nod from our waiter.

CHAPTER FIFTY-ONE

———◆———

E llie agreed to meet us only we felt we needed to go
somewhere other than The Nook since our friendship
with the owners had been revealed the night the insurgents
died at the metal shop. She did not say it, though we got
the impression some people in her agency did not trust her,
most likely the Major's internal followers. She chose a small
coffee shop in a strip mall in Fredericksburg.

"So, you guys been laying low, or are you going to create
more work for us?"

"Why Ms. Ellie, we have no idea what you are referring
to," Kenny said in his best southern accent.

"Yeah right. For the record, your accent sucks."

Seth and I laughed; acting hurt Kenny's head drooped
while his hands covered his heart.

"Do you have any update on Rock?" I asked.

"Pham has been digging only we haven't found much.
He did track down information on the rental car under Ben
Rockford's name like Carli said, it looks like the one he had
when your shooting took place, AJ. The company says the
car has not been returned so Carli's probably right, it's most
likely been chopped."

"Any idea who chopped it?"

"Not yet. I'm pretty sure the guy who arranged it all is a
guy named Dutch. He owns a local junkyard. Our under-

cover guys say Dutch is not dirty, on the contrary he's not squeaky clean either."

"More like a facilitator," Seth said.

Ellie agreed.

"Maybe you need to have a little talk with him," I said. "If he has no direct involvement yet can help our new friend, Greta Meier lock down the insurgent's time in the area, she might be willing to cut him a deal. I'd be willing to bet he mostly dealt with Harbaugh or Rock.

We tell him the truth; she drove Rock's car there, saw the chop shop runners take the car. He doesn't have to know Carli is dead."

"Wait, did you say Greta Meier? Like the Commonwealth Attorney for Stafford County, same Greta?"

"Yeah, same one. If you haven't figured it out, we don't mess around."

None of us gave any indication Greta found us. Not all details need to be shared all the time.

"Wow, Greta's on board. Okay, I'll go there when we leave here."

"In the meantime, you up for a little fun?"

Ellie canted her head, squinting like she thought I might be pulling her leg. A few seconds later, "Maybe?"

"Good. I think Kenny has contacts in every federal agency up and down this coast. Anyway, a couple of his contacts did a financial search of Ava Lloyd, which we shared with Greta. Ava paid a substantial sum to Harbaugh right before the murders of her husband and lover. A couple days later she made another payment, one hundred thousand dollars. Want to guess to who?"

She tilted her head, the wheels turning processing possibilities. She pushed away from the table sitting up straighter, her eyes large, a slight grin forming at the corners of her mouth.

"Please tell me Major Potts?"

We all smiled seeing the joy in her eyes from the realization she might be able to take down the one person who had been gradually taking the department toward being corrupt instead of the upstanding one Ellie hired into.

"Yes, and I'm presuming the enthusiasm on your face means you'll do it?"

"Oh yeah."

"You need to know there is a possibility this could backfire, if it does, you might be looking for a new job."

Without hesitation, she said, "What do you need me to do? I'm ready."

"Ava has hardly left her home; we've been tracking her."

I could see the surprise in Ellie's face about everything we had been up to.

"We'll explain later. We want to wire you along with giving you a means of hearing me without her knowing. We want all of this to look like it is coming from you. We can't be dragged into court or a defense attorney could go after us for...*everything we might have allegedly done.*"

"Sounds simple enough. Still, what makes you think she'll talk?"

"Incentive. Greta knows she would have a difficult time proving a prima facie case against Ava without some help. All the players are dead, except for Harbaugh and Rock, neither of which we know their whereabouts right now."

Ellie's eyes darted between the three of us, obvious enough for even an unseasoned investigator to pick up on.

"What?"

"Uh, I thought you guys had heard. Harbaugh…they found him dead in his hotel room in D.C. No details yet, except for his room had been paid for in advance for a couple of weeks with a message he would be working from his room so not to disturb him. Or so some unidentified source told reporters."

"Rock," Kenny said, no hint of being unsure.

Seth agreed. "Not saying we will although we could probably give the medical examiner a good idea of when it happened based on what Carli told us about Harbaugh supposedly sending a text saying he had to get back to New York thus leaving Rock in charge."

I put my elbows on the table, my folded hands under my chin, taking in the gravity of Harbaugh being dead. The odds of getting any legal justice had narrowed. Looking at Ellie something told me she could pull it off. We had to give it a shot.

"Here's what we do. How about the two of you go talk with Dutch. If he seems like he might cooperate, bring Ellie in to let her take it from there. In the meantime, I need to run everything down to Greta one more time to make sure she wants us to do this given Harbaugh is dead and Rock might be out of the country already."

KENNY PULLED UP TO THE JUNKYARD, WAITING IN THE car with Seth until no one else sat in the parking lot. Ellie pulled up in her car seconds after they entered the narrow lobby with three greasy plastic chairs, a gumball machine in the corner next to a soda machine against the far-left wall.

A man flipping through a large catalog of car parts stood on the opposite side of the counter. He looked to be in his fifties, with salt and pepper hair, a goatee, and matching the description Carli provided.

"You Dutch?" Kenny asked.

Without moving his head, the man raised his eyes to look. "If you're cops I ain't saying nothing without my attorney."

"First of all, we aren't cops, second of all, guys like you don't keep an attorney on retainer."

The man tilted his head, pushing up from the counter to stand straight. His hands slid back to the edge of the counter, cupping the edge with his fingers barely touching the surface.

"You go for the gun under the counter you'll die right there," Seth said, his hand already on the Glock in his waistband. Seth stepped forward, using his six-foot five frame to look down on the man who stood five nine on a good day.

The man looked into Seth's eyes, raised his palms, and stepped away from the counter.

"We are going to make this really simple, Dutch," Kenny said. "Your buddy Harbaugh is dead. Rock, who you know well, did it. Now, Rock seems to be taking out anyone he thinks might have betrayed him. Personally, we think he's gone off the deep end, and in his diminished mental capacity reasoning isn't important. So, you have two choices. You can live or you can die. It's up to you."

"What the hell's that supposed to mean?"

"Good question. Glad you asked. If you want to live you will cooperate with the detective outside, without your fake attorney, hoping the Commonwealth Attorney will cut you a deal. If not, since we are not cops there is nothing unlawful about us putting the word out on the streets about you ratting on Rock, telling the cops you didn't need witness protection to keep a punk like him from trying to kill you."

"That's bullshit. You can't ...."

"Okay."

They started toward the door, keeping an eye on his hands.

"Wait, wait, wait."

Kenny worked his way back to the counter while Seth kept his hand on his Glock.

"All's I've ever done is provide a vehicle when asked. It's an easy grand, the vehicle is always returned, spic and span."

Kenny looked at Seth. "I'm sure him being nervous is why he didn't say anything about having Rock's car taken to the chop shop."

"Whatever," Seth said, a look of disgust on his face staring into Dutch's eyes. "He lies or forgets to tell us something again, I'll text the chick who dropped off Rock's car to be chopped. You heard me, asshole, she's working for us now."

Seth worked on cars in his spare time, so he had been to many junkyards. His gut told him Dutch had no desire to read a newspaper or watch the news, not to mention the articles in the paper about the dead insurgents had been vague. Dutch mirrored the other junkyard owners he had come across. They all had extensive knowledge about car parts, whereas life outside of their junkyards did not matter. They cared about two things, cars and money...in that order.

The tell came when Dutch's shoulders sagged. Looking straight at Dutch, Kenny said to Seth, "Go get the cop. He'll talk to her."

Dutch nodded, he looked down at the floor when Seth turned to go get Ellie.

CHAPTER FIFTY-TWO

———◦———

Greta knew I had no desire to meet in her office, so we met at a small bistro a couple of blocks from her office. At 10:30 a.m. they only had a few customers, so we grabbed a small table in the back corner. Greta had already heard the news about Harbaugh, causing a much more forlorn look than the last time we met.

"I wanted to touch base with you before we send Ellie in to talk with Ava Lloyd. Her career is on the line if she does not have your backing."

Greta took a deep breath, directing it back to me, which surprised me.

"What do you think I should do, AJ?"

I could see the confusion in her eyes, a hesitation about her.

"The prosecution world is often built on a high-win statistic so people like yourself can be reelected. This situation does not lend itself to a high-win probability. If you wanted to bow out most people would accept your decision."

"Most people? Meaning you wouldn't?" she asked, a pained look on her face.

"I'm not like most people," I said.

"My source told me you went after a group of rogue cops in Albuquerque, almost died taking them down. Most people would classify you crazy to go after rogue cops. Tell me, AJ...why did you do it?"

"Right is right, wrong is wrong. Not an overly profound basis…nevertheless it's the reason."

I could see an unsureness about her. Hesitating, she sat deep into her chair.

"I'm not asking as a prosecutor, but…is that how you justify your actions here."

I realized she probably had a good idea what really took place days before at the machine shop. At the same time, I did not sense she had a problem with what had happened, she merely needed answers to help her decide her own position…moral or political.

"Yes, as a matter of fact. The truth is people shooting at you first, regardless of the reason you are there, makes killing them much easier. It may sound strange; I'm glad they did, for the sake of my friend's. They will leave here feeling like dirtbags shot at them, so they dumped them. To be fair, it became obvious early on someone in the Stafford County Sheriff's Office would not allow the good investigators to put the pieces of the puzzle together so they could go after the insurgents. So, I mentally prepared to do what I had to do to stop them from killing my friend, whom they had targeted to be their next hit."

Greta remained quiet, taking a sip of her diet soda. With my cards on the table I wanted to wait…only I couldn't.

"I only have a couple things to say, then I'll leave you to your thoughts. First, think back to what made you want to be the Commonwealth Attorney in the first place. I suspect it had to do with you wanting to protect the good people who reside here, not out of a desire to be political or constantly worrying about conviction rates so you could win the seat again. Second, you brought up Major Potts to us when we first met. You know in your gut he's dirty, you are even concerned he might become one of those rogue cops like I dealt with in Albuquerque. Worse yet, if he becomes Sheriff, the department will gradually become like him. Are you prepared to live with the outcome if we don't at least give it a shot?"

I stood, laid a ten-dollar bill on the table and walked out. I began to sense our work here might be done when I heard my name. Turning I saw Greta taking long, confident steps towards me, a look of determination in her face.

"Let's do this," she said.

Guess I might have been wrong.

IN THE PAST WEEK AVA HAD NOT LEFT HER HOME BEFORE ten a.m. We got Ellie prepared in our hotel room, tested all the equipment and went over the basic plan several times until she began to look comfortable talking about the things she would be discussing with Ava. At 8:45 a.m. we headed out in two cars.

Ellie parked in Ava's driveway, we sat idling at the curb four houses down. If Ellie made it inside, we'd pull up in front of the house to increase the probability of success with the electronics. Kenny had put a body wire on Ellie so we could hear and record the conversation, along with placing a mini voice recorder slightly bigger than a quarter in her suit jacket pocket in case we lost connection. The earbud he gave her so she could hear me looked like a miniature hearing aid making it difficult to notice.

Considering most cops knock, Ellie rang the doorbell. Hearing footsteps approaching she whispered, "Here we go."

"You'll be great. I have total confidence in you," I said.

Ava opened the door wearing a light purple robe and matching slippers, her hair in a quick twist bun.

"Mrs. Lloyd…I'm sorry, I know you asked me to call you Ava. Ava, I'm sure you remember me …."

"Yes Detective, what can I do for you?"

"I have some information I thought you might find interesting and wondered if we could talk. I'm not here to arrest you, I promise."

"Yet," Kenny said in the car.

Ava Lloyd stared at Ellie for several seconds, then looked past her to see if anything appeared out of the ordinary in the neighborhood.

"Does Major Potts know you're here? He told me the investigation has already been closed."

"No, Ma'am, he doesn't. If he did, frankly, I could lose my job."

The beauty behind the truth is a person's body language lines up with their words, and right then everything about Ellie indicated she laid the truth on the line.

Ava must have seen it, too. Stepping back, she motioned for Ellie to enter with a sweeping hand.

When the door closed behind them, we coasted up in front of the house and Seth got out to go around back. We did not think Ava would be foolish enough to try to kill Ellie, except why take the risk.

Ava directed Ellie to a chair while she sat on the same couch where she heard her husband being killed.

After five minutes of small talk Ellie sensed Ava seemed ready to throw her out without a compelling reason to let her continue. She needed to shock Ava into letting her stay, so she decided to say something even we did not know.

"Ava, the lab found traces of duct tape on both your husband and Mr. Dignam's faces near their mouths, along with your husband's wrists."

I shot a look at Kenny whose shock mirrored mine. "Great move," I said to Ellie.

Ava started wringing her hands together, the knuckles turning white.

"What…what are you saying?"

"Greta Meier, the Commonwealth Attorney, has attained a search warrant of your financial records showing you have paid large sums of money to Colonel Rich Harbaugh, in addition to one hundred grand to Major Potts."

Ava's lips separated leaving her mouth agape, her face losing color, becoming white like her knuckles. She fell back against the rear cushion of the couch, her wide eyes locked onto Ellie.

"Quick, remind her you are not there to arrest her," I said

After Ellie did what I said, nearly a minute of complete silence followed.

"Tell her Greta is willing to help her if she helps Greta."

Upon Ellie telling her about Greta, Ava sat up again, a sense of hope.

"What does she want…from me?"

The explanation of Greta wanting a full statement of her hiring Harbaugh to go after A-Ray Corporation, what his insurgents did, her paying him extra to have her husband and lover killed, caused Ava to lose color once again.

"If I do it, what do I get?"

"She is willing to help you reduce your prison sentence. More importantly, she is willing to give you an opportunity to get out of prison with some quality time left if you are willing to take an active role in bringing down Major Potts."

"She's going after Potts?"

"Yes, she is. With your help she believes …."

"I'll do it. He's a damn weasel. After he told you to leave the room, he blackmailed me for a hundred thousand. Here's the thing, he did it with such self-assurance, a smugness about him, I knew right then he had done it before…I am *definitely* not the first. He said it would be a one-time thing. No way, the greedy look in his eyes told me the bastard would come wanting more. You tell Greta Meier, if she makes it worth my effort, hell yeah, I'll help her take his ass down."

CHAPTER FIFTY-THREE

———◆———

After several rounds of negotiations Ava had a deal sweeter than expected, completely contingent on her success with Major Potts. Greta quietly arranged for the probation office to put an ankle monitor on Ava since putting her in the county jail meant Major Potts would know. We feared he would have her killed in the jail or given something to render her unconscious before making her death look like an Epstein suicide via hanging.

Over the next several days Ava cooperated, though we all knew once Harbaugh's death had gone public, she could fudge details and we had no way of confirming them. On the other hand, she had no way of knowing we lied to her about having one of his insurgents in protective custody, a common police tactic for the greater good.

We prepared her no different than we had Ellie. With her buy-in, in addition to bugging her home we set up video cameras inside at all angles in case Potts did not want to sit where Ava directed him.

We agreed to let Potts leave her home once he finished. Knowing politics would become a significant defense, we would seek a signed arrest warrant with a judge validating probable cause. Everything legitimate, or within reason given the circumstances.

Ava placed the call asking Potts over to her house around 6 p.m. so they could discuss "the murder of my poor husband." Potts sounded upbeat, almost excited about the opportunity to see Ava again, agreeing without hesitation.

At six o'clock sharp Potts knocked on the door. We had taken our position in what used to be Danny's home office with the doors closed. Unlike Ellie, Ava refused to have an earbud with me talking to her. She convinced us she would not be able to think straight if she had to listen to a question I formulated, then try to act natural asking it. With absolute conviction she assured us she would get what we needed.

"Major, thank you so much for coming over. Please come in."

Potts smiled. "No problem, Ava."

The inflection in his tone using her name stopped her. When she looked at him, he winked, a perverted smile plastered on his face. Ava forced a grin, even though his demeanor served to solidify her internal conviction to nail the bastard.

Instead of sitting in one of the two chairs across from the couch Ava had tried directing him to, he sat on the couch next to her, patting her thigh once they settled in. Without realizing it, Major Potts fueled Ava's desire to take him down.

"Major, I wanted to make sure we are in agreement of what we actually settled on the other night. I mean, the shock of it all, right, regardless of how things went down with Danny and Keith."

"I'm glad you called Ava. We do need to discuss our agreement, along with some additional things we did not cover initially."

He laid his hand on her thigh.

Ava looked at his hand, then into his eyes.

"Major, you came into my husband's office, told Detective Svenson to leave, made sure to close the door, then you told me if I gave you one hundred thousand dollars you would make my husband's and Keith's deaths go away as a double homicide. You remember, don't you, Major?"

"Yes, of course I remember. I received your wire transfer of the money, for which I am grateful. I'm not sure if this is the right time…it seems like we failed to iron out all the details, if you know what I mean."

His smile bordered between lust and greed causing Ava's blood to boil. She took a deep breath to allow her brain to override her anger.

"What I know is you and Colonel Harbaugh conspired together on this whole fiasco," she said, intentionally not identifying what exactly they worked on. "I'm sensing the two of you are alike, squeezing money out of someone once you have them caught in your trap."

Potts chuckled.

"Now, Ava, it's not like you didn't get anything out of the deal. We took care of your husband and lover; you gave each of us money to do so. I will say, taking care of the initial outcome of the investigation versus making sure things like evidence do not come to light are totally different matters. Besides, it does not have to be money exactly. You are an extremely attractive woman…I could be convinced to substitute a little personal entertainment in place of cash."

Ava stared at him while he rubbed her thigh. Her desire to put him away for good escalated.

"You've done this kind of thing before, haven't you?"

"What do you mean?"

"You've blackmailed other women, for sex or money. I'd guess mostly victims of domestic violence. You probably offered to make sure their husbands went to prison in exchange for their money or their services. That's what I mean."

Potts pondered the accusation.

"I know you're not working with law enforcement otherwise you would be looking at life in prison for the hiring of two murders. So yes…your description, while not exactly accurate, it's close enough. I must say though, like you, every one of those women got more from me than I did from them."

Ava stood and walked over to one of the kitchen drawers where she pulled out a full sized lined yellow pad and a pen. She returned to her seat, close enough for her leg to touch his.

Handing him the items she said, "Major Potts, I am a businesswoman, not unaccustomed to negotiating. Neither of us wants to go to prison, and both of us deserve to profit in our own way. Still, I will not be taken advantage of again and again. So, I am prepared to make you an offer. I will not accept a rebuttal; you take it or leave it."

Potts tilted his head and grinned. His entire perverted demeanor switched to that of a child bound to receive the Christmas gift he had asked for.

"Please, go ahead."

"Very well. You write down everything that happened between us in the office on the night of my husband's death. Include my paying you, you receiving it and your solemn promise you will not come after me for my husband's or Keith's deaths. If you do what I'm asking, I will agree to have sex with you one night a month for one year. At the end of the year you can do with the document what you want. Burn it for all I care. Once a month, one year, nothing more."

Having been around men like Potts before she knew the thought of sex would take away his ability to reason. Knowing camera positions could not capture everything she slid her hand under the pad he held to his inner thigh. With one rub closer to his growing desire she helped him lose sight of her making a copy of the document a potential point of contention. She counted on him thinking with the wrong head.

Potts didn't know whether to smile at the thought of sex with such a beautiful woman or be afraid of putting something in writing.

"How do I know you won't show this to someone or use it against me somehow?"

"Major, don't be a fool. Tell on myself? Seriously? I told you, I'm a businesswoman. I have no intention of being extorted forever. If you try to screw me, no pun intended, I will take it to the FBI. Otherwise, why in the world would I want to bring attention to all the illegalities we have done?"

Her little finger under the pad helped emphasize her feigned desire to work with him.

Nodding, Potts put the pen to the pad. Ava went to the kitchen to allow him to quit thinking of sex long enough to write. Similar to most police officers, he wrote a detailed factual account without any fluff, handing it back to her twenty minutes later.

She read it, specifically checking for the legibility of his signature and the date, then set it on the counter.

When she turned around Potts had a huge grin, patting the couch beside him.

"I'm sorry, Major. I'm right in the middle of my period. I'm not about to have sex with you while I'm cramping and bleeding like a stuck pig."

She wanted to gross him out...it worked.

Potts stood, the evidence of his excitement pushing outward. "Will next Wednesday work for you? My wife is in a bridge club, so I'll be free."

"I'll be sufficiently horny come next Wednesday. I promise to give you something you've never had before." Ava smiled, putting one hand on her hip and winking.

Major Potts made the universal uncomfortable erection waddle to the door; a huge smile plastered on his face. Ava watched through the peephole to make sure he left.

You are going to get screwed Potts, except some guy in prison is going to be the one doing it you piece of shit.

When she turned around Greta Meier held the pad in an evidence bag, smiling at Ava.

Pleased with herself, Ava returned the smile.

CHAPTER FIFTY-FOUR

———◆———

Greta Meier held off making phone calls to the press until 8:30 a.m. to prevent information leaking out early. She scheduled the press conference for an hour later in front of the Stafford County Courthouse down the road from the Sheriff's Office. During the calls Greta hinted to her media contacts they may want to set up in the parking lot at the Sheriff's Office before 9:00 a.m., suggesting they return to the courthouse before she started.

Shortly before 9:00 a.m. the Sheriff received a text from his secretary. He asked the Assistant Sheriff and Major Potts to excuse him while he spoke with her. He dialed her number from the desk phone sitting on the conference room table.

"Yes, go ahead, send them in," the Sheriff said.

Ellie and Sergeant Carothers walked into the conference room.

"What are you two doing interrupting this meeting?" Major Potts asked, a harshness to his tone. "I've told you never to interrupt me in Command Staff meetings."

"I authorized it," the Sheriff said.

The Sheriff looked at Carothers who did a quick side nod toward Ellie. The Sheriff extended his open hand toward Ellie giving her the floor.

"Major Potts, I have a warrant for your arrest, for the extortion…and murder of …."

"Murder?" Potts yelled. He jumped to his feet sending his chair flying. "I never murdered anyone."

As uniformed deputies filed into the room to handcuff Potts, the Sheriff said, "Be careful, Major. That might be construed an admission of guilt for extortion." Turning to Ellie, he said, "Detective, I'm sorry I interrupted you. Please continue with the reading of his Miranda rights."

Ellie read Major Potts his rights while the deputies escorted him handcuffed out of the conference room.

The Sheriff sat and looked at the Assistant Sheriff, his long-time friend.

"Well, I guess this means I need to stick around a little longer," the Sheriff said. "Want to postpone your retirement for a little while?"

The Assistant Sheriff grinned. "Since he's no longer part of the management team, I'd be happy to."

Major Potts continued declaring his innocence the entire trudge through the Sheriff's office building. He garnered two nods from sympathizers, although a dozen disgusted personnel shaking their heads outnumbered them.

"This is all your fault," Potts said trying to turn to look at Ellie who followed the deputies escorting him. "You lousy bitc ..."

The deputy on the left did a quick backhand fist to Potts's groin, nearly doubling him over. When the deputy looked back Ellie mouthed a thank you, drawing a grin in return.

The parking lot already had several reporters and television crews, with more pulling into the lot when deputies escorted Potts out. Most prisoners get transported in a patrol car, sitting on hard plastic behind a cage. The Sheriff had instructed Potts be transported in one of the detective cars, feeling sad for the man he had worked alongside for nearly three decades.

The deputies slowed the pace, inwardly enjoying their providing Potts his couple of minutes of fame. Meanwhile, Potts knew deputies could not give him a nut shot again in front of cameras, although slowing down even more would be much worse.

"Major Potts, did you do what they are arresting you for?" a woman reporter asked, extending her mic without attempting to go past the wall of deputies.

Potts yanked one elbow away from an escort deputy, pivoting toward her.

"I'm innocent. These are trumped up charges trying to keep me from becoming Sheriff. Justice will prevail, and I'll see to it heads roll for this."

"Yeah, yeah," one of the escort deputies said in a low tone. He put his free hand on Potts's head, pushing him down into the back seat of the sedan.

Ellie got in the right rear side after the deputy closed Potts's door. Carothers took the driver's seat then slowly accelerated for the five-minute trip to the Rappahannock Regional Jail.

"Major, you said you understood your Miranda Rights, though you've never said if you will talk or not, nor have you asked for an attorney. Would you like one, an attorney?"

"I didn't kill anyone, and you know it. What's more, all monies I have received have been campaign contributions. You both best be looking for new jobs."

Driving past the courthouse Carothers let the car slow to a coast. Potts looked out his window at the crowd forming near the courthouse steps. Greta Meier walked up to the podium at the top step, with four of her top attorneys flanking her.

"She's probably the one spearheading this witch-hunt.

Everyone in the county knows the polls have shown her approval rating is down to forty percent. When I'm done with her, she ain't gonna have her cushy job no more."

Carothers turned on to Jefferson Davis Highway, accelerating to stay with the flow. Ellie figured time might run out or Potts would lawyer up, so she decided to go for it.

"So, Major Potts, are you aware of the suicide note Colonel Harbaugh left? Greta Meier's investigators spoke with the DC detectives." She recalled AJ's comment about fifty percent of what perps say in a statement being true, except she used the concept against her perp. DC detectives had been contacted, yet Harbaugh's death had not been classified and no note existed.

Potts looked at Ellie, his eyes wider than normal. "Uh, no I had no idea."

"From what the investigators learned, the note is pretty extensive. Anyway, some of the basis of your arrest is the conspiracy he detailed."

Potts began to get pale, the whiteness standing out against his purple shirt and dark charcoal suit.

The vehicle slowed as it approached the private road leading to Rappahannock County Jail, however, Potts lost focus of the outside, his wide eyes still focused on Ellie. Completing the turn, Carothers saw Potts in his rearview mirror almost ready to say something. He took his foot off the accelerator, drifting at fifteen mph.

"I knew…Harbaugh told me his insurgents planned on killing those two men …."

The .30-06 bullet shattered the back window striking Potts behind his right ear. Shattering glass and brain matter hit the back of Carothers head, the bullet narrowly missing him.

Ellie saw half of Major Potts's head explode in front of her causing her mind to do something she had never experienced…processing every detail, almost in slow motion. The entry point behind his right ear meant the shot came from the tree line behind and to her right. Hoping to save Carothers, Ellie bailed out. Rolling on the pavement she heard the accelerator kick in.

On instinct Carothers punched the accelerator to the floorboard, grabbing the radio mic. Negotiating the inverted C curve of the private road with his left hand, his right clicked the mic to let the dispatch center know shots had been fired, one person had been hit and to have the Jail open the Sally-Port door so he could drive in.

Ellie got to one knee, her Glock pointed at the trees. The sunlight hit something smooth causing an instant flash. She fired two rounds of suppressive fire hoping Carothers could get away. She fired two more rounds feeling her partner might make it to the building. Her mind processed move or die, so she pushed off like a sprinter, racing to the tree line. She never heard another shot and her mind returned to normal speed, transitioning to finding the shooter. Moving in the general direction of Jefferson Davis Highway from fifteen feet inside the tree line, she began looking for any movement, stopping sporadically to listen for what she couldn't see.

THE SHOOTER KNEW THE ACCURACY OF THE .30-06 RIFLE with the high-power scope, having fired six rounds on the property of the owner from which he stole it. He recalled the elderly man said he lived alone and when asked about rifles he mentioned he used a .30-06 for hunting.

The elderly man showed the shooter where he kept the rifle and when he turned to grab the box of bullets the shooter slit the man's throat. The shooter took the rifle and bullets out back, shooting at a tree one hundred yards from the man's back porch. In six shots he felt comfortable with the scope and the trigger pull and confirmed the elderly man's death at the same time he took the grease rag hanging half-out of the man's pant pocket. He wiped the few things he had touched, pushed the knob locks on the front and back doors, then walked back to the stolen Toyota Corolla he parked a quarter mile from the man's house, the rifle and bullets in tow. Driving away he tossed the rag into the tree line.

The shooter almost had a twinge of remorse for the old man, until the dark sedan pulling onto the private road toward the jail interrupted his thought. For reasons he would never know the scenario began to play into his hand. The sedan slowed, Potts turned, looking to his right at the detective in the backseat. Despite the shooter believing the first round struck Major Potts, he rapidly slid the bolt action back, jacking another round in the chamber, firing an upper torso shot into Potts's slumping body.

Almost exactly at the time he fired the second round he saw the female detective bail out of the right rear door, rolling twice before coming up to a kneeling position with her service weapon. The shooter held the rifle stock, barrel pointed skyward. He saw the flash from the detective's weapon, two of her rounds coming in his general direction. When she took off for the tree line after firing two more rounds, he set the rifle at the base of the tree, with the box of ammo next to the butt of the gun.

The shooter took off in a northeasterly direction toward The Log Cabin parking lot where he left the stolen Toyota. When the parking lot came into view he stopped, and with the heel of his boot he made a four-inch divot in the ground. He took off his latex gloves, rolled them into a tight ball, laid them in the divot, then concealed it with dirt and pine needles over the top. He made it to his car without seeing or hearing the detective again.

The shooter went north on Jefferson Davis Highway for a short distance, turned left, crossing the southbound lanes and onto a dirt road. He went far enough for the car not to be seen from the highway then pulled off and wiped his prints clean. He walked further up the dirt road and came to a Chevy Traverse he had previously stolen parked facing the highway.

He got to the highway and turned south. Hearing sirens and seeing emergency lights in his rearview he pulled to the right like the two cars in front of him, waiting for the ambulance and two sheriff's patrol cars to go by. Seeing them all turn right towards the jail the shooter pulled back onto the highway. When he neared The Log Cabin restaurant, he saw the female detective talking on a cell phone and slowed. Passing the entrance road to the jail he smiled at the havoc he caused.

Another threat silenced, he thought.

Continuing southbound he felt secure in the knowledge it would take some time for authorities to figure out who the rifle belonged to, find the dead owner, and hope they had a witness. He had used gloves when he took care of the weapon and ammunition, wiping off the few things he touched in the man's house and the stolen Corolla. The fact he now headed the opposite direction in a different car would leave future investigators little to go on.

GRETA MEIER HAD BEGUN THE PRESS CONFERENCE FROM the steps of the courthouse. Having finished outlining the arrest of Major Potts and the basis of the charges levied against him, Greta paused, preparing to articulate the investigators breadth of work piecing together the larger puzzle beyond the deaths of Danny Lloyd and Keith Dignam. Before she could say another word an intrusion of gunshots heard in the distance stopped her.

A buzz rapidly grew amongst the throng of news personnel, along with their uncomfortableness on whether to stay or follow the sirens to the new story.

"Excuse me, Counselor, we are hearing someone fired shots at the police vehicle transporting Major Potts, can you update us on that developing story?" one of the reporters asked excitedly.

Greta tried to maintain composure. Except the real problem had nothing to do with her composure…it had to do with the lack of information.

How the hell am I supposed to know, she thought.

Glancing right she noticed the Stafford County Sheriff sliding toward the mic and gave him full access.

"Ladies and gentlemen, we can confirm there have been shots fired on the grounds of the Rappahannock County Jail. Details are still filtering in therefore I would be remiss to say anything further."

"Did Major Potts get shot?" the same reporter yelled, wanting to be heard over her peers.

The Sheriff stopped mid-turn, looking at the reporter. His voice remained silent, yet in contrast, his body language confirmed what he could not bring himself to say.

A male voice in the crowd said, "Oh my God." Reporters and television crews began running to their vehicles, their brighter futures from being on the cutting edge of a breaking news story hanging in the balance. Amidst patrol cars from all surrounding jurisdictions the two-mile race to the county jail had begun, leaving Greta and her fellow attorneys standing alone.

Nobody wanted to acknowledge the mileage toward reelection Greta could have gotten from prosecuting Major Potts, a strategy most likely dead...right along with Potts.

Greta turned and took up a brisk pace going inside straight to the conference room next to her office. Once the doors closed Greta took a deep breath to calm herself, then turned to look at her most trusted underlings who had followed like lemmings.

"I'm sure you all had the same impression of the Sheriff's failure to answer—Potts is probably dead," she said. "I'll make some calls, until we hear otherwise presume he is. We need to work together, and we need to be quick about it. All suggestions are viable. Resolute...we need to appear confident and unshaken. We are going to put a positive spin on this so help me God."

Greta left the room, barking at her secretary to cancel all meetings before the door slammed behind her.

CAPTER FIFTY-FIVE

Tom and Luci agreed to let us have a private meeting at The Nook at 7 p.m. They wanted to participate, or at least listen in, except Kenny convinced them Greta Meier would never agree to it.

The three of us sat at a table minutes before Greta and Ellie arrived. Lucy had made fresh coffee and stocked the refrigerator with beer before she and Tom left. Kenny sat at the table with his beer after serving everyone.

"Interesting spin you put on the whole thing for the media," I said, looking at Greta.

She shrugged.

"Basically, we decided who could, or would, refute it. H&P are dead. Eight of Harbaugh's insurgents are dead, leaving one alive that we know of. What are the chances he comes forward to say we have it all wrong?"

Nobody said anything.

"Exactly," Greta said. "Ellie said Potts had begun admitting knowledge of murders about to take place at Ava's house when a bullet went through his brain. He may not have provided the perfect admission, yet under the circumstances we felt we had enough to validate our legal position."

"And politically," Kenny added.

"That too," Greta said, a huge grin on her face.

"What about Ava Lloyd?" Kenny asked, looking at Greta.

"I trust you will all understand when I say I lack a true witness and physical evidence for me not to stick with the deal we offered her. Honestly, I'm happy considering without the deal I don't think we put her in prison at all."

"Did you guys get any evidence of the shooter?" Seth asked Ellie.

Shaking her head, she said, "Not really. The rifle belonged to a sixty-three-year-old widower who lived about five miles up a dirt road. We found him dead...his throat slit. We found both front and back doors locked and things inside his place seemed wiped clean. The rifle appeared to be wiped clean of prints except a partial we think he missed, although there are enough points of comparison, we believe it's the owners. We found the rifle lying next to the tree we believe the shooter stood next to when he shot Potts. At the time I tried to get into the trees to locate him, except I never did."

"Leaves two options the way I see it," I said. I pulled a Kenny and made them wait a few seconds.

"Rock seems like the obvious answer, right?" I hesitated to watch them look at each other. "Except, is he?"

"Around here there's enough dark blue or black Tahoes and Suburbans, it could be any number of agencies needing to make sure Potts didn't say something he shouldn't," Kenny said.

"Rock's motive to make sure nobody is alive who can implicate him specifically seems pretty strong though," Ellie said.

"I agree," Seth said. "Although, if he is still around, I would think he would be going after a certain group of people, no names mentioned of course, who got them before they got anyone else. Not to mention targeting AJ, who according to Carli, Rock hates for killing his best friend, Dingo."

"Having been a former federal prosecutor, trust me, I've seen lots of crap fly under the radar around here. If some black ops group wanted Potts dead, we'll never know who or why. And, in that same vein…I personally appreciate each of us having our own vested interest in keeping certain bits of information to ourselves, for the greater good, of course."

Greta grinned bringing one to each of us.

Raising my cup of coffee, I said, "Here's to good people doing what's necessary for those who can no longer do it for themselves. Right is right, and wrong is wrong. What we've done here is right, I'm certain of it."

"Here, here," they all said, raising their beer bottles.

THE FOLLOWING MORNING SETH AND I SAID OUR GOOD-byes to Tom and Luci since Kenny would be taking us to the airport. The Lloyd's company appeared to be listing like a ship taking on water with no captain to lead the crew. Conversely, Andy had returned to work half-days, unable to leave his children parentless for long hours. Ironically, A-Ray Corporation's importance in the industry catapulted to the top after what transpired with the owners of Dall Industries. Death did not slow criminals or terrorists, and many agencies looked to A-Ray's for answers and required their expertise. Ric had made a positive turnaround and would be okay so Kenny would be staying back to help him and Andy in any way he could.

Walking in front of the restaurant I received a text from an unknown number, something I usually sent straight to trash. The message hung on the screen for a brief second.

Something told me to open it based on the first two words: Black suburban.

I stopped to open the text and to give me privacy while they kept walking.

> BLACK SUBURBAN. I KNOW YOU HAVE SEEN
> US WATCHING FROM A DISTANCE. IMPRES-
> SIVE—PULLING THAT OFF WHILE KEEPING
> LOCAL AND FEDERAL AGENCIES FROM GET-
> TING IN YOUR WAY.

I debated whether I should respond, though the investigator inside me wanted more information.

> WHAT AGENCY?
> NOT THE COMMON ONES.

I figured the NSA might be the strongest possibility, or some black budget group well hidden in the DOD. *Unless it is some kind of shadow group,* I thought.

Still, using texting to try and lock it down might only serve to end the connection. Even though I presumed their phone, whoever they were, would be destroyed after the conversation, I wanted more.

> HARBAUGH ONE OF YOURS?
> YES…AND NO. YEARS AGO.
> GO OFF THE RESERVATION?
> PERCEPTIVE. GREED.
> ELIMINATE HIM?
> DIDN'T HAVE TO.
> WHY NOT ELIMINATE US? CLEAN UP LOOSE
> ENDS.

A long pause ensued, enough for me to begin thinking I asked the wrong question.

> RIC! HIGHLY DECORATED SOLDIER. MANY TOP-SECRET MISSIONS. YOU PUT HIM IN FRONT OF YOUR OWN SAFETY. YOU THREE DESERVE MEDALS—NOT ELIMINATION. UNFORTUNATELY, YOU WILL NEVER BE RECOGNIZED AND CAN NEVER TELL ANYONE. I'M WILLING TO TRUST THAT WILL HAPPEN. YOUR TRUST WILL NOT BE BROKEN.
> I COUNTED ON THAT.
> NICE WE DON'T HAVE TO BE LOOKING OVER OUR SHOULDERS.
> NOT FROM US—ROCK??? I'LL BE IN TOUCH.
> WAIT! IN TOUCH FOR WHAT?
> YOU'LL SEE.
> WHAT DO I CALL YOU?
> YOU DECIDE.
> I'M THINKING...PUPPET MAN.
> YOUR CHOICE.
> WHAT ABOUT POTTS?

Another long interlude.

> PUT YOUR PHONE ON THE SIDEWALK AND CRUSH IT. YOUR BANK ACCOUNT TELLS ME YOU CAN AFFORD A NEW ONE.
> YOU KNOW EVERYTHING?
> YES.

Out of my peripheral vision I caught something dark moving. I saw a shiny black Suburban creeping along the curb one hundred feet down on the opposite side of the street.

I smiled, tipped my phone in the Suburban's direction, then crushed it on the sidewalk. The headlights on the Suburban flashed on and off before it made a U-turn and drove out of sight.

Looking over I saw confusion on Kenny and Seth's faces.

Kenny said what they both had on their minds, "What the heck is that all about?"

Smiling, I said, "Top secret. I'd have to kill you."

"What the hell? You know I've got top-secret clearance."

"Seth doesn't. What's more, apparently yours isn't top secret enough."

Seth's laughing caused me to join him. I planned on telling them everything, though for now messing with Kenny all the way to the airport would be fun.

Before we got halfway to the airport the radio DJ announced, "The shooting deaths of a retired Army Colonel in Washington DC and a Major at Stafford County Sheriff's Department might have connections. Police are not disclosing much, although reporters for Action 13 News say their sources are saying it's a conspiracy gone wrong. More on News on the Hour."

CHAPTER FIFTY-SIX

———◦◦◦———

I borrowed one of Kenny's burner phones to call Celia. I had not been able to get through to her for several days and thought she might still be touchy about me putting myself at risk. I texted first to let her know I had to use a different phone. I looked forward to telling her about me coming home, hoping the use of the word let her know wherever she lived I would call home.

She did not answer on the first two attempts, so I waited until we made it through security at the airport. When I tried again the ringing stopped although seconds of silence greeted me.

"Celia, it's AJ. I'm at the airport, I'm coming home. I'm so excited to see you and Brooke."

The silence continued for what seemed an eternity. I wondered what she must be thinking and almost said something, except the clearing of a throat stopped me. It sounded like she had been crying, trying to gather herself before she spoke.

"AJ...it's Brooke. Please hurry ..."

I heard sobbing and a voice in the background I did not recognize saying she would talk to me.

"Hello, AJ? My name is Carolyn. I'm a hospice nurse ...."

"Hospice? What's going on? Where's Celia and why is Brooke crying?"

"AJ, there is no easy way to say this. I'm sorry...Celia has stage IV ovarian cancer. She and I have had several conversations, many about you. Suffice it to say, she would not let anyone contact you or let you know. She said your helping a friend and the people being terrorized back there held more importance considering you could save people from dying. She knew you could not do the same for her, and she made us promise."

"She had to have known before I left."

"I believe so."

"It makes sense now. I thought she had been mad at me for coming here."

"No, not at all. She admires how you always try to help people in danger."

"How long, Carolyn?"

"She has gotten worse pretty quickly this last month. Although there is no way to know for sure, it's been my experience she'll hold on knowing you're coming home. I can tell her you are on your way, correct?"

"Yes...yes, of course."

"When do you think you'll get here?"

"We're almost ready to board. I should be there around seven tonight."

"I'll tell her. I know she's been hoping you would make it. We'll talk more after you get here."

"Okay," I managed to say before she disconnected.

I had no idea how long I stared at the phone. Seth putting his hand on my shoulder brought me back.

"AJ, what's wrong?"

I looked into my friend's eyes and felt the tears in mine building.

"Celia...cancer...she's dying," is all I could say, tears ran down my face.

Seth helped me to a seat before walking over to the attendant using the mic directing passengers to board.

"AJ, you need to get on the plane. It's too late for me to change planes. I can't come with you. I've asked them to keep an eye on you, but you need to get on. They're almost ready to close the door."

Heading toward the door, I said, "Seth, can you call Mac, in Albuquerque? I'll need a ride."

"You got it."

He hugged me and watched me amble down the ramp.

Turning the corner, I saw a flight attendant who looked a few years older than me, her eyes slightly watered.

"Sir, you can have the entire back row to yourself so nobody will bother you. If there's anything we can do …."

I knew if I tried to speak I would break down, so I mouthed the words, *Thank you.*

The first three rows of people overheard the flight attendant and could tell something happened. Fortunately, nobody beyond them knew a thing. I slid into the window seat in the last row, put my seatbelt on and laid my head against the hard-plastic wall.

I never heard the announcements or had a clue we had taxied to the runway. The takeoff brought me out of my fog, and I looked around. People existed in their own worlds, many asleep or watching something on their iPad.

Before long, my mind left the plane and went to Albuquerque, recalling all the time I had spent with Celia, our conversations, and our growing fondness for each other. I replayed each of them several times in my mind, my mental transportation to Celia, Brooke, and me…a true blessing which helped me not to focus on the clock.

I am not sure at what point in the flight it happened, still I found myself thinking of what Carolyn said about people holding on for an important reason. I recalled Mac's grandmother, Oma, had done something similar, openly saying she wanted to see her granddaughter get married. Shortly after the wedding Oma passed. I had heard similar stories over the course of my time in the detective bureau and all of them seemed to provide some type of solace.

Despite my effort not to, I could not keep from thinking about whether I would be too late once again. When my fiancé, Bethany had been kidnapped and murdered a few years before, I did not realize the imminence of her death while I had her on the phone, instead I attempted to convince her I would be there soon. I did not arrive in time, nor did I have the opportunity to say goodbye. Though I tried to pray for a different outcome, thoughts of being late crept in once more.

MAC AND SAM, THE TWO MEN I GREW UP NEXT TO IN Albuquerque and called my brothers, picked me up at the airport. Both knew Celia and Brooke well having spent quite a bit of time together. I put my bags in the trunk and hopped into the back seat. Both turning to look at me told me they must have known the question at the forefront of my mind.

"She made us promise not to call you," Sam said. "I know she could see it's been tough for us, yet she still made us promise every time we went to see her to help out around her house."

Not only could I see the sincerity in their eyes, I knew their integrity would never let them lie to me, much less break a promise they made to Celia.

In many respects the drive to Celia's house seemed to take longer than the flight, my mind wandering through the past having ended. Right before we got there, I put my hand on Mac's shoulder.

"You're not saying much. For years we've been able to read each other, even without saying anything. Somethings on your mind, what is it?"

"We're almost there. We can talk later. Really, I promise we'll talk."

My eyes went to Sam who quickly looked away. Although I had no doubt something needed to be said, I trusted Mac's sense of priority, especially being less than two blocks from Celia's house .

As we turned onto her street, I closed my eyes and said a quick prayer, asking God to let me be strong for the sake of Celia and Brooke.

CHAPTER FIFTY-SEVEN

———◆———

B rooke burst through the door when we pulled to the curb. She jumped into my arms before I had the car door closed, and buried her tear covered face in the crook of my neck. I stood twisting from side-to-side, rubbing her back for close to a minute. Her world had to be caving in and her heart broken, her father being killed the year before and now her mother dying from cancer. My heart ached for her searching for the right words to say.

She wiped her eyes on my shirt and lifted her head, looking me in the eyes.

"I don't want to go live in Little Rock with my uncle. He's mean, he doesn't like kids."

"I've never heard your mom talk about him."

"He beat up his wife and went to jail for a long time. He's mean, AJ."

She started crying again and buried her head.

"Let me go in and talk with your mom," I said, rubbing her back again. "We'll talk about this again. I promise."

She nodded without lifting her head, making no attempt to get down. I carried her to the front door where the woman I presumed to be Carolyn met us.

"Hi AJ. I'm Carolyn. Brooke honey, why don't you come with me. Let AJ and your mom have some time."

Brooke got down and Carolyn wrapped her arm around

Brooke's shoulder while they walked to the backyard.

"AJ, do you want us to wait here?" Mac asked.

"I don't know, Mac. To be honest…I'm not sure about anything right now."

"We'll wait."

They made their way into the living room and sat.

Reading between the lines, I thought, that's Mac's way of saying the end is near.

I took a deep breath then headed down the hall.

When I walked in the bedroom I almost gasped. Celia had not been a large woman in the first place, yet in the several weeks I had been gone she lost an incredible amount of weight. She had depressed cheeks, and her eyes had dark circles, creating a more sunken look than her cheeks. I walked to the side of the bed, taking her hand in mine and placing my other one on her forehead.

Celia opened her eyes and a tear formed in the corner.

"I'm sorry, AJ. I so wanted to spend our lives together."

"Oh, Celia …" I kissed her on the cheek, then wiped the tear with the back of my finger. "Is this why you wanted to take things slow?"

She nodded, then closed her eyes for a good fifteen seconds to garner energy. I sat on the bed next to her and leaned into her shoulder, my arm up on the pillow around the top of her head. When she laid her head into my chest, I laid mine on her forehead.

"I love you, Celia. I have almost from when I first met you. I'm sorry I did not say it earlier. I wanted to give you space, give you time to deal with Peter's murder." I kissed her forehead, holding my lips there for several seconds. "I love you so much."

"I love you, too, AJ. I wrote you a letter when I still had

strength. I couldn't be sure you would be back in time. Please don't be angry, I wanted you to help your friend, not sit here watching me wither while danger existed for him. The letter explains everything."

I leaned up to be able to look into her eyes.

"I would never be angry with you. I love you too much to ever let that happen. When I read the letter, I promise I'll trust your judgement."

I softly laid my hand on her cheek and felt the slight pressure of her leaning into it. Celia closed her eyes again, nearly double the length of time.

Opening her eyes once again, Celia said, "I want to talk about one thing. It's important, and I…I don't have much time."

"Whatever you want, sweetheart."

I stroked her cheek once again.

The corners of her lips raised, a caring look in her eyes when she focused into mine.

"I want to talk about Brooke."

"She told me she has an uncle in Little Rock. She says he's mean. You never told me about him."

"He's ten years older. Drug addict, spent time in jail, never came to either of our parent's funerals."

"Brooke mentioned he has a wife."

"Divorced. Almost killed her. Prison. Two years."

"Brooke cannot go there."

"I don't have any other living relatives. Her dad's only living relatives are cousins. Worse than my brother."

Celia closed her eyes needing a rest. She tried to take a deeper breath, then opened her eyes. "AJ, would you …"

"Yes, unequivocally, yes. I'd consider it an honor to raise Brooke."

Tears came to Celia's eyes, then she whispered, "Thank you so much. She loves you, too. Thank you, so, so much."

I knew then why Mac held off saying anything.

"Mac already has all the paperwork drawn up, in case I said yes. Right?"

Celia nodded. "Please, get the others to come in?"

I kissed her forehead, then went and got the others: Brooke, Mac, Sam, and Carolyn.

When Celia told her, Brooke started crying, laying on the bed next to her mother resting her head gently on Celia's shoulder.

I could see Celia's energy waning.

"Brooke, I would love to adopt you…only if it's what you want, too."

Brooke lifted her head and looked at me, a half smile on her face. "It is. I prayed you would say yes. Thank you."

I looked at Mac who nodded. We had two witnesses along with my friend the former judge who had been Celia's quasi-attorney, or at least put her in touch with one. I mouthed, *Thank you*, and the three of them quietly left the room.

With the little strength she had left, Celia imparted her motherly wisdom on Brooke to make sure Brooke knew her parents loved her with all their hearts.

"We will be watching you. You can talk to us; we'll always be with you and watching the beautiful woman you become. And I promise, we will be there when you get married."

Brooke nodded and wiped tears away with her shoulders.

"Can you do me a favor?"

Brooke nodded again.

"When AJ finds a woman he loves and wants to marry, please be kind to her and do your best to let her be like a mom. AJ will not marry someone unless he knows you are okay with it, so can you do that for me?"

Brooke looked over at me and thinly smiled, and then said, "I promise."

"I love you both, so much."

Celia then closed her eyes.

Brooke and I laid with Celia and I could feel her tension release once the important things had been taken care of and she had the opportunity to tell us she loved us one last time.

Brooke put her hand in mine above Celia's head and we stayed there until Celia took her last breath.

CHAPTER FIFTY-EIGHT

———◆———

A blur adequately described the next few hours. Carolyn, Mac and Sam took care of things like calling the mortuary and cleaning Celia's room. The coldness in my core from the reality that I could not avoid the inevitable slowly dissipated, though the heaviness of the final emotional hours remained.

Brooke could hardly let go of me and when she did, she remained attached. For a long time, we sat out on the back porch, her on my lap, her head on my shoulder. I knew Brooke would have questions at some point, though for now she seemed content to sit quietly and let what had to happen in the house go forth without us.

By the time everyone left it seemed later than eleven o'clock. Brooke fell asleep from pure exhaustion and I carried her to her room. I took off her shoes and pulled the cover over her, kissing her on the forehead.

"We'll get through this little girl…together."

When I walked back into the living room the pictures on the hutch drew my eyes in. I recognized the several I had seen before with Brooke and her parents, the numerous ones of Brooke at different ages, and several of Celia and Brooke together. One particular picture sitting in the middle of them all caught my attention, one I had never seen there before. The three of us stood together with

Brooke in the middle, all smiling. I remembered when Mac's girlfriend had taken it at a barbeque a few weeks before I went to Virginia. I smiled for a myriad of reasons, though mostly due to our being together and happy, a positive memory preserved.

I went to the kitchen pantry and got a bottle of red wine and poured a glass, then went to Celia's desk to get the letter she wrote me. I took it to the back porch and settled into a chair and removed the letter. Celia normally had beautiful handwriting, yet I could see the unevenness of the letters with the variance in pressure, signs she probably wrote it only a day or two before.

Taking a few sips of wine to garner strength, I focused on the letter.

My Dearest AJ,

I am not sure if you will make it here before I'm gone. I so admire your willingness to put others first before your own safety. I knew you belonged there helping Kenny. Even though friends wanted to let you know, I asked them not to. Please do not be angry. I would rather you remember the woman you kissed before you left, not the way I am today.

Thank you for coming into our lives when things seemed so bleak. Your helping to restore Peter's good name and strong character meant so much to Brooke and me.

I know now the pelvic and abdominal pains I ignored for so long proved to be the cancer. They started a few months before Peter's death. Things increasingly became stressful while he gathered infor-

mation on the corrupt cops at the police department. Then they killed him. We had minimal insurance, I had little money, and I convinced myself everything I felt had to be stress related. For months, those corrupt cops kept intimidating and scaring us, so the stress remained. Apparently, when you came along the cancer must have been well on its way.

I am sorry I kept you at bay about a relationship. You remained so patient and so willing to wait, and still helped us get back on our feet. I knew I began falling in love with you, I also sensed my own physical problems. I got scared, I'm sorry. I want you to know I do love you and I wanted so badly to have a life with you. You're an incredible man!

I need to ask a favor of you I know is not fair. I also know in my heart you will be great at it. I need someone to help Brooke through this terrible time, and more importantly to raise her. She loves you AJ, and neither her father nor I have family who we would trust to raise our daughter. I trust you, and I know Brooke does too. I have worked with Mac and an attorney he set me up with so you can adopt Brooke if you are willing. PLEASE CONSIDER IT.

When someone murdered your fiancé, Bethany you went through tough times. Then your life got better, and we found each other. I know you will get through this. What I am afraid of is you blaming yourself in some way as though two women you loved died on account of you, which you know is not true. Do not let fear keep you from being open to falling in love again. I know Bethany would want you to, and I most definitely want it for you. You deserve a good woman to be in your life.

Thank you, AJ. You helped me to climb out of the gloom and enjoy life again. You helped Brooke and I smile again and enjoy being together. That will be so important for her to be able to remember some good times, and she will thanks to you.

You mean the world to me. I love you with all my heart.

Celia

WHEN BETHANY DIED, I STRUGGLED WITH NIGHTMARES for months over not being able to save her, and on a more personal level for not getting to say goodbye. Somehow, I knew the same would not be true now. Being able to see Celia and talk with her, now reading her poignant letter, together they would be the difference in how I moved forward.

Like Bethany, Celia could read right through me. She could not have been more accurate about my immediate thought upon hearing of her cancer and being on her death bed. She knew my thoughts would center on the women I love dying, along with my being at fault somehow. Strangely, when I read her words…*which you know is not true*…I had the feeling she lightly laid her hand on my cheek and looking into my eyes she pleaded with me to trust her.

Sipping on my wine my thoughts went to the honor Celia bestowed on me to raise Brooke. I had no clue how to do it or where to start, yet I sensed her love in her willingness to allow me such a privilege.

Thank you, Celia, for loving me. I will always love you.

CHAPTER FIFTY-NINE

---·◆·---

C elia's funeral drew many attendees. The parents from Brooke's gymnastics team, her fellow interior design students along with the instructors, and many police officers and their families with whom her husband had worked.

Brooke wanted to speak so we put together some thoughts the night before. The tears in my eyes when she spoke of her parents revealed my pride in the eleven-year-old girl I would now call my daughter. Her parents had done an outstanding job raising her and I vowed internally while I listened to her to do my best to continue what they started.

Hours later toward the end of the reception, I felt the vibration in my pocket from my new cell phone. I almost ignored it yet at the same time I had a strange feeling I should look.

I made my way into the backyard and walked away from where a small group chatted. Alone I pulled out my phone and one message showed. It did not have a contact name, although the phone number began with the DC area code.

> SORRY TO HEAR ABOUT CELIA'S PASSING. MY
> CONDOLENCES.
> THANK YOU.
> YOU OKAY? CAN I DO ANYTHING TO HELP?

I hesitated, caught off guard.

DOING OKAY. THANKS, NOT RIGHT NOW.

IF YOU DO, ASK. CONCERNED.

ABOUT?

ROCK. YOU HAVE BROOK TO CONSIDER NOW.

YOU DO KNOW EVERYTHING.

Somehow, I knew after several seconds of no response there wouldn't be one.

HOW WOULD I CONTACT YOU?

KEEP THIS NUMBER. PERSONAL USE ONLY.

NOT TRACEABLE. DON'T TRY.

NO DESIRE TO.

QUESTIONS OR CONCERNS ABOUT BROOKE

FEEL FREE TO ASK.

THANKS AGAIN.

Puzzled, I held the phone staring at the last message regarding Brooke.

Putting the phone in my pocket I contemplated George Orwell being correct, Big Brother is always watching. I turned to head back to the house and froze.

Puppet man? Or is it …

THE END

Made in the USA
Monee, IL
18 August 2022

11879254R00204